"I have come to hol[d] [you in the highest] possible esteem and I hope you will permit me to pay my addresses, not as your employer but as...a suitor for your hand."

"I am honored you would think of me in such a connection, but I have made no secret of my attitude toward marriage," Leah replied.

"You have expressed it...in most vehement terms. But I hope," Hayden continued, "that you might permit me to attempt to persuade you otherwise."

"I do not believe my opinion of marriage is likely to change, but perhaps it would be worth...testing to be certain."

This was more encouragement than Hayden had expected. "I can ask no more than that."

His obvious satisfaction with her answer seemed to cause Leah some dismay. "I hope you will make no more of it than I have said. I should be very sorry to injure your feelings if, as I expect, I cannot give you the answer you wish."

Of course he would be disappointed, for Kit's sake, if he could not induce Leah to accept his eventual proposal. But that was all.

Still, it might not be the best strategy to inform a prospective bride that he intended to guard his heart.

Books by Deborah Hale

Love Inspired Historical

The Wedding Season
  "Much Ado About Nuptials"
*The Captain's Christmas Family
*The Baron's Governess Bride
*The Earl's Honorable Intentions
*The Duke's Marriage Mission

*Glass Slipper Brides

DEBORAH HALE

After a decade of tracing her ancestors to their roots in Georgian-era Britain, Golden Heart winner Deborah Hale turned to historical romance writing as a way to blend her love of the past with her desire to spin a good love story. Deborah lives in Nova Scotia, Canada, between the historic British garrison town of Halifax and the romantic Annapolis Valley of Longfellow's *Evangeline*. With four children (including twins), Deborah calls writing her "sanity retention mechanism." On good days, she likes to think it's working.

Deborah invites you to visit her personal website at www.deborahhale.com, or find out more about her at www.Harlequin.com.

The Duke's Marriage Mission

DEBORAH HALE

HARLEQUIN® LOVE INSPIRED® HISTORICAL

Recycling programs for this product may not exist in your area.

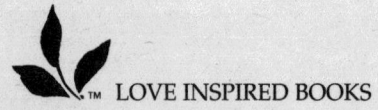 LOVE INSPIRED BOOKS

ISBN-13: 978-0-373-82989-7

THE DUKE'S MARRIAGE MISSION

www.Harlequin.com

Printed in U.S.A.

Now the Lord is the Spirit, and where
the Spirit of the Lord is, there is freedom.
—*2 Corinthians* 3:17

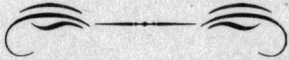

To all the parents who want to protect
our special needs children while still fostering
their strength and independence.

Chapter One

Somerset, England
July 1816

Should she have accepted a position as governess at this secluded country estate rather than helping her friends establish a new charity school? Second thoughts nagged at Leah Shaw as she stood before the imposing front entrance of Renforth Abbey.

She could not deny it would have been a stimulating challenge to seek suitable premises, hire teachers and otherwise prepare to educate the orphaned daughters of clergymen. But her friend Evangeline would be much better suited to such tasks than she. No doubt it would be a fulfilling project to create a compassionate, well-run alternative to the miserable institution she and her friends had endured.

But an equally vital mission awaited her *here,* Leah reminded herself. Somewhere in this vast, splendid house was a child who needed the kind of help she was uniquely qualified to provide.

"Is this all the luggage you've got, miss?" The cart driver who had conveyed her from the village unloaded her trunk and two boxes. "Or will there be more coming?"

"This is the lot." Leah fished in her reticule for some coins to pay him. "I prefer not to encumber myself with too many worldly goods. They would only weigh me down and make it difficult to move from place to place."

After spending so many years as a virtual prisoner of that horrid Pendergast School, Leah could never bear to remain in one place for long. Besides what did it matter how many possessions she owned? The true measure of a life well-lived was in experiences accumulated—sights seen, books read, friends made. Those she would carry with her in the bottomless portmanteau of her memory. It would not need to be re-packed next year when the time came for her to leave Renforth Abbey.

The massive oak door opened to reveal a vexed-looking servant, whose severely erect posture made him look taller than his actual height. He eyed Leah and her small amount of baggage with a critical scowl. "May I inquire your business here, miss? I fear you have come to the wrong house."

Refusing to be intimidated, Leah fixed him with her brightest smile. "If this is Renforth Abbey then I am in exactly the right place. My name is Leah Shaw.

I have been engaged as a governess for Lord Renforth. And you are…?"

"Adolphus Gibson, butler to His Grace, the Duke of Northam," he announced as proudly as if the peerage belonged to him. "I beg your pardon, Miss Shaw, but I was not aware a governess had been engaged for young Lord Renforth."

"No need to apologize, Mr. Gibson." Leah breezed past him, tugging off her gloves and untying her bonnet. "I am certain if you'd known I was coming you would have arranged a much warmer reception. But I am not one to stand on ceremony. If you would kindly direct me to the nursery to meet my new pupil, I can make the acquaintance of your staff later. I suppose it takes a great many servants to run a place this size. What an immense responsibility it must be for you."

The butler's severe expression eased. "The staff is indeed numerous, Miss Shaw. It is an honor to supervise a house of such long and noble history."

"You must be frightfully good at what you do." Leah swept a glance around the entry hall as she strode through it. Though the room looked scrupulously cared for, it seemed strangely neglected, too, as if it did not get much use. "Most butlers in great houses are considerably older than you by the time they reach such a position."

She pointed to an elaborate staircase of gleaming reddish-brown wood. "Is this the way to the nursery?"

"Indeed it is." The butler started to close the door. "Allow me to escort you. Then I shall inform His Grace of your arrival."

"That would be very kind of you, Mr. Gibson. Might I also prevail upon you to have my belongings brought in and taken to my room?"

"Of course, Miss Shaw. I must see to that immediately." He sounded scandalized by the thought of her bags sitting outside, as if Renforth Abbey were some common rooming house. "If I may ask you to wait a moment…"

Leah waved him away. "Do not trouble yourself about me, sir."

The moment he was out of sight, she headed up the stairs. As she'd expected, there were plenty of servants going quietly about their work from whom she was able to ask directions.

At last she located the nursery and marched in. After one look, she nearly turned around and walked out again. Surely this magnificent room could not be the nursery—even if it belonged to the heir to a dukedom. The massive bed was nearly as large as some rooms Leah had occupied in the past. The hearth was equally imposing and looked to be made of marble. The walls were hung with tapestries showing fantastical beasts and birds, though they were not easy to see in the dimness. The thick curtains that draped the windows did a thorough job of keeping out the summer sunshine.

"Is that you, Papa?" A small voice emerged from within the cavernous bed. "Is my rest time over yet? I hope so, because I haven't slept a wink."

The child's words woke a housemaid who had been dozing in a chair near the bed. "What is it, Master Kit? Can I fetch you something?"

The girl sprang up when she spied Leah. "Who are you, miss, and what are you doing here?"

"I am his lordship's new governess." Leah twitched the window curtains open. "And I have come to meet my pupil. I'm dreadfully hungry after my journey. Would you be so kind as to fetch me something to eat?"

The girl blinked rapidly as if wondering whether she might be only dreaming Leah's sudden arrival. Then her training took over and she bobbed a curtsey. "Yes, miss. Right away."

"Governess?" piped the small, clear voice from the bed. "What is a governess? Tilly, if you're fetching biscuits, I want one, too."

"Yes, Master Kit," called the maid as she rushed away.

Leah dropped her bonnet and gloves on the nearest chair.

"*I* am a governess." She pulled back the bed curtains so she could get a look at her new pupil. "*Your* governess. A governess is a lady who teaches children in their homes. My name is Leah Shaw. You may call me Miss Shaw or Miss Leah if you prefer."

She smiled down at the boy who lay in the bed. His hair was dark and close-cropped. She had been told he was almost eight years old. Though he appeared smaller than most boys of that age, his thin face and the dusky shadows beneath his blue-gray eyes made him look older than his years, until he smiled back at her. There was such a winsome air about that expression, it immediately dispelled her doubts about accepting this position.

"Welcome to Renforth Abbey, Miss Leah." The boy greeted her with quaint formality for his age. "I am Christopher Latimer, Lord Renforth. But everybody except Dr. Bannister calls me Master Kit. I wonder why nobody told me I am to have a governess. Perhaps they thought it would excite me. Dr. Bannister says it is not good for me to get excited."

"Nonsense!" Leah did not care for the sound of Dr. Bannister. She had rebelled against too many people like him over the years. "A little excitement now and then never hurt anybody."

No wonder the poor child looked so pale and peaked—trapped in this room with nothing to do but lie about and be tyrannized by a repressive old physician.

Kit's smile widened and a silvery twinkle kindled in his eyes. "Do you mean it?"

Leah gave a vigorous nod. "For a start, let's get you out of that bed. It is a fine day outside, one of the nicest we've had all summer. Would you like to see?"

"I would." Kit sighed. "But I cannot walk. There is something the matter with my legs—they are very stiff and will not bear my weight."

"I know." Leah tried not to make too great a matter of his difficulty. "But your arms work well enough, don't they?"

When Kit nodded, she twitched back the covers and lifted him to the edge of the bed. "I can carry you on my back if you put your arms around my neck and hang on tight."

"I can do that," said Kit, latching on to her.

"Very good." Leah brought his stiff, thin legs out on either side of her waist, hooking her arms around them for additional support. "Are you ready for your ride?"

Kit chuckled. "Let's go."

As she got to her feet, Leah was surprised by the child's light weight. It took almost no effort for her to whisk him over to the windows.

The view from there was splendid indeed. Wide terraces planted with a vivid array of flowers lined the gentle slope that tapered down to a lush green lawn in front of the great house. A pair of ornamental lakes spread on either side of the wide, smooth lane. A picturesque stone bridge spanned the narrow stream that ran between them. An elegant folly crowned the top of a low hill that overlooked one of the lakes. Leah had worked in some fine houses before but none could begin to compare with this.

"The sky is so big and blue." Kit sounded delighted by the simple act of looking out a window. "The flowers are very pretty. I have never seen so many at once. Mostly I only see a few in a vase."

The child's reaction convinced Leah this must be the first time he had been allowed to look out his window. The repression she had suffered at the Pendergast School was nothing compared to that!

They talked for a while about the things they could see but eventually Leah's arms grew tired. "I believe it is time I got you back to bed."

"Oh, no, please," Kit begged. "Let me stay a little longer."

Leah had handled enough children over the years to

have learned a trick or two about getting them to cease an activity they were enjoying. "Shall we pretend you are a cavalry officer and I am your horse? Perhaps you are riding back to your tent after a long day scouting. Does that sound like fun?"

She started toward the bed with a trotting step and gave a rather good imitation of a horse's whinny.

Kit chuckled, his reluctance apparently overcome as Leah had hoped. "I shall call you Shawberry. Do you like that name?"

"I do. It is very clever. You can say giddyap to make me go faster or whoa to make me stop. But do not strike me with your whip or I might rear up and throw you."

As she spoke, Leah heard the nursery door open. It must be the maid bringing refreshments. That should encourage Kit to leave off their riding game without a fuss.

She did not expect a harsh voice to crack through the air like a lash. "What are you doing with my son? Get him back to bed this instant!"

The shock of that unexpected sound made Leah start and lose her balance. As she began to topple, a wave of panic engulfed her. What if she landed on top of this fragile child and injured him worse than he was already?

A blaze of protective anger seared through Hayden Latimer when he spied a strange woman prancing about the nursery with his son clinging to her back.

Who on earth was she and what did she want? She had bluffed her way into his house by pretending she'd been engaged as Kit's governess. But that was a wicked lie.

When he heard her threaten to throw the child, paternal instinct overcame his manners.

He moved toward her just as disaster struck. The woman reared like a real horse that had been reined in too hard. She lost her balance and fell backward.

Hayden lunged forward, catching her and Kit before they hit the floor. A wave of relief crashed over him when he realized he had averted one of his most feared calamities. But it did not quench his dread of what could have happened or his rage at the person who had put his son at risk. He despised the flicker of satisfaction it brought him to have his arms around a woman again after so many years. He had no business thinking of *anything* but keeping Kit safe.

Resisting the odious urge to linger near her, Hayden wrenched his son away and cradled the child in his arms. "Do you hurt anywhere, Kit? What did this woman do? Did she frighten you?"

Before his son could answer, the woman spun around to confront Hayden. "I could not have frightened him half as much as you did with your shouting. And I would not have lost my balance if you hadn't startled me."

In a grudging tone she added, "I *am* grateful to you for catching us, though."

As Hayden bore Kit back to the safety of his bed, the woman straightened up and smoothed out her skirts. They were white, sprigged with pale green that matched her fitted spencer. Her rich, dark brown hair was gathered in a wild cascade of curls, some of which had come loose when she had fallen. With a traitorous pang, Hayden noticed she was quite pretty, in a lively, vibrant way he wished he did not find so appealing.

Her accusation unsettled him nearly as much as her appearance. Had *his* actions placed his son in jeopardy? His conscience forced him to admit it was possible.

Guilt made him defensive. "How else was I supposed to react when I found a strange woman in my son's nursery, cavorting with him in such a dangerous manner?"

The poor little fellow was clearly shaken by the experience. His eyes, so much like Celia's, looked larger than ever and his pale cheeks were flushed. His thin chest rose and fell rapidly beneath his nightshirt.

"Please, Papa." The child shrank from him when Hayden ruffled his hair in a reassuring caress. "Don't be angry with us. Miss Leah only wanted to show me how fine a day it is outside."

"You see?" The woman's tone roused Hayden's antagonism. "*I* am not responsible for frightening him. The two of us were enjoying a pleasant time until you barged in, snapping and snarling. Don't fret, Kit. Your father is not vexed with *you*."

The gall of her! Offering his son words of comfort as if there could be any possibility his anger was directed at the child.

"Of course I'm not angry with *you,* Kit." He tucked the bedclothes around the child. "I was only worried that some harm might come to you, as it nearly did.

And I was shocked to find a stranger here with you instead of Tilly."

"Miss Leah isn't a stranger," Kit protested. "She is my new governess. She's going to teach me here at home because I cannot go to school."

The note of eagerness in his son's voice struck Hayden a blow. Even if the child were strong enough to undertake a course of study, this woman possessed none of the qualities he would require in a governess.

"We'll see." Hayden knew better than to deny Kit any odd thing that took his fancy. The child had inherited a measure of his late mother's willfulness and could make himself ill with fretting when thwarted.

Hayden had received enough warnings from the doctor about keeping his son calm and quiet. Over the years he had learned to delay giving an answer until Kit forgot his request. Now, much as he wanted to insist that pigs would fly before he allowed this heedless creature to teach his invalid child, he resorted to the usual evasions.

"*Miss Leah* and I should talk it over." It felt odd to refer to this odious stranger in such a familiar way—sweet and sour at the same time. "Did you get any sleep while I was away meeting with Mr. Forster?"

Kit shook his head. "I wasn't tired. The time dragged until Miss Leah came."

"Then perhaps you should try to sleep now," Hayden suggested, "while I talk to...her. By the way, where *is* Tilly?"

What had possessed the nursemaid to desert her post at such a time?

"She went to get us some biscuits," replied Kit. "We were hungry."

"*You* were hungry?" Hayden doubted that. His son never had much appetite. It took every ounce of persuasion he could muster to get the child to swallow a few spoonfuls of broth or porridge.

"Only a little," Kit admitted. "But I wanted to keep Miss Leah company and she is hungry after her long drive. Perhaps I should go for a drive so I will be hungry, too."

A *drive?* This fragile child jolted about in a carriage pulled by large temperamental horses that might bolt without warning? The mere thought gave Hayden chills. This woman was filling his son's head with all manner of dangerous fancies. He must get her away from Kit before she suggested the boy should slide down the staircase on the butler's tray!

Just then Tilly returned with the refreshments she'd gone to fetch. Hayden supposed he could not blame the girl for being caught off guard by the stranger's sudden appearance and taken in by her flagrant deception. He would have a word with her later and make it clear she was not to leave Kit alone after this, except on his express orders.

"Tilly, I need you to sit with my son for a bit longer. He may have something to eat if he wishes, though nothing that will upset his digestion. Meanwhile I shall take this lady away for a private…chat."

He scowled at the interloper and gave a curt nod toward the door. She had the temerity to smile at him, her hazel eyes dancing.

As he strode toward the door, Hayden heard Tilly ask what Kit would like to eat.

"Nothing for now." The boy sounded far too cheerful to suit his father. "I shall wait for Miss Leah to come back. Then we can eat together."

His son would have a very long wait, Hayden reflected as he held open the nursery door for the woman who had thrown his calm, orderly household into turmoil. He intended to send her packing, with a warning never to darken the threshold of Renforth Abbey again!

Her introduction to the duke could have gone better, Leah admitted to herself as he hustled her out of his son's nursery.

It was a shame such a handsome man should spoil his looks with that severe expression. He acted as if he had caught her trying to murder his son rather than giving the poor child a much-needed taste of freedom. True, her efforts might have had unfortunate consequences, but everything had turned out well in the end. Why fret about all the terrible things that *might* come to pass if they never did?

"This way." The duke's tone was nearly as stiff as his posture as he strode down the wide, paneled corridor, clearly expecting her to follow.

He cut a fine figure, tall and spare with broad shoulders. Leah tried to dismiss the unsettling sensation that had come over her when he caught her and Kit. The first grasp of his arms had conveyed dependable strength with gentle protectiveness. For as long as she could recall, Leah had made her own way in the world and treasured her independence. But for that fleeting instant, she'd relished the sensation of having someone to lean on.

Of course, the duke had spoiled it the very next moment by tearing his son away and blaming her for what had happened, when it was at least as much his fault. His ungracious behavior reminded her that having someone to rely on often came at a cost of rules and restrictions she could not abide. No doubt she was about to learn the rules of Renforth Abbey straight from its formidable master.

"Is it much farther, Your Grace?" she inquired as she trailed him down the broad staircase. "As Kit mentioned, I am rather hungry. A truly gracious employer would have invited his son's new governess to eat before dragging her away to discuss her duties."

The duke halted at the foot of the stairs and turned on her so swiftly that she barely managed to keep from bumping into him. As it was, she teetered on the second last step, precisely at eye level with His Grace.

At that intimate distance, she was struck by the color of his eyes. His incisive blue gaze seemed to pierce the armor of her bravado and see her more clearly than she cared to be seen. There was something else about his eyes that unsettled her. Dusky shadows beneath them and crinkled lines radiating from the corners made him look tired, as if he had not enjoyed a truly restful sleep in years.

That thought provoked Leah's sympathy, something she did not want to feel for a man who clearly regarded her with loathing.

"You may dispense with the deception, Miss… whatever your real name is. You might have succeeded in fooling my butler, the nursemaid and my son, but *I* would certainly remember if I had engaged a governess for Kit. I have done nothing of the kind, nor do I intend to. I cannot fathom your motives in coming to Renforth Abbey but I am certain they cannot be good."

How could he say such insulting things while looking so vexingly attractive? Leah considered that most unfair. The duke's chestnut-brown hair was clipped short, like his son's, perhaps to keep it from ever appearing untidy. His jutting nose and the crisp line of his jaw gave his face a severe look. The generous fullness of his lower lip contrasted with that, as did his mobile brows and high forehead, which seemed inclined to settle into lines of bewilderment or worry. The combined effect was altogether too compelling to suit Leah. She did not want to feel even a flicker of admiration for such a harsh, repressive man.

"My real name is the one I told everyone I've met so far at Renforth Abbey—Leah Shaw." She exaggerated the pronunciation. "I have done nothing to deceive anyone. You may not recall hiring a governess for your son, but have you forgotten asking your sister to find a suitable person to instruct him and supervise his care? I am surprised Lady Althea did not write to inform you when I would be arriving. I assumed she had."

"Althea?" The duke's eyes widened and he took a half step back, as if Leah had pushed him. "My sister sent you here?"

"Is that not what I said?" It was difficult to stay

vexed with the duke when he appeared so confused. "Perhaps you remember now. Things sometimes slip my mind, too, though not often anything this important. My previous employer recommended me to Lady Althea. She thought I would do very well for your son. Having met Kit, I agree he needs someone like me… in the beginning at least. As I told your sister, I do not care to remain in one position for more than a year. I hope that will not be a problem."

"Not in the least." The duke made an obvious effort to marshal his composure. "But there has been a misunderstanding. I apologize for accusing you of deliberate deception. Once you have learned the circumstances, I believe you will agree I had grounds for suspicion. When it comes to the safety of my son, I cannot be too careful."

He drew back, giving Leah room to descend the last two stairs. She rather wished he had not, for it meant he towered over her again…not that she was the least bit intimidated. "That was a very lukewarm apology, considering the dreadful things of which you accused me. What is this *misunderstanding* you feel excuses your incivility?"

Clearly the duke was not accustomed to having his conduct questioned. No doubt his word was law at Renforth Abbey and he was free to treat his servants as he wished. Moving from one position to another so often, Leah had learned not to put up with such nonsense from her employers. Once she made that clear, she seldom had any further trouble. For his son's sake, she hoped the Duke of Northam would be equally sensible.

He seemed to debate whether to rebuke her for addressing him as she had, but decided against it. Instead, he began to walk down the ground floor corridor. This time he did not stalk off and expect her to follow, but strolled by her side like an escort. "Perhaps I deserve that, Miss Shaw. But what was I to think when I knew neither of your coming nor that my sister had engaged your services? If she told you she was acting on my behalf then it was *she* who deceived *you*."

Now it was Leah's turn to be taken aback. Was it possible she had misunderstood Lady Althea?

The duke paused before a set of elaborate double doors. "Let us continue our discussion in the privacy of my library."

He opened one door and ushered her in. Leah stifled a gasp at the magnificence of the room. Everywhere she looked were vast shelves, some built into the walls, others jutting out to create interesting alcoves. All were filled with a fortune in finely bound volumes. Her friend Marian would be in her glory with such a library at her disposal!

Leah expected the duke to invite her to sit in one of the handsomely upholstered chairs grouped around the room. Having been told she was hungry, perhaps he might ring for tea. Instead he strode to a substantial writing table and stood behind it.

Planting the tips of his fingers on the edge of the tabletop, he fixed her with an icy-blue gaze, which reminded her of the most tyrannical of her teachers at the Pendergast School. "Let us get one thing clear, Miss Shaw. I did *not* authorize my sister to find a governess for Kit. She told me that was what I should do. When I refused, she must have taken matters into her own hands."

Leah cringed to reflect upon her earlier actions—barging into Renforth Abbey, ordering the servants about. More importantly, she wondered what would become of that poor child if he was not to have a governess. Now that she had met Kit, she was more anxious than ever to teach him.

Until recently Leah's vocation had been a means to fund her plans for the future. Having been left a small inheritance, she did not have the same concerns as her friends about saving every penny to support herself when she could no longer work. If she chose, she could afford to take a lease on a cottage in the country, hire a widowed companion for the sake of propriety and live a retiring life. But that prospect did not appeal to her in the least.

Instead she preferred taking temporary teaching positions, which gave her the opportunity to see new places and meet new people while saving money toward her dream—a tour of the Continent. The salary she'd been offered for this position would have made it possible for her to go abroad far sooner.

But it was not the thought of her plans being dashed that dismayed her at the moment. If the duke meant to send her away, she had nothing to lose by speaking her mind. She strode to the writing table and planted her hands on the opposite side, mirroring his stance. "I happen to agree with Lady Althea, sir. It is clear your son wants and needs a governess. Since I have come all this way, why not let me stay for a while, on trial, and see how it works out?"

"Stay?" The duke's fingers pressed hard upon the writing table. "Out of the question! I am quite capable of providing my son with the care he needs. I see now why my sister sent you here. She thought once you got your foot in the door, I would not be able to send you away. Let me assure you, she was mistaken."

When he drew a deep breath to continue, Leah seized the opportunity to get a word in. "Don't be ridiculous! I have no intention of staying where I am not wanted. But what could it hurt to do what I have proposed?"

What could it hurt? If the matter had not posed such a threat to his son, Hayden might have laughed at Leah Shaw's preposterous question. He scarcely knew where to begin to enumerate the possible consequences.

At the same time he could not dismiss his suspicion as to why Althea had selected this particular woman. His sister must have thought he would fall under the sway of Leah Shaw's lively beauty and want to keep her at Renforth Abbey under any circumstances.

As he stared across the table at her, Hayden could not stifle a pang of impatience with himself. This was the first time in years that he had been so conscious of a woman's appearance. Leah Shaw's fine dark brows were mobile and expressive, reflecting her changing mood in the blink of an eye. Her lips had a similar mercurial quality, though he sensed their most frequent expression was a winsome smile.

Reminding himself it was not her fault he found her attractive, he strove to moderate his tone. "Miss Shaw, I regret that our acquaintance began with such an unfortunate misunderstanding, entirely the fault of my meddling sister. Althea has been trying to run my life ever since our nursery days. She had no business sending you here without my approval, but you are not to blame for that. Nonetheless, I know what is best for my son. As you have seen, his needs are different from those of other children you may have taught. His health and well-being are my primary concerns. I fear his constitution is too delicate to allow him to undertake a rigorous course of study."

"Nonsense!" she snapped. "The right sort of teaching need not tax Kit's constitution. On the contrary, it would provide him with some much-needed diversion. From what I have seen, the worst threat your son faces is being bored to death under your stifling regime."

What had made him suppose this woman could be reasoned with? No one who would romp about with a frail, disabled child on her back could have any sense worth appealing to. Hayden knew some people, women especially, were motivated by impulse and emotion rather than good judgment. Such people were a danger to themselves and everyone around them. He had seen proof that Leah Shaw was one of those people.

"*I* will decide what is best for my son!" He was not accustomed to being put in his place with such insolence. "Not my sister and certainly not a stranger who never set eyes on Kit until an hour ago."

When she tried to interrupt, he silenced her with a stern glare. "It is too late in the day for you to leave Renforth, so I will order a room prepared for you. I also intend to pay you half of whatever annual salary my sister promised. That should keep you until you secure a new position."

"That is generous of you sir, but—"

"I offer this settlement on the condition that you leave Renforth Abbey tomorrow morning without any further fuss and never return. Is that clear?"

"Perfectly clear. However, my silence is not for sale at any price. I appreciate your civility in offering me a bed for the night, but I refuse to look the other way when I am certain you are making a grave mistake, for which your son will pay."

Her reply left Hayden momentarily speechless. It had never occurred to him that Leah Shaw might reject his offer. Though it vexed him to be thwarted, he could not stifle a flicker of admiration for this infuriating woman that had nothing to do with her attractive looks. In spite of her brief acquaintance with Kit, she must care a great deal about his welfare or she would not decline such handsome compensation.

How could he fault her for that? Yet he dared not follow the perilous course she proposed. Years of caution argued strenuously against it.

"I understand your concern for your son's well-being." Leah Shaw continued, clearly determined to have her say, for which she would pay such a high price. "And I commend you for it. But is it necessary to keep your child alive by depriving him of everything that makes life *worth* living? Has he ever looked out that window before today? Has he ever been allowed to leave the confines of that bed, or is it a splendid prison cell?"

Her impassioned words went far beyond mere impertinence. They verged on brutality. Every one struck Hayden a painful blow. But when he tried to rally his defenses and strike back, a traitorous part of him inquired whether some of what was said might be true.

"If I were obliged to endure such a solitary, monotonous existence…" her voice faltered "…I would go mad. I beg you, sir, if you do not consider me suitable, hire someone else to be Kit's governess. But do not permit your dislike of me to deprive your son of the joy of learning!"

He did not *dis*like her. Hayden bit down hard on his tongue to keep from admitting it. The trouble was, he could easily come to like her *too* well. From there it would be but a short, treacherous step to caring about her opinion of him. That was a weakness he could not afford with his son's welfare at stake.

"I have heard quite enough!" He cut her off with a slashing motion of his hand. "If you will not accept the compensation I have offered, that is your choice, Miss Shaw. But I will not risk my son's health on the advice of someone who knows so little of Kit's situation. Contrary to what you may believe, I love my son with all my heart and I am confident I know what is best for him. Nothing you can say will alter that. Good day and farewell to you!"

With that, he turned on his heel and stalked out of the library, torn between relief and regret that he would never set eyes on Leah Shaw again.

Chapter Two

That infuriating man!

As Leah watched the duke march out of the library, she found herself torn between acute frustration and intense relief. How could he not understand the intolerable conditions to which he was subjecting his young son? It reminded her of her blighted youth at the Pendergast School—the dank, dark rooms, the stultifying routine and stifling conformity. She had rebelled against it by every means she could devise, outrageous humor being the most effective weapon in her arsenal.

If only His Grace would give her a chance, she was confident she could brighten Kit's life and broaden his horizons, which were even more severely restricted than hers had once been. At least she'd had the stimulation of her studies and the companionship of her friends.

Yet much as she wanted to stay at Renforth Abbey for Kit's sake, Leah would not be sorry to escape having to deal with his imperious father. Though she had been impressed by the duke's offer of such liberal compensation, she resented his assumption that she could be bribed into silence over something as vital as the welfare of his child. Since leaving that wretched school, she had never encountered such a stubborn, shortsighted despot!

Scarcely aware of what she was doing, Leah began to rub the palms of her hands against her skirts. No indeed, she did not relish the prospect of constant battles she would have to wage with Lord Northam to get him to ease the restrictions on his son. And yet, she could not deny something about their verbal sparring had stimulated her.

"I beg your pardon, Miss Shaw." The butler's voice jolted Leah from her silent fuming. "His Grace informs me you will be staying the night at Renforth. He requested I provide you with tea. Would you care to take it here, or in one of the sitting rooms?"

How many sitting rooms did this house have?

"Here in the library will do very well, thank you, Mr. Gibson." Leah tried not to let her annoyance with his master affect her courtesy toward the butler.

"As you wish. If you would care to take a seat, I shall return shortly."

So the duke had paid attention when she told him she was hungry. Leah considered his unexpected gesture of hospitality as she took a moment to appreciate the muted grandeur of her surroundings. Above the lofty bookshelves hung centuries-old portraits in gilt frames. A collection of delicate Oriental vases lined the mantelpiece while a finely crafted table globe stood nearby. Three groups of chairs and sofas occupied different areas of the room without appearing crowded in the least.

After a good look around, Leah took a seat on one of the brocade armchairs clustered around a low table near a tall bank of windows. She had scarcely gotten settled before the butler reappeared, bearing a tea tray.

"I am sorry to hear you were mistaken in thinking you had been engaged as a governess for the young master." The butler sounded sincerely sympathetic as he offered Leah a bounty of sandwiches, biscuits and cakes that made her mouth water.

"You cannot be half as sorry as I am." She heaped her plate. "For the boy's sake, more than mine. I cannot imagine how the poor child bears it, being confined to that bed day after day. How can his father do that to him?"

"I beg your pardon, Miss." The butler glared down at her. "But you would be wrong to presume His Grace's actions arise from anything less than the tenderest devotion to his son. He scarcely leaves the young master's side except to snatch a few hours' sleep and to attend to the most pressing business of the estate. He spends hour upon hour reading to the boy and amusing him by every means he can contrive."

The bite of buttery biscuit in Leah's mouth suddenly lost its flavor, as she chided herself for her harsh rush to judgment. She of all people should understand the willingness to surrender all one's time and energy in the service of a loved one. But she had done everything in her power to *preserve* her grandmother's independence, Leah's conscience protested. She would never have locked Gran away from the world, no matter how much safer that might have been.

"Do you not think the child would benefit from exposure to more varied society and the opportunity to learn?" she asked as much to soothe her self-reproach as anything. "His legs may not be capable of taking him places other children can go, but surely his mind should be allowed to range freely and undertake challenges."

"There are some in His Grace's household who would agree with you." The butler's solemn expression made it impossible to guess whether he might be among that number. "Certainly Lady Althea has expressed that opinion often."

"Why does her brother refuse to heed her?" Leah thought she might know the answer even before the butler replied.

The duke's sister had a very forceful personality and she was clearly accustomed to getting her way by whatever means necessary. Leah resented the way she had been misled and manipulated by her ladyship. Whatever the duke's faults, at least he was forthright in his opposition.

"Her ladyship was not here the night her nephew was born." The compulsion to defend his master seemed to get the better of Mr. Gibson's discretion. "The midwife thought the child was stillborn. But His Grace insisted every possible effort be made to revive his son. He was warned that even if they succeeded, the child might be weak, perhaps a lifelong invalid. His Grace paid them no heed. He has nursed his son through several bouts of illness over the years. He has devoted his life to the child. I believe that gives him the right to decide what is best for his son."

"I have no doubt His Grace is acting out of concern." Leah could not stifle a flicker of admiration for the duke. "But I am still convinced he is wrong in this instance."

The butler looked as if he would have liked to debate the matter further, but realized he had already revealed too much about his master's private business. "If you do not require anything more, I shall leave you to enjoy your tea, Miss Shaw. Then I will show you to your room."

After Mr. Gibson had gone, Leah started on her tea. She found her appetite rather blunted by what the butler had told her about Lord Northam and his son. Given their history, perhaps it was not surprising the duke had reacted excessively to her actions in the nursery. If she had not been so impulsive, might His Grace have been more receptive to the possibility of hiring a governess for his son?

By the time the butler returned, Leah's hunger was appeased but not her conscience. She refrained from making any more critical remarks about the duke as Mr. Gibson led her past many enormous, handsomely decorated rooms. They ascended a different staircase than the one Leah had taken to reach the nursery.

"This will be your room for the night, Miss Shaw," the butler announced as he opened a door and ushered her in. "I trust you will find it to your satisfaction. Dinner will be served at eight."

For a moment Leah was too awestruck to reply. She was accustomed to staying in plain, cramped little rooms near the nursery. This airy, elegant chamber, decorated in shades of cream and coral, looked more suited to a princess than a humble governess.

"Will His Grace be dining with me?" She would welcome the opportunity to apologize for not being more careful with his son.

The butler shook his head in a decisive manner that sank her hopes. "His Grace eats in the nursery with his son."

"Of course." Leah experienced a sharper stab of disappointment at the news than it merited. "In that case, you need not trouble your staff on my account. I am quite content to take a tray in my room."

"It will be no trouble," Mr. Gibson insisted. "The staff will enjoy an opportunity to prepare and serve a proper meal."

"Very well, then. If you are certain." Leah glanced toward the window. "Since I will not be staying on at Renforth Abbey, might I look around the house before dinner? I have never visited a place so fine."

"If you wish." The butler sounded uncertain whether to treat her as an honored guest or a glorified servant who had just been dismissed.

"I promise I will stay out of the duke's way," Leah assured him.

"That should not be difficult," the butler replied, "provided you keep away from the new range, which houses the nursery and His Grace's bedchamber."

"Does he truly spend *all* his time there?" The very

thought made Leah feel as if the walls of this spacious room were beginning to close in on her.

The butler nodded. "Except for meetings with the estate overseer and his man of business. And on rare occasions when Lady Althea pays a visit."

"Poor man." The words rose instinctively to Leah's lips, though she reminded herself it was the duke's choice to live that way.

After Mr. Gibson departed, she set off to explore the house. As she strolled from one grand room to another, all so rich in history, Leah found herself with many questions she wished she could ask someone. Which artist had painted the imposing portrait of a gentleman on horseback that hung above the mantel in the blue drawing room? What was the story behind the magnificent tapestries in the great hall? Had the house originally been a monastery as its name suggested?

Finally, eager for a breath of fresh air, she took a stroll in the gardens. The mingled scents of many different flowers perfumed the summer dusk. Looking back at the house, she glimpsed the duke staring down at her from one of the upper windows.

"Can you not see?" she whispered, wishing that he could hear her. "*You* are as much a prisoner of that gilded cell as your poor child?"

When was the last time he had indulged in the simple pleasure of a walk in his own garden?

As Hayden watched Miss Shaw stroll among the shrubberies and flower beds, he tried to recall the smell of the air on such an evening and the high-pitched chorus the frogs sang from their lily pads on the ornamental lakes. Those gardens belonged to him and yet they might as well have been as distant as the moon for all the opportunity he had to enjoy them.

That was *his* choice, the strong voice of parental responsibility reminded him. He had a duty to the child he had helped bring into this world, a child who had not asked to be born frail and motherless. A son who needed him in a way few children needed their fathers.

On the day of Kit's birth, he had made his son a promise, and he was more committed than ever to keeping it. The loss of a little freedom was a small price to pay. At least he had his liberty to lose. It was a luxury his son would never know. One he could not afford if he was to survive.

"What are you looking at, Papa?" asked Kit in a tone that sounded both plaintive and petulant.

"Nothing in particular." It troubled Hayden to give his son a less than honest answer. But he feared any mention of Miss Shaw would only upset the child, and she had done enough of that already. "Shall I read you another story? Or shall we play with your little people?"

Kit shook his head. "I want to look out the window again. Miss Leah let me. She pretended she was my horse. She carried me over so I could see the garden."

"She almost fell while carrying you." Hayden's annoyance with the woman sharpened his tone. "You might have been badly injured if I had not caught you. There is nothing much to see out this window, especially now that it is growing dark."

He jerked the curtains closed.

Was he wrong to have denied his son a glimpse of the grounds and gardens? Hayden tried to stifle a pang of conscience. The doctor had insisted it was better if the child did not see what lay beyond the safe boundaries of his nursery. It might only promote dangerous discontent, making Kit yearn for liberties that could pose a danger to his fragile health. How could he reject the counsel of a man to whom he owed Kit's life?

Hayden had never questioned the wisdom of his decision, until Leah Shaw came barging in, flinging about words like *solitary, monotonous* and *stifling.* He told himself the woman meant well, she simply did not understand the seriousness of his son's condition.

"Will you take me to the window tomorrow morning, when it is light again?" Kit pleaded. "You are bigger and stronger than Miss Leah. You will not let me fall."

"We will see about that tomorrow," replied Hayden as he strode back to his son's bed.

"No, you won't." Kit pouted. "You never do when you say that. When is Miss Leah coming back? I like her. She is going to be my governess and teach me lots of new things."

Why had she blurted all that out to his son? Hayden silently fumed until his sense of fairness intervened. Why should Miss Shaw have kept quiet about something she believed to be true? Still, he wished she had shown a little more discretion. Now he would be obliged to inform his son it had all been a misunderstanding.

He tried to break the truth to Kit gently. "That has not been decided for certain. I fear you are not yet strong enough to study with a governess. It can be difficult and tiring. Wouldn't you rather listen to stories and play games with me?"

The child thought for a moment. "Couldn't I do both? I could study with Miss Leah until I grow tired then you could read to me while I rest."

Kit's pale little face seemed to glow with satisfaction that he had come up with such a clever plan on his own. Hayden's sense of fairness urged him to admit it sounded like a good compromise. But life was not fair and fate was not fair. Hayden barely managed to stop short of thinking God was not fair.

He did not blame the Almighty for what had happened to Celia and his son. That had been *his* fault for not protecting his wife from her own impulsive nature. If he had kept her from traveling when she was so close to her confinement, she might not have gone into early labor. She might have survived Kit's birth and his son would likely have been born healthy.

After all that he did not deserve Divine mercy, yet the Lord had heeded his desperate prayer and spared his infant son. As the parent of an ailing child, Hayden had come to rely more than ever upon the strength of *his* Heavenly Father. Now he lifted a silent prayer for reassurance that he was doing the right thing and inspiration for the proper words to explain his decision.

Kit seemed to attribute his father's hesitation to a different cause. "Do you think I am not clever enough to learn from Miss Leah? Just because my legs don't work properly, do you think my mind is weak, as well?"

"Kit, how can you say that?" Hayden groped for his son's hand. "I think no such thing! It is obvious you are very bright for your age."

He strove to infuse his words with the force of certainty. If he did not fully succeed, it was only because there had been a time when no one could assure him what his son's mental capacity might be. Though he would have loved Kit no less, he had been overjoyed for the child's sake when he began to speak at an early age and otherwise demonstrate that his wits were not impaired.

"You don't mean that!" Kit pulled his hand away from his father's and shrank from him in a way that tore at Hayden's heart. "You think I'm like Elsie who works in the scullery. I hear the servants talk about her. They say she walks with a limp and she's slow-witted. They laugh about the mistakes she makes."

Outrage roared through Hayden, setting his face on fire...or so it felt. "No one should laugh at the girl or treat her unkindly. Nor will they under my roof if they wish to remain here, I will see to that! If she cannot walk or reason as well as they, all the more reason they should treat her with kindness."

He knew how cruel people could be to anyone with a weakness. He never wanted his son hurt by that kind of mockery. He would speak to Gibson at once and make certain his instructions were clear. "But Elsie's troubles have nothing to do with my reluctance to have Miss Shaw as your governess."

"What is it, then?" Kit sounded as if he doubted his father would tell him the truth. "Don't you like her?"

"Not especially." The words rose to Hayden's lips by a kind of defensive instinct he did not fully understand. Yet they tingled upon his tongue with a sour tang of untruth. The fact was he found Leah Shaw far too engaging, when she was not challenging his judgment. "What I mean is, I am not certain she is the right sort of person to have in charge of you. She lacks the proper sense of caution, for one thing."

He could not afford any partiality toward a person who opposed his manner of raising his son. He knew Miss Shaw meant well, as did his sister. They simply could not understand how much Kit meant to him. Not having children of their own, they had never experienced how a tiny hand could hold a parent's heart or how much stronger that bond grew the more a child depended upon its parent.

In spite of all that, Hayden could not entirely disregard the things Leah Shaw had said. Was Kit's safe, quiet life a kind of imprisonment?

"I don't care!" The child's defiant tone troubled Hayden. "I like Miss Leah and I want her to stay. She makes me smile and forget I don't feel well."

The lady had made *him* forget his troubles, too, Hayden was forced to admit. Even when they argued it had made him feel more truly alive than he had in quite some time.

But how could he allow her into his home and into his son's life? Until now he had been able to control Kit's small world to make it a place of comfort, safety and acceptance. Leah Shaw would be a disruptive influence. Already she had introduced an element of dangerous discontent into Kit's relationship with him that might smolder into outright rebellion if he did not quench it at once.

"Miss Shaw came to Renforth by mistake." He set about patiently trying to explain to Kit how his Aunt Althea had hired the lady without consulting him.

When he reminded his son of the harm she could have caused by carrying him to the window, Kit refused to listen. "Even if I fell and got hurt it would have been worth it to see the grass and the flowers and move about out of bed!"

The last words came out in a sob, which set him coughing. It chilled Hayden to the depths of his heart to see his son's thin shoulders heave beneath his nightshirt. Leah Shaw had caused this, he fumed as he strove to quiet the child.

He rejected the cruel irony that she might be the only remedy.

"Hush, now, hush." He stroked Kit's dark hair. "Perhaps I can speak to Miss Shaw to see if she would be willing to stay for a little while."

The son's coughing began to ease. "Do you… promise?"

He'd only meant to divert the child as he had so often before, but what could he say that would not provoke a worse coughing fit? "I promise, though I would not be surprised if she refuses. I am not certain she thinks any better of me than I do of her."

Kit immediately began to breathe easier. His face

lit up with the brightest smile Hayden had seen from him in a very long time.

"She will stay. I know she will," the boy announced with happy certainty his father did not share.

She had always preferred temporary positions to longer ones, Leah reflected the next morning as she drove away from Renforth Abbey. But staying less than twenty-four hours was by far her shortest.

It could also have been her most lucrative position yet, if she had accepted the duke's offer. Since it had been clear nothing she said would change his mind about hiring her, why could she not have saved her breath and taken what he had been prepared to give her?

"I do *not* regret rejecting his insulting offer!" she muttered out loud, the better to convince herself.

She hoped her refusal had convinced the duke she was not speaking from motives of self-interest. She truly believed Kit needed someone to teach him, to amuse him and to advocate for him with his overprotective father. The boy needed someone who would treat him as a *child* rather than an object of pity.

Peering out the carriage window, Leah took her final glimpse of Renforth Abbey and sent a dark scowl in the direction of the new range. Was His Grace standing at one of the windows this very moment, watching with an air of gloating triumph as his carriage whisked her out of his son's life?

Where would she go once she reached the village? Leah wondered as the trees closed in on either side of the lane, blocking any further view of the great house. She knew any of her friends would be happy to extend her their hospitality until she found a new position. But she hated to impose on them. Hannah and Lord Hawkehurst would still be on their honeymoon. Marian would be occupied with her precious baby while Rebecca and Grace were both expecting. Besides, Leah feared they would try to persuade her to change her mind about helping Evangeline set up their school.

It would be better if she went to London and found temporary lodgings. From there she could write to her previous employers, inquiring if they knew of a family looking for a governess. All that would take time, though—time with no money coming in, only bleeding out of her savings, pushing her travel plans further and further into the future. For a moment Leah's natural optimism deserted her. She leaned back in the handsomely upholstered seat in the duke's fine carriage and heaved a sigh.

But no sooner had it left her lips than she heard the muted thunder of galloping hooves and caught a fleeting glimpse of a horseman overtaking the carriage. Immediately, the vehicle began to slow and finally came to a halt. Leah was about to open the carriage door to ask what was going on when it flew open and the Duke of Northam climbed in.

The poor man was the picture of exhaustion. In spite of her annoyance with him, Leah could not stifle a pang of sympathy. His eyes were bloodshot, and the dusky smudges beneath them darker than yesterday. His face was unshaven, the dark stubble further accentuating his pallor. Strangely, it made him more appealing rather than less.

"Your Grace." Instinctively she reached toward him, fearing he might collapse at any moment. "What are you doing here? Whatever is the matter?"

The duke avoided her outstretched hand and hurled himself onto the seat opposite her with a sigh that echoed her recent one. "*You* are the matter, Miss Shaw. You have filled my son's head with the notion of having a governess and he will not rest until I persuade you to return to Renforth Abbey. I have been up half the night with him, only to fall asleep while you prepared to leave."

He looked as if he could sleep for a solid week without relieving his bone-deep weariness. Mr. Gibson had claimed the duke spent nearly every waking hour with his son. Did he also sit up with the child at night when he was ill or fretful? His present appearance suggested so. Leah had never met a father whose devotion ran so deep.

"Name your price," the duke demanded in a breathless voice as if he had chased the carriage down on foot. "And I will double it."

Double whatever sum she named? Leah's cherished dreams of travel and adventure, which had seemed shattered only moments ago, suddenly glittered brighter than ever. "You truly want me to take charge of your son?"

"Of course not!" His Grace flared up. "There is nothing I want less. But Kit wants it and I dare not refuse this fancy of his no matter how little I like the idea. So tell me your terms of employment and I will tell you my conditions."

His hostility to the notion of having her as Kit's governess stung Leah harder than she expected.

"I believe we should do it the other way around." She crossed her arms in front of her. "*First* you tell me your conditions then I shall decide what amount of compensation I require to comply with them."

The duke scowled only to have his forbidding expression spoiled by a wide yawn.

"Very well," he agreed once it had passed. "For my son's protection I must set firm limits on what you can and cannot do with him. No more cavorting around pretending to be his horse. Kit will remain safely in his bed. You may work with him for one hour in the morning and another in the afternoon. You will cease at once if he seems tired or unwell. You will not stir up discontent with his situation or the precautions I must take for his safety."

Leah's spirits sank. If she accepted the conditions His Grace demanded, she would never be able to help Kit break out of his stifling prison. Instead, *she* would end up bound hand and foot by the duke's rigid limits.

"In that case, sir," she replied, "I fear there is no salary I could name that would render such a situation tolerable to me. I am sorry you have gone to so much trouble to hire me back, but I must decline. I could not teach under such conditions."

She was taking a risk, she knew, in rejecting the duke's offer. Perhaps that had been his aim, to present her with conditions she would be forced to refuse.

Then he could place the blame for Kit's disappointment on her. But if the duke truly was prepared to go to any lengths to insure his child's wellbeing, he would be obliged to compromise.

Hostile silence bristled between them as His Grace considered her refusal and his response.

What could he be thinking? Was he weighing the danger he feared she might pose to Kit against the torment of more sleepless nights trying to comfort a disappointed child? Or had some part of him begun to recognize the consequences his excessive protectiveness might have upon his son?

"Tell me then, Miss Shaw, under what conditions *would* you be prepared to accept a position as my son's governess?" A glint of steely determination in his tired eyes warned Leah against pressing too far with her demands.

"What about this?" she proposed. "I will do my utmost to avoid anything that might bring harm to your son. In return, you must promise not to interfere with my methods of teaching. That is a reasonable compromise, surely?"

The earl's brow creased in a dubious frown. Or perhaps it was only a look of deep thought.

"And your salary demands?" he asked, giving her hope that he meant to agree.

"I make no demands." She strove not to take offense at the way he had phrased his question. If she were as weary as he appeared, she might be hard-pressed to maintain proper civility. "I ask only that you honor the terms I accepted from your sister."

"Very well, then." The duke thrust out his hand. "We have a bargain."

Leah reached out to grasp his hand only to hesitate at the last moment. "There is one more matter we should settle."

"What is that?" His Grace sounded suspicious of this last-minute provision.

"It is something your sister agreed to when she engaged my services. I mentioned it earlier, but I want to be certain you understand. It is not my practice to stay in one position for more than a year. When the time comes for me to leave, I will help you secure a replacement. Would that be agreeable to you?"

A year would give her plenty of time to persuade His Grace that more freedom could only benefit his son. After that, another governess would be able to follow the trail she had blazed.

The tension in the duke's posture and expression eased. He closed the final inches between her fingertips and his to shake her hand. "A one-year position would be entirely agreeable to me, Miss Shaw."

Clearly the one thing he approved about her taking the position was the prospect of being rid of her in twelve months.

That was one matter on which they could agree, Leah told herself in an effort to stifle a flicker of doubt.

Chapter Three

One year. Could he abide having Leah Shaw under his roof for that long? Hayden asked himself that question as he rode back to Renforth Abbey behind the carriage.

One year was a distinct improvement over having her there for an indefinite period. And at the end of that time, the decision to leave would be *hers,* not his. Kit was clever enough to realize that no amount of pleading with his father was likely to make his governess stay, so there should be no repetition of last night's upset.

Though Miss Shaw had offered to assist him in finding a replacement governess when the time came, Hayden had no intention of permitting any such thing. If he decided his son would benefit from further instruction, *he* would hire someone more suitable. But if this experiment proved to be nothing but a disruption, he and Kit would return to the routine that had served them well enough for the past several years.

In the meantime, Hayden knew he would have to be vigilant to prevent Leah Shaw's presence from putting his son's health at risk. Not to mention keeping Kit from becoming too attached to his new governess. Which of those would be the most difficult, he could not predict. Miss Shaw was headstrong and impulsive, but she also possessed a certain charm that he feared might prove equally hazardous…and not only to his son.

That fear was confirmed when the carriage halted at the entrance to the house and his butler greeted the lady as if she were a long-lost relative. "It is a pleasure to welcome you back to Renforth Abbey so soon, Miss Shaw. Do I take it you will be staying somewhat longer this time?"

"I hope so, Mr. Gibson." She gave a melodic ripple of laughter that Hayden resented, though he could not fathom why. "At least long enough to make a proper acquaintance of the place."

As Hayden dismounted, the butler turned toward him. "Now that Miss Shaw will be staying, shall I find her more suitable quarters, Your Grace?"

Quarters nearer the nursery, for instance? Hayden did not want that. Leah Shaw might begin poking her pretty nose in more often than he wished. "What is wrong with the room she had last night? Put her back in there."

"I couldn't," she protested. "It is too grand. You might need that room for—"

"Guests?" Hayden interrupted her with a derisive chuckle. "I am not in the habit of hosting house parties, Miss Shaw. The only person who comes to visit is my sister, who descends periodically without invitation or warning. There are plenty of other rooms we can place at Althea's disposal. I insist you keep your present quarters."

He ignored the butler's doubtful look, but found it impossible to do the same with Leah Shaw's engaging smile of gratitude. "That is very kind of you, sir. It is a lovely room. I have never had one half so fine before."

Her gratitude troubled Hayden, knowing how little he deserved it. Yet he hoped it might make her feel obliged to comply with his wishes, if she believed he had granted her some sort of honor.

"I trust you will be comfortable there." His reply came out more like an order. "Now, if you will accompany me to the nursery, my son will be pleased to learn you have accepted the position."

"Of course, Your Grace." Miss Shaw hurried to keep up as Hayden strode into the house. "Would you like me to begin his lessons right away?"

"Indeed not." He steeled himself against the charm of her eagerness. "Kit will be tired out from last night, if he has not made himself downright ill. We will postpone any lessons until he is fully recovered. I only hope the assurance that you have accepted the post will relieve his anxiety and allow him to get some rest."

"You make it sound as if it is *my* fault your son was upset," she said as they ascended the main staircase toward the new range. "If you recall, I came here yesterday with every intention of being his governess. It was your initial refusal to let me stay that disappointed Kit."

Coming on the heels of too many other sleepless nights, his most recent one had worn Hayden's patience threadbare. He resented Miss Shaw's accusation that he was responsible for distressing his son to the point of illness.

But he could not deny it.

"What does any of that matter now?" he demanded. "It is settled that you are staying. Who decided what and when is of no consequence."

"It is of consequence to me." Leah Shaw spoke quietly but with firm insistence that warned Hayden he would have his hands full during the next twelve months. "I would never do anything to upset your son."

"But I would?" Hayden shot her a glare as she tried to keep up with his long-striding pace. "Is that what you are saying? I will have you know—"

What he would have her know must wait, it seemed, for they had reached the nursery. Hayden did not want to risk a confrontation with Miss Shaw where his son might overhear.

With considerable effort, he moderated his tone. "I beg your pardon, Miss Shaw. I did not mean to imply that you were responsible for my son's distress. But surely you can understand why the start of his lessons must wait until I am satisfied that he is well enough."

The lady accepted his apology with a gracious smile that held a vexing suggestion of triumph. Even so, the way her full, mobile lips curved upward, bracketed by winsome dimples, was too appealing to suit Hayden. He could not risk falling under her charm for fear she might use it to persuade him to relax his vigilance over his son.

"Perhaps we should decide together when Kit is

ready to begin," she suggested. "I assure you, I do not mean to subject him to a rigorous course of study that might tax his strength. I only want to provide him with an agreeable diversion, so he will be less inclined to dwell upon his limitations. I hope that will make him *less* prone to upsets and restless nights, which would benefit you both."

Without awaiting his reply, she pushed open the nursery door and entered.

"Is that you, Papa?" Kit demanded, his voice thin and fretful. "I heard you talking outside my door. Did you catch Miss Leah before she left? Did you ask her to stay and teach me?"

"He did, indeed," Miss Shaw piped up brightly as she approached Kit's bed. "And very persuasive he was, too. I have promised to stay for a year then I will help your father find a new governess to take my place."

Hayden gritted his teeth. He wished she had not blurted out that information to Kit right at the outset. She had sworn she would do nothing to distress his son and he believed her. The problem was, she did not seem to anticipate the effect her words or actions might have on the child.

"A year is a very long time." Kit seemed to take the news well, much to his father's relief. "Can you teach me everything there is to learn in one year, Miss Leah?"

She laughed, not in a way that mocked the child's ignorance, but as if they shared an amusing jest. Her laughter seemed to waft through the room like a fresh summer breeze. "I am certain you are very clever and I am an excellent teacher, but there is far more to know in the world than I could teach you in twenty years."

She perched on the right-hand side of Kit's bed... where Hayden usually sat. "I am not certain even your wise father knows *everything*."

Was the impudent creature teasing him? Part of Hayden was inclined to take offense. But another long dormant part actually enjoyed it.

Her young pupil had been right about one thing, Leah decided a few days later. A year could be a very long time. Especially a year at remote Renforth Abbey, with so little to occupy her.

The duke had decided his son needed at least two days of rest before any instruction could begin. Even then, he would only permit her two hours a day with the child. His Grace had given her strict orders not to tire or overstimulate his son. Did he not realize that half of Kit's trouble stemmed from being understimulated for so many years?

Difficult as it was for her, Leah managed to stifle an impudent reply. She did not want to antagonize the duke for fear he might further restrict her time with Kit. Instead, she resolved to make the most of each hour, so he would see how much good her lessons did the child.

"So tell me," she asked Kit as she sat beside him on the bed for their first lesson, "can you read any words at all?"

Before the boy could answer, the duke spoke up

from his chair on the opposite side of the bed. "He does not need to read for himself. He has me to do it for him."

Leah's hand ached to pluck a pillow from behind her back and hurl it at Lord Northam. Much as she chafed under the other limits he had imposed upon her, she most resented his insistence on being present during his son's lessons. How could she do her job properly with him sitting there glowering at her, providing disagreeable answers to the questions she tried to ask his child?

Reminding herself not to antagonize him, she turned a deaf ear to his words. She spoke to Kit in an even brighter tone, which she sensed annoyed his father. "You would *like* to learn to read, though, wouldn't you?"

"Yes, I would," Kit answered quickly, before the duke had an opportunity to express a contrary opinion. "Very much."

She glanced down at him and they exchanged a grin of mischievous conspirators.

Then his expression grew anxious. "How will you teach me to read, Miss Leah?"

"Your father has already made a fine start." Leah took care to speak loud enough for the duke to hear.

"He has?" Kit's eyes widened in surprise and his brow creased, perhaps wondering whether she might be joking. "How?"

"By reading *to* you." Leah hoped a dose of approval from her might lead the duke to relax his suffocating vigilance. "In my opinion it is the very best way to start. Now I reckon you are ready to take the next step."

"What is that?" The boy's eyes fairly glittered with hunger to learn.

A good number of Leah's previous pupils had viewed their lessons as a disagreeable chore, undertaken with the greatest reluctance and shirked at the slightest opportunity. She had been obliged to exercise all her powers of invention to interest them in learning anything at all. This little boy, whose world was so much more limited than theirs, seemed to recognize the many doors an education might open for him.

"You will see," she teased, to whet his curiosity. "Tell me, what is your favorite story? The one your father has read to you most often. One you practically know by heart. Is there a book like that?"

The child gave a vigorous nod. "*Gulliver's Travels.* It is the book I always choose if Papa asks which one he should read."

"An excellent selection!" Leah reached for his thin hand and gave it a squeeze. The waxen coldness of it chilled her. "That is a favorite of mine, too. I like to imagine what it must be like to visit all those fantastical lands. Which would you most like to explore if you could?"

Kit had obviously given that question a great deal of thought already, for he replied without hesitation, "Lilliput, of course."

"I thought you might say that." What an engaging prospect it must be, for a child so weak and dependent on the care of others, to appear large and powerful to the tiny inhabitants of that land.

"Would you like to go there?" Kit asked.

"Of course." Leah chafed his hand gently in an effort to warm it. "I would like to visit all those realms."

It would represent the ultimate freedom—to voyage far beyond the limits of any map, to places where horses could talk, islands could fly and mice could grow as big as horses.

"I cannot take you to any of the others," the child spoke in a tone of wistful regret. "But we can visit Lilliput."

Before Leah could ask how that was possible, Kit called out to his father, "Will you bring the box, Papa, for me to show Miss Leah?"

"I thought this was lesson time, not playtime." The duke's gruff tone sounded strangely defensive.

"But I want her to see them." Kit thrust out his lower lip in a pouting frown. "You can fetch the book, too, so Miss Leah can teach me to read it."

When his father did not stir at once, he added in an imperious tone, "Now."

"Very well." The duke's obvious reluctance was tempered with something that sounded like fear. "Do not fret yourself. I will fetch them."

A moment later he appeared at his son's bedside with a well-worn volume of *Gulliver's Travels* bound in red leather. He also brought a wide but shallow wooden box of the kind Leah had seen used to store chessmen. It was closed with a finely wrought bronze clasp.

Once Kit got his way, his disposition became all sweetness again.

"Thank you, Papa. Put it here." The child gestured to his outstretched legs covered with bedclothes. It was impossible to mistake his rising excitement, which Leah feared would not please his formidable father.

But the duke obeyed his son's orders without a murmur.

Kit quickly unlatched the box and threw back the top with a flourish. "These are my Lilliputians. What do you think of them?"

"I think they are marvelous." Leah reached to pick up one of the tiny figures nestled in the box, to examine more closely. At the last moment, her hand froze. The little people in that box were so skillfully crafted that they looked as if they might squirm or protest if she tried to touch them.

Kit was clearly accustomed to playing with his Lilliputian figures and had no such qualms.

"Papa gave me some of them as a present on my birthday, then more for Christmas and more for my next birthday." Kit plucked one of the figures from the box and held it closer for Leah to inspect. "This is Emperor Mully Ully Gue. See his gold helmet with the plume and his sword?"

Leah nodded and peered closer. The figure appeared to be carved out of wood and painted, with the addition of metal embellishments, which Kit had pointed out. If she had needed any further evidence that the duke would take infinite pains for his son, this thoughtful gift certainly provided it.

"The emperor looks just the way he is described in the book, down to his arched nose and olive complexion. Who else have you got there?"

The child rummaged through his collection and

drew out two more figures. "This is Gulliver's friend, Reldresal, and *this* is his mortal enemy, Skyresh Bolgolam."

"He does have a very disagreeable look." Leah squinted to make out the high admiral's carefully painted features. His thick black brows were drawn together in an unmistakable scowl.

Kit chuckled. "Papa gets that look sometimes."

"Indeed I do not!" the duke protested, which only made Kit laugh louder and Leah join in.

"You have it now, Papa!" the child squealed.

Leah nodded. "If you could see yourself in the mirror, Your Grace, you would be obliged to admit your son is correct."

The duke dismissed them both with a gruff, "Humph! No wonder Bolgolam was vexed to have a giant suddenly wash up on the shore of Lilliput and turn everything in the kingdom upside down."

Was he talking about Lemuel Gulliver in Lilliput or the new governess at Renforth Abbey? Leah wondered as Kit showed her more of his little figures. If he meant the latter, she could only observe that some things in his household needed to be turned on their heads.

She might not be a giant, like Gulliver, but she had the power of right on her side. What could stand against that?

Did his son truly see him as some sort of sour-faced petty tyrant like Gulliver's enemy, who would tie him down with a thousand small, annoying threads?

Hayden had done his best to stifle that thought for

the past week. But now, as he listened to Kit's afternoon lesson, it ambushed him again.

Miss Shaw was reading part of the story about the ridiculously long list of restrictions set upon Gulliver's freedom. Did the new governess consider *his* rules regarding her position equally restrictive? And perhaps equally ridiculous?

"'If an express require extraordinary dispatch…'" she read, "'the Man-Mountain shall be obliged to carry in his pocket the messenger and…' what is the next word, Kit?"

"'Horse,'" the child responded immediately.

"Very good." Miss Shaw continued reading. "'The messenger and horse a six days' journey, once in every…'"

"'Moon'!" Kit supplied the next word before she could even ask.

"Well done! 'And return the said messenger back (if so required) safe to our Imperial Presence.'"

Let Miss Shaw think what she liked! Hayden crossed his arms tightly over his chest and shifted in his seat. The rules he had put in place were for his son's protection, so Kit did not overtax his strength or get too excited. No doubt Skyresh Bolgolam believed he was protecting the citizens of Lilliput from the potentially dangerous actions of the giant castaway. Actions that might seem perfectly innocent to Lemuel Gulliver if he were home in England could have dire consequences on an island populated with inhabitants only a few inches tall.

Drat it all! He was doing it again. Hayden made a conscious effort to relax his scowling features.

By the time the governess finished reading the whole list, with some help from Kit, Hayden could no longer keep his thoughts to himself. "Perhaps the reason Bolgolam seems so disagreeable is because Gulliver gets to tell the story. The reader knows Gulliver's intentions toward his hosts are entirely benevolent. But how could the high-admiral know that? Surely he was right to be wary of a creature that posed such a grave threat to the kingdom?"

The silence that greeted his outburst felt charged with ridicule.

"It is only a story, Your Grace," Miss Shaw said at last.

Hayden could picture her exchanging mocking looks with his son. That added fuel to his outrage. Was Leah Shaw trying to turn Kit against him?

"I *know* it is a story," he snapped. A story that contained unsettling parallels with his own life.

"Now, Kit, let's see how well you remember your numbers." Miss Shaw addressed the child in a tone of feigned cheer that seemed designed to exclude his father from their conversation. "How many soldiers has the high-admiral set to guard Gulliver?"

Hayden heard the rattle of toy figures being taken from their box, then Kit began to count, "One…two… three…"

On he continued, all the way to nine—a considerable accomplishment for a boy who had only begun learning his numbers the previous day. Hayden's heart swelled with pride, though he could not stifle a pang of regret that he had let his son reach the age of seven without learning to count.

He tried to justify himself with the excuse that a bedridden boy had no need of such knowledge…except perhaps for the self-respect that came from mastering a skill other children his age took for granted.

"Very good, indeed," Miss Shaw commended her young pupil. "Now what if Gulliver sneezed and three of the soldiers ran away in terror? How many would be left to stand guard?"

Kit considered the question for a moment, perhaps counting the remaining figures under his breath. Then he announced in a triumphant tone, "Six!"

"Correct! It seems you are naturally clever with numbers."

Hayden knew Kit's governess must be smiling down at him with warm admiration that no male could resist, be he seven years old…or seven and thirty. No doubt the boy was gazing back up at her with the eager devotion of a puppy, prepared to do anything she asked.

"Now try this one," Miss Shaw continued. "If the emperor decided the conditions placed upon Gulliver's release were too numerous and removed the last five, how many would be left on the list?"

Again Kit silently pondered the question. As the pause stretched longer and longer, Hayden grew increasingly anxious. It was not a fair question at all. How could a child who had only begun to count be expected to subtract such a sum? Was Miss Shaw deliberately trying to discourage him? Hayden began to mouth the answer, hoping it would somehow communicate itself to his son.

At last he could stand it no longer. "Four, Kit. The answer is four. Nine items on the list minus five. It was far too difficult a question for you."

"No, it wasn't!" the child protested. "I was about to say four when you shouted it out first. Truly I was, Miss Leah."

"Of course you were, Kit. It is always a good idea to think carefully about a question before you give an answer. Your father was a trifle impatient, that's all." Mild as her words sounded, Hayden felt the sting of her reproach.

"Papa thought I could not figure it out on my own," Kit complained bitterly. "He does not believe I can do *anything!*"

"Now, son." Hayden rose and approached the bed. "You know that is not true."

"It is!" Kit glared at him with stormy defiance that smote Hayden a cruel blow. "I wish you would go away and stop interrupting, Papa. These are *my* lessons, not yours."

"Of course they are, son. I only meant—"

"Pardon me, Your Grace." Miss Shaw cut him off. "But perhaps the two of you could settle this later, after Kit and I are finished our work."

He would not be ordered about in his own house by this interloper!

"You *are* finished, Miss Shaw. At least, you should be." Hayden stabbed his forefinger in the direction of the mantel clock. "This lesson has already run a quarter of an hour past its time. Every day this week your lessons have exceeded the time we agreed upon. Every lesson has gone on longer than the last. Keep it up and you will have my son working 'round the clock."

Leah Shaw thrust out her pert chin. "I only extended my teaching time to compensate for *your* constant interrup—"

"It will not do." Hayden broke in before she could finish. "Today's lesson is over."

"That's not fair, Papa!" Kit pushed the box away, scattering his Lilliputian figures over the bedspread. A few tumbled onto the floor. "I enjoy my lessons. I don't want to stop!"

"Hush now, Kit." His governess tried to soothe the boy. "We can continue our work tomorrow."

"Tomorrow is Sunday," Hayden reminded her. "At Renforth Abbey, we keep the Sabbath. There will be no lessons on Sundays."

"Is that because of God?" Kit demanded. "Then I don't like him! He made me a cripple and now he won't let me have my lessons."

"Kit!" Hayden was not certain which dismayed him more, his son's rejection of the Almighty or his use of that horrible word.

"Now, Kit." Miss Shaw persisted in her effort to calm the tempest she had provoked. "I am certain you don't mean that."

"I do! I do!" Kit pounded on the bed with surprising strength and his eyes began to fill with tears.

Hayden knew he was in for another tantrum. The

prospect threatened to overwhelm him. "Please go, Miss Shaw."

In spite of the *please,* it was not a request.

"No!" Kit wailed. "I want her to stay. *You* should go away, Papa, not Miss Leah!"

"But, Kit—"

"*Now,* Miss Shaw," Hayden insisted as his son burst into angry howls.

With obvious reluctance, she obeyed.

He had hired the woman, against his better judgment, in an effort to prevent this sort of outburst, Hayden fumed as he struggled to settle his son. If it was going to happen either way, why should he bother to put up with Leah Shaw's disruptive influence?

Chapter Four

Kit's cries pursued Leah as she fled the nursery, even after she pulled the door shut behind her. Who would imagine such a delicate child could produce such a commotion? Vexed as she was with Lord Northam's stiff hostility and smothering interference, she could not help but pity him for having to listen to those deafening shrieks.

"It is his own fault!" she muttered as she returned to the peace and quiet of her distant room. "If he would just let us be, Kit and I would get on perfectly well. I thought we had a bargain."

She had assumed, when the duke agreed to hire her, it meant he was willing to give her a fair opportunity to teach his son. If she had known he intended to hover in the nursery, watching and criticizing her every move, she would never have consented to stay. Even when the duke was not openly finding fault with her, she was all too aware of his brooding disapproval.

When she reached her quarters, Leah shut the door

behind her with a bang, but it did little to relieve her feelings. More offenses rose in her mind, stoking her resentment of the duke.

If he felt he *must* interrupt his son's lessons, did he always have to sound so gruff? Not since leaving the Pendergast School had Leah felt so restricted in her actions or held in such severe contempt, no matter what she did. It made her respond the way she had at school—by employing impudent wit to lift the spirits of her fellow pupils and make them part of a covert rebellion against the forces of authority.

Another reason she'd made light of the duke's behavior was to disguise the true severity of their antagonism from his son. Today she had not been able to hide her mounting irritation. She'd allowed the veiled hostility between Lord Northam and her to spew forth. The result had been to upset Kit, which was precisely what she'd been trying to avoid.

Leah flounced over to the window, where she planted her elbows on the sill and cradled her chin between her clenched fists. Perhaps if the duke was made to reap what he had sown, he might think twice about interrupting Kit's lessons after this.

On reflection, she knew it was foolish to hope Lord Northam might recognize that *he* was responsible for upsetting his son. Instead he would likely blame her and redouble his interference. Could she remain at Renforth Abbey under such intolerable conditions?

No sooner had that thought blazed through her mind than Leah began to laugh at herself. "What would my friends think of me if I were to write them with complaints about my position here? I have been given a generous salary, an elegant room and the finest dining in exchange for two hours work a day and only a single pupil to teach. This is most governesses' idea of paradise!"

Counting her blessings helped to take the edge off Leah's frustration, though not as much as she wished it would. The trouble was, she did not care about creature comforts as much as some people. The cold and hunger she'd endured at school had mattered less to her than the tyranny of the staff and the deadly dull routine. Long hours of idleness were no boon, either. Much as she sometimes pitied Evangeline for having charge of such a full nursery, Leah would have gladly changed places with her friend. How swiftly the days must fly for her friend with so many duties to occupy the time. And Evangeline would never want for company.

Even the wretched Pendergast School had been superior to Renforth Abbey in that respect. There she'd had friends to commiserate with and younger pupils to defend from bullies. Here, she had no one to talk to for hours on end.

She'd tried making friends with some of the maids, but they always seemed too busy to chat with her and she did not want to interrupt their work the way Lord Northam did hers. Mr. Gibson firmly discouraged her attempts to socialize with his staff. Perhaps because of the fine room the duke had assigned her, the butler seemed to believe she should be treated as a guest of the house.

That left Leah with only two occupations to fill her

interminable hours of leisure—writing letters to her friends and wandering the halls and grounds of Renforth Abbey. Though she had found many sights of interest during her rambles, she feared she would grow vastly tired of the place long before her position ended.

In an effort to vent her feelings, Leah took up her pen and began a letter to Grace, the most sympathetic of her friends, who now lived in Berkshire with her husband and three delightful stepdaughters. As she scribbled away furiously, Leah fancied she could hear her friend's gentle voice, urging patience and forbearance. But those virtues were not an essential part of her character as they were of Grace's.

Yet, by the time she had finished her letter, Leah's raw indignation felt somewhat relieved.

A few hours later, as she finished her solitary dinner, Mr. Gibson inquired, "Will you be joining the rest of the household for matins in the chapel tomorrow, Miss Shaw? Or does His Grace wish you to attend the young master while he is at worship?"

Leah shook her head and tried to make a jest of the situation. "Lord Northam seems to feel it would be an offense against the Fourth Commandment for me to teach his son anything on a Sunday."

The butler did not seem amused. "In that case, we will see you in the chapel tomorrow morning at ten o'clock."

"Where would I find the chapel?" Leah asked, rather surprised she had not stumbled upon it during any of her explorations.

The butler provided her with directions then bid her good evening.

Perhaps she ought to see if she could find the place while Mr. Gibson's directions were still fresh in her mind, Leah decided as she rose from the table. She wanted to be sure she knew her way so as not to risk being late for the service. Such a blunder would not impress the duke.

Hard as Leah insisted to herself that His Grace's opinion of her did not matter, deep down she feared otherwise. She had grown accustomed to being respected and valued by her employers, though she knew she had been more fortunate than some of her friends in that regard. By contrast, the duke's air of suspicion and ill will bothered her more than she cared to admit.

After only one wrong turn, Leah managed to locate the cloisters which led to the chapel. Long ago, when Renforth was an abbey, the cloisters had been an open, roofed walkway for the monks. At some point since then, the sides had been enclosed with tall, narrow windows installed between the stone pillars.

Her footsteps barely made a sound as she padded over the stone floor. When she reached the door to the chapel she eased it open with quiet reverence. Leah knew her friend Grace would urge her to pause and say a prayer for help and guidance. Communing with the Lord might give her a more charitable perspective on her troubles, and perhaps help her feel a little less isolated at Renforth Abbey.

Candles flickered within brass lanterns on the altar, casting just enough light for Leah to make out the vaulted ceiling and an intricately carved rood screen of dark wood. As she paused to get her bearings in the dim stillness, she realized she was not alone.

It was more than the abiding presence of God, though she sensed that, as well. The chapel had another mortal occupant, kneeling in one of the pews, so deep in prayer that he seemed unaware of her arrival. She had only to hear a few words he spoke aloud to the Lord, to realize that man was the Duke of Northam.

"Seven years ago, Lord, You spared my child's life as I begged you." His fervent words echoed through the small stone chapel. "I have never ceased to give You thanks for that blessing. But now I wonder if I was unpardonably selfish to keep my son from the joy of heaven to endure the trials of this world."

The pain in the duke's voice was so raw, it seared away all the resentment Leah harbored toward him, leaving only ashes of pity. Was it any wonder he clung so tightly to the child he had come so close to losing?

"Heavenly Father," the duke continued, "grant me the strength and patience to do my best for Kit, to keep him safe, healthy and happy."

Leah began to back away. She should not be here, eavesdropping on the most intimate communication between a man and his Maker.

In spite of her good intentions, the duke's next words stopped her in her tracks. "Help me have patience with Kit's new governess, Lord. I fear she is right that I should have found someone to teach him long before this. I know she thinks I am an unfeeling tyrant, but please do not let her turn my son against me."

His words hit Leah like the stinging stroke of a switch across her palm. Before she had time to remember where they were, a fierce denial burst from her lips. "I am *not* trying to turn Kit against you! I would never do anything so wicked! It is *you* who are blighting his affection for you."

Her outburst spun the duke around and brought him to his feet. "What are you doing here, woman? What right have you to spy upon a man at prayer?"

That was a charge against which Leah could not defend herself. Her conscience reproached every bit as indignantly as His Grace did. Part of her wanted to turn and flee, but that had never been her way. Now that she had glimpsed what lay behind the duke's hostility toward her, she could not permit it to go unchallenged... no matter what the consequences.

Was it not enough that Leah Shaw had made his son view him as some kind of ogre? Now the woman had stolen into his private chapel and listened in on his prayers!

Never in his life had Hayden felt so dangerously exposed.

Like a lion tormented by a thorn in its paw, he reared up roaring accusations, desperate to frighten her away and perhaps make her forget what she had overheard. Any of his servants would have turned tail at once and not stopped running until they reached the village.

Miss Shaw flinched from his outburst, but held her ground until he paused for breath. Then, instead of bolting back to her room and barricading the door, she thrust out her chin and stepped up to confront him. "I did not mean to spy on you, sir. I came here to pray, as well. I had no idea anyone would be here until you spoke. I was going to go away quietly until I heard you say I was turning Kit against you. I could not let you go on believing anything so ridiculous."

Hayden seized upon the word. "Ridiculous am I? Perhaps I seem that way to one who makes a joke of everything. You may be able to make light of my son's condition and the measures I take to protect him, but I cannot."

As he spoke, Hayden scuttled sideways toward the centre aisle where he would not be hemmed in by the pews. Miss Shaw continued to approach until they were nearly toe to toe.

"I do not *take* your son's condition lightly." She stared up at him defiantly. "I try to *make* light of it so he will not feel sorry for himself or use it as an excuse to do less than his best. Fortunately Kit does not seem inclined to do either. He is a fine boy. In a great many ways you have done an admirable job of raising him."

She spoke in such a rebellious tone it was difficult for Hayden to recognize the praise her words contained. "I...have? Admirable?"

Leah Shaw gave an emphatic nod that made her dark curls dance around her face. "Very admirable. Even if you were not, I would never seek to turn a child against a parent. I beg you put that thought out of your mind at once."

Hayden wanted to believe her. When she turned those wide hazel eyes upon him, it was difficult to resist her entreaty. But there were facts he could not altogether dismiss. "Before you came here, my son never spoke to me the way he has of late. We were perfectly content."

"You might have been, but was he?" Though her tone and stance betrayed no hostility, her words challenged Hayden nonetheless. "Kit is no longer an infant and I am not convinced his health is as fragile as you believe. I suspect he would soon have begun to crave more freedom. My coming only set the spark to some very dry tinder."

"That is not true!" Hayden spoke louder than he'd intended, perhaps to drown out the insidious whispers of doubt in his mind. "You set him a bad example by making me the butt of your jests, laughing off everything I say as if it is contemptible."

At last something he said seemed to make a serious impression upon this infuriatingly lighthearted woman.

"Is that how it appeared to you?" She took a few unsteady steps and sank down onto the nearest pew. "Believe me, Your Grace, I never intended to mock you in front of your son."

She sounded sincere, but Hayden had suffered too many pinpricks from her rapier wit to be easily persuaded. "Then why did you make me the butt of your fun?"

Kit's governess hoisted her shoulders. "That is what I have always done when I feel oppressed."

Something about the way she spoke suggested it had been a frequent occurrence in her life. That thought made Hayden feel strangely protective toward her, something he had not felt for anyone but his son in a very long time. Suddenly his grievances against her no longer seemed to matter so much.

With a flick of his hand he signaled her to budge over in the pew. Then he slid in beside her. "Is that why you only take governess positions for one year, because you have been mistreated by your employers in the past and fear it will happen again?"

She clearly considered him another such tyrant. Hard as Hayden tried to dismiss that possibility, when he looked back on his actions, he could not.

"My past employers have allowed me considerable latitude." Miss Shaw answered his question without telling him what he wanted to know. "I had no quarrel with any of them."

"If not them, who was it that oppressed you?" Hayden persisted even though he could tell it was not a subject she cared to discuss.

"What possible bearing can that have on our present situation?" She wrapped her arms around herself as if to ward off a chill, though the summer evening did not merit it.

"I suspect it may have a considerable bearing upon our…difficulties."

Miss Shaw defied him with silence until he was almost prepared to abandon his questioning. Then, in a convulsive movement, she wrenched her arms from around her torso and raised her hands so he could not avoid looking at them. "If you must know, I rebelled against my teachers at the charity school where I was sent. Jests were a little safer than outright defiance. But not entirely."

Hayden looked closer at her palms and saw they were crisscrossed with fine lines, paler than the surrounding flesh. Scars like that must have taken a good many thrashings to form. The thought sickened him with outrage.

Before he could respond, Leah Shaw whipped her hands out of his sight and shot to her feet. "Perhaps now you will understand why I cannot abide anything that smacks of repression."

She turned away from him and sought to exit the narrow pew at the other end.

Hayden scrambled up and flew to intercept her. He reached the chapel door ahead of her, blocking her escape. But when he glimpsed the defiant look in her eyes he sensed it would be a terrible mistake to detain her that way. An appeal might work better.

He stepped aside, allowing her free access to the door should she wish to leave. "Please stay, Miss Shaw. We have too little opportunity to talk without my son present. I should be sorry to lose this chance while he is asleep."

Leah Shaw cast a longing glance toward the door but held her ground. "Whose fault is it that Kit must witness all our conversations? That is another reason I have tried to make light of all your fault-finding during our lessons. I did not want to trouble him with the hostility between us. However much you detest me, I must ask that you treat me with respect in front of him."

"I do not *detest* you!" Hayden protested even as his

conscience questioned how she could be expected to know that.

"Indeed?" She crossed her arms in front of her chest and gave an exaggerated scowl. Hayden feared it was an all-too-accurate imitation of how he had looked this week during Kit's lessons. "If we are quibbling over a choice of words, how *would* you describe your attitude toward me? Contempt? Loathing?"

An unexpected hint of vulnerability behind her challenge forced Hayden to confess the truth. "Threatened."

The instant that word left his mouth he wished he could take it back. But Miss Shaw's bewildered silence urged him to explain himself. "I am afraid Kit will prefer your company to mine. Your way of teaching makes lessons more diverting than play."

"Do you mean that?" His grudging admission seemed to moderate the worst of her defensiveness. "You interrupted so often, I was certain you must disapprove of my methods."

"Quite the contrary," he muttered, driven to confess by a growing sense of shame. "I interrupted because I was drawn into your lessons. None of my tutors ever engaged my interest in learning the way you have Kit's…and mine."

For the first time that evening Miss Shaw's lips broke into one of her infectious grins. "Neither did any of my teachers. That is why I am so determined to take a different approach."

Hayden began to understand her mysterious motives at last. "So every day you teach is an act of rebellion against *them?*"

A mischievous spark kindled in her eyes. "You are a dangerously perceptive man, Your Grace."

Others might wonder how perception could be considered dangerous, but Hayden thought he knew. There was something else he now understood, as well. Leah Shaw did not mean to defy *him* but rather those grim teachers who had tried to make her youth a misery. But she had refused to let them. Her humor and high spirits had been a means of rebellion.

Who could not admire that kind of courage? Hayden found it impossible.

"This conversation has been most enlightening, though I am not certain a chapel is the best place for it." The duke motioned toward the door. "May we continue out in the cloisters?"

Leah thought for a moment then nodded. Knowing the duke felt threatened by her connection with his son shed an entirely different light upon his recent actions. No parent would want to lose their child's affections to a newcomer. She regretted giving Lord Northam cause to fear that might happen, and even more to think she meant to ridicule him in Kit's eyes.

His Grace pulled open the chapel door and motioned her into the cloisters. This would be a better place for them to converse, Leah realized. Not squared off opposite one another, fixed in their positions, but moving forward side by side.

She had only taken a slow step or two when the duke caught up with her.

"I hope you know I would never harm anyone the

way you were." He sounded as if he expected her to doubt him.

"Of course, I know it." She answered more sharply than she meant to.

What had compelled her to show him her scarred palms and tell him how she had come by those scars? She was not at all comfortable having him see a side of her that she had hidden for so many years behind a protective mask of vivacity and rebellious high jinks. But since he knew, should she risk disclosing more about her past if it might benefit his son?

"The punishments I received were not the worst thing about the Pendergast School, you know."

"There was *worse?*" The duke sounded outraged on her behalf, as if he longed to confront anyone who had ever wronged her and bring them to account.

That notion stirred something in Leah. "Not worse in the way you may think. But I would have happily borne a thrashing every day of my school career if only I had been allowed more freedom to do what I wanted rather than what I was ordered to do."

Their footsteps made a steady, soothing murmur on well-worn stones. The duke's silence made Leah wonder if he could comprehend her feelings any better than the holy brothers who had once tread these cloisters.

Upon entering the order, those men would have surrendered their freedom to own personal possessions and act contrary to the orders of their superiors. They would have given up even the basic freedom to love. Had it been a constant sacrifice for them to live according to those vows? Or had they found peace and fulfillment in subduing their individual wishes so completely to the will of God?

That thought troubled Leah. Did it make her any less a child of God because she treasured the freedom she had always considered one of her Creator's greatest gifts?

"So you think I am a tyrant like your teachers." The duke sounded more grieved than angry. "Because I will not allow Kit to do whatever he likes in spite of the consequences he is too young to appreciate?"

"Of course not." Leah's hand tingled with the urge to clasp his and give it a reassuring squeeze. But that was a liberty she did not dare take. Her association with the duke had barely begun to thaw. The last thing she wanted was to give him cause to take offense. "I believe you are an excellent father in a great many ways. It is obvious you care deeply about Kit and would do anything in your power to protect him and make him happy."

"Of course I would," His Grace replied without an instant's hesitation. "My responsibility for my son is one from which I would never want to be free. It is not a burden but an anchor—a fixed, lasting connection I cherish above all else. Without it I might be free, but that would mean nothing for my life would be empty."

When he put it that way, the duke's argument was most persuasive, Leah had to admit. But how could two people with such contrary beliefs both be right?

Perhaps the key to working together for Kit's welfare lay in concentrating on their areas of common ground, however small. "The Lilliputian figures you had made for Kit are the most splendid playthings I have ever seen. How did you think of them?"

"I hardly remember now." Her praise seemed to catch the duke off guard, though Leah sensed it pleased him. "Kit loved the book and talked of how he wished he could visit Lilliput. Then it occurred to me that I might be able to bring Lilliput to him."

By now, in spite of their leisurely pace, they had reached the archway where the cloisters joined the house. Leah stifled a foolish pang of disappointment that their stroll and conversation must come to an end.

Then, without seeming to be aware of what he was doing, the duke turned and started back the way they had come. "You make excellent use of those little figures and the book to teach him, Miss Shaw. I never thought I would live to hear a child demanding *more* lessons."

Now it was Leah's turn to be gratified, nearly to the point of embarrassment. "Learning can be a joy and it should be. Whatever ails your son's legs there is nothing wrong with his mind. A proper education can bring the rest of the world to him, the way your little figures brought him the land of Lilliput."

The duke gave a slow, pensive nod. "I had not thought of it like that. I suppose if Kit wants more study time, it would do no harm to extend his lessons a little."

That was a start. Leah allowed herself a tiny smile, but turned her face away from Lord Northam so he would not think she was gloating.

His concession emboldened her to try for more. "I am not certain he needs quite so much rest time. He seems to find it passes slowly with nothing to do. Perhaps we could use some of it for lessons instead."

"He has complained about his rest time." The duke's gaze strayed toward the grounds of Renforth Abbey that lay beyond the cloister windows. "But I need those free hours to attend to estate business. My steward already finds that time is not enough to get through all the matters we need to discuss."

How could she phrase her request in a way that would not offend the duke? "I am not suggesting you take time away from your duties, sir. Could you not trust me to teach Kit without your oversight?"

"It is not a matter of trust," the duke insisted until she shot him a dubious look, softened with a smile. "Very well, perhaps it is, a little."

Leah sensed his reluctance. It was a stout barrier. And yet, the duke's love for his son was a powerful force. "Believe me, sir. Kit's affection for you will not be diminished by a little time spent apart. Indeed, I believe he might enjoy your company more if he did not have it in such abundance."

"Is that a polite way of saying you want me to push off during Kit's lessons and allow you to do your job without having your every move scrutinized and every other sentence interrupted?" Lord Northam glanced toward her, his handsome features set in a dark scowl.

But was that a silvery twinkle she glimpsed in his blue eyes? And did one corner of his frowning mouth twitch as if barely restrained from curling upward?

Those subtle signs of amusement provoked her to

risk a blunt reply. "Yes, Your Grace, that is exactly what I am trying to say."

She sought to soften the sting her words might inflict with a teasing tone. "I reckon it would do *both* you and your son good to spend more time apart. What is it that prevents you, besides mistrust of me?"

The duke pondered her question. Though she found it difficult to keep silent, Leah did not pester him for an immediate answer.

After a moment His Grace halted and turned toward her. "The night Kit was born, I prayed as I have never prayed before or since. I implored God with all my heart and soul to let my son live."

With the fresh memory of what she had overheard in the chapel, Leah could picture that desperate paternal plea.

"He was such a fragile little scrap." Lord Northam continued, "I vowed I would care for him and do everything in my power to keep him from harm. But I had no idea how all-consuming it could be to tend an infant. I began letting the nursemaids take more and more responsibility for him. When the problem with his legs was discovered, I knew I had let my son down."

"It is *not* your fault Kit cannot walk. The stiffness in his legs was not a Divine judgment on you for letting a nursemaid change his linen now and then." It was a feeble jest, but Leah hoped it might help the duke see how foolish it was to blame himself for his son's condition. "Mr. Gibson told me Kit suffered a difficult birth. The trouble with his legs must have been there all along, only no one noticed until he was old enough to begin walking."

"Perhaps." The duke's mouth was set in a rueful line. Clearly her words had not eased his guilt. "But it was a reminder of the promise I had made and that my duty would be a lifelong one. I have not shirked it since and I do not mean to now."

"It is not shirking your duty as a father to give Kit a little time away from you," Leah insisted. "It is natural to want to protect those we care about and hold them close. But we must be careful not to cling too tight or we may…crush them."

For a moment, she thought she might have persuaded him, but then he shook his head. "I am sorry, Miss Shaw. But I cannot agree to what you ask. If you had a child of your own like Kit, perhaps you could understand."

He turned on his heel and stalked toward the house, leaving Leah frustrated that she had come so close to winning his cooperation, only to fall short.

"Wait!" she called, running after the duke.

When Lord Northam's only response was to quicken his pace, she put on a burst of speed and caught him by the hand. He spun around abruptly, fixing her with a glare that seemed to hold more surprise than anger. Had any person in his employ ever dared lay a restraining hand upon him?

Before he could reproach her, Leah gasped out the only words she could think of that might change his mind. "I do understand…better than…you might suppose."

Chapter Five

How could Leah Shaw understand about having a child like Kit? Her words shocked Hayden even more than her sudden seizing of his hand.

"What do you mean by that?" He turned toward her but made no effort to shake off her intrusive touch. "Did you bear a child out of wedlock and place it in fosterage somewhere?"

Others might condemn her and think she'd gotten what she deserved. If it was true, Hayden felt only pity for her…and an odd sense of disappointment.

His question made her features go slack in an expression of astonished dismay. It also seemed to remind her that she was still clinging to his hand, for she released it abruptly.

The shock did not strike her dumb, however. Hayden wondered if anything was capable of that. "Child out of…? Of course not! How could you imagine such a thing? Do you assume that because I value my freedom, I care nothing for right and wrong or my self-respect?"

What an unaccountable evening this had been, sending his emotions reeling from one extreme to another and back again. It taxed Hayden as if he had exerted muscles stiff from long disuse. And yet, it made him feel as if he was fully awake and alive after a long, numb half sleep.

"I think no such thing," he assured her with complete sincerity. "But what other conclusion was I to draw from your extraordinary statement?"

Leah Shaw inhaled a quick breath and opened her mouth, as if she meant to rattle off a dozen innocent explanations. But no words came out.

After an awkward pause, her features twisted into an almost comical expression of chagrin. "You do have a point, sir. But if you will allow me to explain…"

A strange sensation afflicted the corners of Hayden's mouth, almost like an itch. It could not be relieved by scratching, but rather by grinning. He tried to resist the impulse. "Not only would I *allow* you, Miss Shaw. I would positively encourage you to enlighten me."

Once he had declared himself willing to listen, the contrary damsel seemed to grow reluctant. To his surprise, Hayden found he could sympathize. It had not been easy for him to disclose the painful events of his son's first struggle for life and the wrenching discovery of Kit's disability. Yet, confiding in Leah Shaw had brought him an unexpected sense of relief. Was that because he knew life had dealt harshly with her but had not managed to break her spirit?

After a brief struggle that played out on her expressive features, Miss Shaw forced herself to speak. "Before I was sent away to the Pendergast School, I was raised by my grandmother, my parents having died when I was very young. In her last few years, Gran began to go blind. I had to do more and more to help her and look out for her. She may not have been a child, but I was every bit as devoted to her as you are to your son. And she was every bit as dependent on me as Kit is upon you."

The thought of a young girl caring for her blind grandmother took Hayden aback. Was it any wonder Leah Shaw prized her freedom if she had carried such a weight of responsibility on her shoulders at that age? Yet she did not sound as if she'd begrudged that duty any more than he resented caring for his son.

"I do not doubt how strong such a bond can be, Miss Shaw. My sister and I were raised by our grandmother after our parents died. She was devoted to us and we… that is…*I* to her. It is difficult to imagine having her dependent upon me as yours was upon you. She was a rather formidable lady. But near the end of her life, when she needed my help, I tried to care for her as much as she would permit me."

"What about your sister?" Leah Shaw picked up on his verbal slip, much to Hayden's annoyance. "Was she not devoted to your grandmother? I find that difficult to imagine."

He had already told Kit's governess more about his personal history than he cared to, but he supposed one more disclosure would hardly matter. "You have met Althea. Perhaps you will understand when I tell you that she and my grandmother were too much alike in temperament to be compatible."

The notion seemed to puzzle Miss Shaw. "Gran and I were a good deal alike—both adventurous and talkative and inclined to look on the bright side of things. No one understood me the way she did. But I suppose if Lady Althea and your grandmother were both strong-willed and anxious to have everything their own way, it could not have made for an easy relationship."

In spite of the serious subject of their conversation and the uncomfortably strong emotions this evening had provoked, Hayden found he could not suppress a chuckle. "That is a charitable way of putting it. The truth is, my sister and grandmother got along like sparks and gunpowder."

"With you often caught in the explosions?" asked the governess with an unsettling flash of perception.

Hayden replied with a rueful nod. "By times."

Discretion urged him to say nothing more on the subject, but the lady's intuitive grasp of his family's complicated dynamic drew him out in spite of himself. "Every rule Grandmother set, Althea was not content until she had pushed or broken it. I tried to tell her some of them were for her own good and kicking at the traces would only make Grandmother clamp down harder."

Miss Shaw gave a sympathetic nod. "Did you sometimes think that if your grandmother had only eased her restrictions, it might have made your sister less determined to rebel?"

"Quite often, but I knew better than to express that opinion." Caught up in his memories, Hayden spoke without thinking. But as soon as the words were out of his mouth, he detected a change in Leah Shaw's demeanor.

She was no longer a disinterested listener, but one who recognized an opportunity she could not resist exploiting. "Your Grace, I see the same situation beginning to develop between you and Kit. I dare to express my opinion because I know how much you care for your son and want him to be happy. I believe that is more important to you than being right or exerting your authority."

"Of course it is," he replied without hesitation, gratified that she recognized the sincerity of his motives.

He knew what she was going to ask…again. This time, he would find it difficult to refuse her as readily as he had before. What had changed in such a short time to make that possible?

When Miss Shaw started to speak, he raised his hand to bid her be silent until she had heard him out. If he must back down, he would do it on his own terms. He also wanted to make it clear she would not be allowed to take a mile simply because he had given her an inch.

"I know what you are going to say. You believe Kit will be less antagonistic if I leave the two of you alone during his lessons. I am still not entirely persuaded it is a good idea, but I reckon I owe it to us both to try."

The way her face lit up brought Hayden an unaccountable rush of satisfaction. His sense of caution warned that it could be dangerous for him to become anxious to please this woman. Who knew what disturbing changes in Kit's nursery routine she might propose if she gained that power over him? That stern admonition did little to quench the warm, buoyant feeling that swelled in his chest.

"Thank you, Your Grace!" Leah Shaw looked as if she meant to clasp his hand again. She managed to stop herself at the last minute, rather to his disappointment. "You will not regret your decision. I will see to that."

Hayden affected a grave look to mask his unsettling feeling of vulnerability. "I wish I could share your optimism, Miss Shaw, but I do not. If you give me the slightest cause for second thought, I will not hesitate to revoke my decision, no matter how strenuously you or Kit object. I also have a condition to impose."

"What might that be, Your Grace?" His words dimmed the eager luster of her eyes but did not extinguish it altogether. She seemed prepared to accept that she could not have *everything* her own way.

"At least once a week, I wish to be included in Kit's lessons. Not as a barely tolerated observer, but as an active participant, so I can get a taste of what you are teaching him. Are you willing to grant that concession?"

He expected Kit's governess to betray her distaste for the idea, while grudgingly accepting it as a necessary evil.

To his surprise, her face brightened again. "That is an excellent suggestion, sir! I'm certain it will do Kit good to have you show such an interest in his studies. And I believe he will enjoy having you for a classmate."

It was not a *suggestion* but a *condition*. Hayden reflected on the difference but decided it was not worth arguing over. He felt rather suspicious of anything Miss Shaw agreed to so readily, yet he could not deny that part of him looked forward to sharing Kit's lessons with the boy's spirited governess.

Three weeks after her confrontation with Lord Northam had shattered the peace of the ancient chapel, Leah savored her victory as she conducted a lesson with Kit and his father. She sat on one side of the boy in his enormous bed while His Grace sat on the other.

She handed the child his copy of *Gulliver's Travels*. "Perhaps we can start by showing your papa what fine progress you have made in reading this week."

Kit took the book from her and addressed his father as he flipped the pages. "You must listen, Papa and not interrupt me. If I have trouble making out a word, don't tell me what it is right away. Give me time to figure it out for myself."

"As you wish," replied the duke with a hint of asperity. "Am I permitted to offer a correction if you get a word wrong?"

The boy considered his father's question for a moment then glanced up at his governess. "Would that be alright, Miss Leah?"

Over his son's head, the duke shot her a significant look. It was not the baleful glare she recalled from her first days at Renforth Abbey. She had not received one of those from him recently. His present level gaze informed Leah that he recognized Kit was parroting *her* instructions. Fortunately, a twinkle in his eyes suggested he did not resent it.

"Perhaps your papa could give you a signal if you have made a mistake," she suggested. "He might shake his head or give a little cough, but not correct you right away. I feel certain you can come up with the proper word on your own."

"What if I can't?" Kit's question betrayed a lack of confidence in his abilities that Leah was endeavoring to remedy.

Years of being coddled and having the simplest things done for him had left the child easily frustrated by failure and sometimes reluctant to attempt new tasks. Seeing that gave Leah renewed appreciation for her own upbringing. When she'd told the duke about the Pendergast School and her early years with her grandmother, his face had radiated pity for her. But she knew those early challenges had fostered resourcefulness, resilience and gratitude for the smallest blessings, all of which had served her well ever since.

"If you try as hard as you can, but still are not able to figure out the word, you may ask your papa for help. But he should not tell you the correct one unless you ask him."

Kit seemed reassured by the idea of having assistance if he requested it. He gave a thoughtful nod. "That sounds like a good way, doesn't it, Papa?"

"I believe it does." The duke's words rang with sincerity, which pleased Leah.

Of late, he seemed to have accepted her presence in

his house and the changes she was making. Soon, she might be able to push for a little more freedom for Kit.

"Now," His Grace continued, "shall we get on with your reading so I can hear how well you are doing?"

Kit inhaled a deep breath and began to read. To Leah's immense satisfaction, the duke managed to refrain from correcting his son, except upon request. There could be no question Lord Northam was learning some valuable lessons from her.

Against her expectations, she was learning a thing or two from him about patience, selflessness and all-consuming devotion. Accustomed to having his own way so much, Kit could be demanding and uncooperative at times, yet the duke never had a cross word for his son. Leah did her best to emulate him, but it was not always easy.

His example made her wonder how her life and character might have been altered if her parents had not succumbed to consumption before she was old enough to remember them. How would it have affected her to grow up protected and nurtured the way Kit was? Perhaps she would not have become so independent and spirited, but might she feel more contented and secure?

She would never know. Leah dismissed such fruitless speculation. Since the past could not be changed, it did no good to dwell upon what might have been.

"Very well done, Kit." The duke's voice roused Leah from her musing. The warm approval of his tone seemed to extend to her as well as his son. "I cannot get over how quickly you have been able to learn so much."

Perhaps concerned that the child might mistake the

remark for doubt of his abilities, Lord Northam added, "It took me months, even years, to learn what you have in a matter of weeks."

Kit beamed with pride in his accomplishments. This was clearly an unaccustomed feeling for him, but one he liked a great deal. Yet he did not gloat or take all the credit for his achievement. "Don't mind about that, Papa. You're very clever, but you did not have a good teacher like Miss Leah."

Once again she and the duke exchanged a look over his son's head. This time, both their eyes sparkled with amusement at Kit's well-meant, but rather condescending remark. Both pressed their lips together to keep from laughing, lest it injure his feelings.

The duke mastered his merriment first. "Indeed I did not have a teacher like yours who makes studies so interesting. If I had, who knows what a brilliant scholar I might have become?"

His words brought a warm flush to Leah's cheeks and made her lower her gaze, though she did not altogether understand why. Was it so the duke would not see how much his praise pleased her?

"You gentlemen are determined to give me a very high opinion of myself." Instinctively she sought safety in jest. "But I must not let myself get too toplofty or my head may swell up too big for my bonnet!"

Father and son joined in laughter at the comical picture she painted. Their amusement brought Leah a familiar sense of satisfaction that nothing else in her life had ever been able to match. She'd never possessed the power or fortune to indulge the generous impulses that filled her heart. But she had always been able to bring a smile to the dear faces of Gran and later her school friends. For moments at a time, she had been able to relieve them of their cares. What gift could be better than that?

"Shall we return to our lessons?" she suggested when their mirth subsided. "As clever as Kit is at reading, his grasp of arithmetic is even better. Your Grace, would you kindly fetch his Lilliputian figures to assist us? They are such excellent teaching tools. They deserve more of the credit for your son's astonishing progress than I do."

"With pleasure." The duke produced the box of wooden figures from a small bedside table. "It never occurred to me how these might be used to teach Kit. I commend you on your resourceful methods, Miss Shaw."

"Thank you, Your Grace. A governess is obliged to adapt her materials according to the circumstances of her pupils." The duke's praise gratified Leah, though not for her own sake. Instead she viewed his approval as an asset she could call upon to gain the next step in his son's liberation. "Now, Kit, I am going to set you a more challenging problem than any you have tried before. Do not be daunted, though. I am certain it is within your capability."

The remainder of the lesson proceeded well. Leah was forced to admit she enjoyed having the duke take part in his son's education...on her terms. He now seemed to accept that additional study time was having a positive effect on Kit. Did he also recognize the benefits to *his* well-being of having more time to himself? Perhaps not, but she certainly did.

The duke seemed more relaxed of late, readier to smile and even laugh on occasion. The shadows of exhaustion beneath his eyes had begun to fade and his step had grown lighter, as if part of a crushing burden had been shifted from his broad shoulders. Leah observed all these small changes with a warm sense of fulfillment, much like she'd experienced as a child when she made her grandmother laugh.

There was another reason she welcomed the duke's participation in his son's lessons, though she was reluctant to acknowledge it. The fact was, she craved the stimulation of adult company. The Renforth servants still seemed alarmed by her efforts to make friends. She would have given anything if Hannah or Rebecca lived near enough to meet for a chat over tea. Being able to talk and jest with Lord Northam during some of his son's lessons went a little way toward filling that void in her life.

Once Kit's lessons were concluded for the day, Leah took a long walk in the gardens then wrote a reply to Grace's recent letter. Having already given an account of her arrival at Renforth Abbey and a description of the estate and family, there was little news to report in this one.

When the clock struck eight, she started and threw down her pen. "Oh, dear! I haven't time to dress for dinner or I'll be late."

What was the point of dressing up to dine all alone? Leah asked herself as she dashed through the echoing corridor then flew down the stairs. She had come to rather dread her solitary meals in the vast dining room, which seemed to highlight her isolation at Renforth Abbey. She would have much preferred to dine on a tray in her room, but Mr. Gibson insisted his staff welcomed the opportunity to prepare and serve a proper meal.

The butler stood waiting just outside the dining room when she arrived, flushed and breathless.

"I'm sorry…to be late," she gasped. "I was trying…to think of…something interesting…to say in my letter."

Before Mr. Gibson could reply, a familiar voice issued from the dining room. "I find it difficult to imagine you at a loss for something diverting to say, Miss Shaw."

As he spoke, Lord Northam stepped into the wide hallway to stand beside his butler. He was dressed in finer attire than Leah had seen him wear since her arrival at Renforth Abbey. His well-cut blue coat emphasized his lean build and the rich frets of chestnut in his dark brown hair. His linen was crisp and spotless. His boots were polished to a dark gleam. Was he going away somewhere or perhaps expecting company?

"Good evening, Your Grace." Suddenly conscious of his rank, she curtsied to the duke for the first time in over a fortnight. "You give me too much credit. It is not easy to generate interesting news when my life is so quiet compared to those of my friends."

"Begging your pardon, Miss Shaw," said the butler, "but the post was late arriving. There are letters for you."

He gestured toward a small silver tray that rested on a narrow table just outside the entry hall.

"*Letters!*" Leah flew toward the table. "More than one?"

"Is that not usually what the use of the plural indicates?" Lord Northam inquired, in what Leah could only conclude was meant to be a jest. "Perhaps you ought to brush up on your grammar by presenting a lesson on the subject to Kit and me."

Leah laughed, more from delight at receiving letters addressed in the familiar handwriting of her friends than because she found His Grace's quip very amusing. Even with their busy lives and exalted ranks, Rebecca, Marian and Hannah had not forgotten her.

As she turned the letters over, fairly caressing the thick paper, the duke spoke again. "My son fell asleep early tonight. Dispensing with his nap and undertaking additional lessons seems to have made it easier for him to settle at bedtime."

"I am pleased to hear it, Your Grace." Leah bit her tongue to keep from reminding him that she had told him such changes might have that benefit.

Now that they were getting along better, she did not want to spoil it by vexing him. Besides, the arrival of her friends' letters made her feel kindly disposed toward the whole world.

"I thought I might join you for a proper dinner," he suggested, "if you do not object."

The duke had dressed up just for...*her?* Flattering

as the notion was, Lord Northam's offer took her aback nonetheless. The letters in her hand called to her the way rich cake might tempt someone faint with hunger. Leah would have liked to bolt her dinner and retire to her room as quickly as possible to read them. Or perhaps she might have taken advantage of her solitude to look them over while she ate. Either act would be inexcusably rude if she were to dine with her employer.

Besides, she would feel so out of place, still in the same plain dress she had worn all day, while he looked so splendid.

But how could she refuse?

As she opened her mouth to reply, it occurred to Leah that cultivating the duke's acquaintance might make it easier to persuade him to loosen his protective grip upon his son. Surely that would be worth a little delay in reading her letters.

What had made him suppose his son's vivacious governess would want to spend her private time in his company? Hayden could not mistake her hesitation when he asked. The lady had made it clear she considered him little better than a jailer who kept his young son imprisoned in a stifling cocoon.

Lately, he'd begun to question whether she might be right.

The extra hours of study which he had feared might tax Kit's strength appeared to be having the opposite effect. His son was sleeping better, eating better and seemed in altogether brighter spirits since he'd been permitted longer lessons with his governess. Could there be other activities Hayden had assumed would harm Kit that might instead prove beneficial?

Perhaps so. But could he afford to take that risk with his child's well-being at stake?

He had taken a different kind of risk coming here this evening in search of pleasant diversion. After a fortnight of uninterrupted sleeps, Hayden felt like a new man—less anxious and irritable, more energetic. But with that energy came a sense of restlessness and a disturbing awareness of how restricted his world had become. He had hoped the novelty of a proper meal in the dining room and a spell of Miss Shaw's lively conversation might take his mind off such troublesome thoughts. But one look at the lady's face told him she found the prospect as appealing as a dose of brimstone and treacle.

"If you prefer to dine in private, I quite understand." He tried to conceal his disappointment, not least from himself. "I can have my dinner later, after you finish."

"You should do nothing of the kind," she cried, much to his surprise. "What objection could I possibly have to you eating in your own dining room? If one of us ought to withdraw, it is I. But since you have kindly invited me to join you, I should be honored to accept."

"Capital!" Her unexpected agreement acted as a tonic upon Hayden's spirits. "It is settled, then."

He turned to the butler, who had remained passive and still during their exchange, almost as if he had not heard a word of it. "You are quite certain, Gibson, that this change in our arrangements will not inconvenience the staff?"

"Not in the least, Your Grace," the butler assured him. "I shall be more than happy to set a place for you at the head of the table again. If you and Miss Shaw will excuse me, I shall attend to it at once."

"The head of the table?" Hayden shook his head. "With Miss Shaw clear down at the other end, we might as well each be dining on our own. We would have to shout ourselves hoarse to carry on a conversation. Set our places across from one another, if you please."

"Very well, Your Grace." Gibson bowed and retreated into the dining room to carry out his master's orders.

Once the butler had left them alone, Hayden found himself suddenly overcome with awkwardness.

"You are certain it will not be an imposition to dine with me?" he asked Kit's governess. "Truly?"

"Truly, Your Grace," she insisted with a persuasive ring of sincerity. "If I gave you cause to think otherwise, I must apologize. Your invitation took me by surprise. I am not attired to dine with a dustman, much less a duke."

She gave a sweeping gesture to indicate her dress, accompanied by a comical grimace that made Hayden smile.

"I see nothing wrong with how you look," he assured her. Privately, he thought the simple style of the garment most becoming on her. "Besides, this is hardly a formal occasion. Are you certain there is no other difficulty?"

Leah Shaw ducked her head, like a child ashamed of some mischief she'd committed. "I must confess,

I *was* anxious to read my letters. It is odd. Only two months ago, I saw most of my dear school friends for the first time in years. Yet I now find myself pining for their company more than I did before."

Was that all? It surprised Hayden to find himself overcome with relief. "I do not think it is odd at all. You must have enjoyed seeing your friends again and now you are more acutely aware of what you've been missing."

Could that be his problem, as well? Had a taste of Miss Shaw's company made him realize how much he missed having a woman in the house?

Hayden roughly dismissed the thought. But another one occurred to him and refused any attempt to put it from his mind. "Besides that, I suppose you have more time on your hands at Renforth Abbey than in your previous positions, and fewer diversions."

Did those disadvantages lead her to view this position as an arduous one, in spite of the generous salary? That possibility troubled Hayden.

"That is true, Your Grace," she admitted with a wistful half smile.

"Then, by all means, go read your post," he urged her. "I will not be offended, I promise you."

Miss Shaw held up her letters. "These are not like milk that will go sour if they sit too long. They will say all the same things if I read them this minute or three hours from now. Dinner with you, on the other hand, is an opportunity that might not come again soon. I should avail myself of it while I have the chance."

Letters going sour like milk? Miss Shaw did have an amusing way of putting things, Hayden had to admit.

As he strove without success to produce an equally witty reply, the butler came to his rescue, appearing in the dining room doorway. "The table has been set as you requested, Your Grace. Shall I inform the kitchen staff that you and Miss Shaw are ready to dine?"

"Please do." He offered his arm to Kit's governess. "Shall we go through, Miss Shaw?"

She might have preferred to read her letters immediately, but the lady had to eat sometime. The pair of them dining together would make less work for the kitchen staff. Yet it was not those practical considerations that made his spirits soar when Leah Shaw smiled at him and took his arm.

As they made their way to the table he said, "This will give us an opportunity to discuss my son's studies without him overhearing."

"An excellent suggestion, Your Grace!" In her eagerness, Miss Shaw gave his arm a little squeeze.

The sensation seemed to travel up his arm and communicate itself to his heart, which began to beat faster and warmer than it had in a great while.

Chapter Six

Not many weeks ago, at her friend Hannah's wedding breakfast, Leah had dined in the company of a baron, a viscount and an earl without the slightest awkwardness. Why did this unexpected invitation to share a meal with the Duke of Northam discompose her so?

When they reached the table, she found herself strangely reluctant to let go of His Grace's arm. And when he held her chair, as if she were a titled lady, her knees grew weak. Rather than sinking onto her seat with elegant grace befitting her surroundings, she dropped like a sack of potatoes.

Might it be because he looked so splendid compared to her—every inch the nobleman? Of course, that must be the reason.

Yet knowing the cause of her strange agitation did not keep Leah's tongue from turning stubbornly mute as she faced Lord Northam across the comparatively narrow width of the long dining table. She hoped he did not expect her to entertain him with amusing conversation. At the moment, she could not think of a word to say, except perhaps to remark on his handsome appearance. Even her lenient sense of discretion warned her that would not be appropriate.

His Grace seemed rather ill at ease, as well, which only made matters worse. Did he regret his impulsive invitation? Had he hoped she would accept one of his offers to reconsider her decision?

As self-conscious silence stretched between them, Leah silently pleaded for the food to arrive, so they would have something to talk about, however commonplace.

As if to fulfill her wish, Mr. Gibson appeared just then, bearing two bowls. With excessive care, he placed one before Leah. Fine wisps of steam rose from the soup, bearing a savory aroma that made her mouth water.

After Mr. Gibson served Lord Northam, the duke picked up his spoon and cleared his throat. Leah awaited some conventional remark that might thaw the stilted atmosphere between them. "Tell me about these friends of yours, Miss Shaw. How many are there? Do you write to one another often?"

His question took her by surprise and loosened her tongue. "There are six of us who have remained especially close over the years. How often we write depends upon how busy we are and whether we have much news to report. In the past, we sometimes wrote serial letters, each adding to the others before sending it on. It saved us time, paper and postage."

Could a man in his position understand the necessity to economize on such trifles? If he thought such a thing, the duke gave no indication of it.

"But you no longer write that way?" He cast his gaze over the small pile of letters on the table beside Leah's place. "Why?"

"There is not the need for economy that there once was." Leah paused to take a sip of her soup, a toothsome blend of shredded vegetables in a thick stock. "Several of my friends have married well. One is now the wife of a sea captain retired from the Royal Navy. Three others are wed to peers. Lady Steadwell lives in Berkshire and Lady Benedict in the Cotswolds. Before coming to Renforth Abbey, I attended the wedding of my friend Hannah Fletcher to the Earl of Hawkehurst."

"Indeed?" The duke seemed surprised by this information, perhaps even disapproving. "I know some of those gentlemen by reputation. But that accounts for only four of your friends. What of the fifth? Is she too plain to attract a husband?"

The notion of Evangeline Fairfax being described as plain was almost enough to make Hannah choke on her soup.

"Nothing of the kind!" Her tongue thoroughly loosened now, she launched into an admiring description of her friend. "Evangeline could have any man she set her cap for, no matter what his rank, if she had any wish to marry."

"But she prefers to remain a spinster? Why?" The duke sounded offended on behalf of all men everywhere.

That amusing notion restored the composure Leah

had earlier misplaced. "If you knew her, you would not have to ask. Evangeline has a very strong will and definite ideas of what should be done and how. I cannot picture her standing at an altar, vowing to *obey* any man."

"And you, Miss Shaw?" inquired the duke. "What is your reason for remaining single while so many of your friends are making brilliant marriages?"

From across the table he cast her a searching look that made her squirm. Not wanting him to guess how much his question flustered her she used humor to parry it.

"For the most obvious of reasons, Your Grace, because no gentleman has ever asked me." There was more to it than that, of course, but Leah had no intention of making it a topic of dinner conversation. She had already told Lord Northam far more about herself than she had disclosed to any of her previous employers.

Anxious to change the subject, she thought of one that would surely divert the duke. "I thought we were to discuss Kit's studies, not the matrimonial misadventures of my friends and me. Are you satisfied with his progress so far? Since he is not present, you may speak candidly."

To Leah's relief, her diversion succeeded. "I would tell you the same thing, whether my son were here or not, Miss Shaw. I am quite astonished at how quickly he is learning to read and do sums. I had no idea Kit was so clever."

By now they had both finished their soup. Mr. Gibson whisked their bowls away then served the fish course, Dover sole in a white sauce seasoned with capers.

With her fork poised over the appetizing dish, Leah paused to ask Lord Northam another question. "Do you find his studies are putting a strain on his health?"

The duke took a bite of fish and chewed on it intently for several seconds. That was hardly necessary, as Leah discovered when her first bite fairly melted on her tongue.

At last His Grace spoke. "You know perfectly well his studies have done my son no harm. I have never seen him so well in…longer than I can recall. Now I suppose I must admit I was wrong so you may have the satisfaction of gloating."

Was that what he thought of her? Leah shook her head in vigorous denial. "The only satisfaction I take is in seeing Kit do so well and seeing you have a little opportunity to rest after all the time you have spent caring for him."

There was still a great deal to be done to give the boy and his father the kind of freedom they both deserved, but they had made a good beginning. Leah hoped the success they'd experienced might make it easier for the cautious duke to take the next step down that long road.

"I never begrudged a moment of that time," His Grace mused aloud. "Now that I have more for myself, I scarcely know what to do with it."

Leah consumed the last of her fish and barely resisted the temptation to lick her plate clean of the tasty sauce. "You must not spend it all on estate business.

Take up some pursuits you enjoy. What sort of things did you like to do before you had a child to care for?"

His Grace considered her question as Mr. Gibson removed their plates and served a chine of beef. "I used to enjoy the company of my wife."

Leah winced at the note of longing in his voice. Could that be part of the reason he had devoted all his time and energy to his son's care—as a distraction from his loss? Now that she had *freed* him from some of his burden, was he feeling his old grief as if it were fresh and raw? He deserved better.

"What sort of things did you and the duchess enjoy doing together?" She tried not to dwell on the duke's loss, the same way she refused to get caught up in pity for Kit. "Reading? Playing cards? Riding?"

"We did sometimes read together, though Celia found it tiresome if it went on too long. She liked to play the pianoforte and she loved to dance when we attended assemblies in London. She enjoyed playing cards, especially for wagers, though that was not a pastime in which I cared to indulge."

It sounded to Leah as if the late duchess had enjoyed more active, social pastimes, while her husband had preferred quieter, solitary pursuits. She could not help but sympathize with Lady Northam. Had she longed to travel and savor the amusements of London while her husband preferred the tranquility of his secluded estate? Might her young son have inherited some of her restlessness? Perhaps it would be best not to dwell on this subject.

"Getting back to our discussion of Kit, sir, it seems

to me there is an important part of his education I have not been able to undertake."

"What is that?" The duke seemed grateful to her for steering their conversation in a different direction. "And why have you been forced to neglect it? Are there particular materials you require? If so, prepare me a list and I shall secure them for you at once."

Leah shook her head. "It is not a lack of materials that prevents me, Your Grace. I assume there are plenty of paper, pens and ink available at Renforth Abbey. I would like Kit to begin practicing his penmanship and learning more advanced arithmetic that will require him to write out the equations. But he cannot undertake written work in bed where ink might spatter on the sheets or spill onto the coverlet."

She rattled on scarcely drawing breath for fear the duke would refuse her before she had a chance to finish. "I know Kit is capable of sitting up. Could we not install a writing table and chair in the nursery where he could take his lessons?"

Concluding her request in a breathless rush, she braced for an argument like the ones they'd had before. At the time, she had rather relished such disagreements, for they injected a bit of excitement into her quiet existence at Renforth Abbey. Now she shrank from the prospect of a hostile exchange with His Grace.

"I fear you have me at a disadvantage, Miss Shaw." The duke did not sound as troubled by it as his words suggested.

"In what way, sir?"

"By compelling me to admit your previous suggestions have not done Kit any harm, you have demolished my arguments before I can make them. It would be perverse of me to claim otherwise."

Had she understood him properly? Leah scarcely dared to hope. "Does that mean you are willing to do what I ask, sir?"

The earl gave a halting nod. "I cannot pretend it comes easy to me, taking any sort of risk where Kit's well-being is concerned. Perhaps I *have* been overly cautious about his health to the detriment of his happiness. You have shown me that if we take small steps, the potential benefits outweigh the risk of harm."

"Thank you, Your Grace!" It was well they had the whole width of the table between them. Otherwise she might have thrown her arms around the duke, so pleased was she with his answer.

Having watched him care for his son, she knew how difficult this decision must be for him. She took it as a rare compliment that he trusted her enough to undertake a course of action that must seem so perilous to him.

She must do everything in her power to make certain he did not regret his decision.

It amazed and touched Hayden how much Leah Shaw had come to care for his son in the two brief months since she had arrived at Renforth Abbey.

As he watched Kit at his writing table, learning to form his letters, Hayden recalled the joyful smile that had illuminated Miss Shaw's face when he'd agreed to give her idea a try. In that moment, it became clear to him that she truly believed greater independence was as vital to Kit's interest as protecting his fragile health. From everything he had witnessed since she'd become the boy's governess, he was gradually being forced to agree.

He roused from his thoughts to find the governess gazing at him with a different sort of smile than the one she'd lavished upon him during their first dinner together. This one might lack the brilliant sparkle of the other, but its soft glow warmed him.

"Your son can make all his letters now, Your Grace," she announced with obvious pride in her young pupil's accomplishment. "He can also form his numbers and write his name in script."

"Well done, Kit!" Hayden strode toward the table to look over his son's latest written work.

"Not my whole name yet." Kit laid down his pen. "Just Christopher for now. But I will soon learn the rest."

Sitting at the writing table with papers and books spread around him, Kit looked like any other school-boy his age, busy doing his lessons. Only his nightcap, dressing gown and the blankets tucked around his legs suggested otherwise. Lately Miss Shaw had begun to advocate that the boy be dressed in day clothes for his lessons.

"I am certain you will master writing your full name before I know it." Hayden patted his son on the shoulder. Was it his imagination, or did the boy's frame feel sturdier beneath his hand? "I have great confidence in your abilities. But you have had enough time sitting up for today. Let me get you settled back in bed, then you can read me a page from *Gulliver's Travels*."

"Not yet." Kit picked up his pen with a defiant air. "I want to try writing Latimer, first."

Before Hayden could reply, Miss Shaw spoke up. "You will have plenty of time to practice your family name tomorrow, Kit. You mustn't tire yourself out."

Hayden shot her a look of gratitude for coming to his assistance. Unfortunately, it was not enough to persuade his son, who deliberately dipped his pen in the inkwell and began to write.

"I don't like to stay in bed so much," the child announced as he tried to form a script letter *L*. "Nobody else at Renforth has to."

His concentration broken by trying to write and talk at the same time, Kit had trouble forming the letter to his satisfaction. Again, he tried, becoming increasingly frustrated.

His governess replaced the stopper in the ink bottle and removed it from the table so he could not continue. "People stay in bed when they are ill or tired and you happen to tire more easily than most."

"No, I don't," Kit insisted with a mutinous scowl. He crumpled up his paper.

"I am certain you are overtired now," Miss Shaw replied briskly as she collected the remaining books and papers from the writing table until it was empty. "Otherwise, you would not be talking this way. Come now, back to bed with you."

She glanced at Hayden and nodded first toward Kit and then toward his bed.

"Miss Leah is right, son." Even in the midst of this disruption, it felt pleasant and natural to refer to her by her Christian name. "You do not want to fall ill and have to miss your lessons for a while."

He slid one arm beneath the child's thin, stiff legs and wrapped the other around his torso.

"No!" Kit struggled against his father's grip as Hayden hoisted him from the chair. "I don't want to go back to bed! I don't want to stay in this room. I want to go somewhere else!"

When his governess tried to calm him, the child hurled his crumpled exercise paper at her. It hit her nose, leaving a streak of black from the ink that had not yet dried.

"You keep me locked up because you're ashamed of me!" In spite of his father's and governess's best efforts to quiet him, the boy began to scream and thrash about.

Hayden feared he might drop his son, or perhaps hurt him by holding on too tight. Was that what he had been doing all these years without realizing it?

In the midst of this turmoil, Hayden was vaguely aware of a knock on the nursery door. Then he heard it open and the butler announce, "Dr. Bannister to see the young master."

Hayden's mounting anxiety and frustration eased upon hearing the physician's name. Dr. Bannister had been away in France for the past three months. Though he had arranged for one of his colleagues to attend Kit if necessary, Hayden had feared his son might contract some serious illness that only his long-serving physician could treat properly.

"What is all this ado?" Dr. Bannister marched into the room, exuding his accustomed calm competence. "How often have I stressed the necessity for preventing my young patient from becoming overexcited?"

"Doctor." Hayden breathed the word like a sigh of relief as he finally managed to deposit his son back in bed. The sound of the physician's voice alone quieted the worst of Kit's struggling. "As usual, you have arrived just when you are needed most."

It was Dr. Bannister who'd worked over the waxen mite Celia had borne with nearly her last breath. He had rubbed the tiny chest and limbs, blown puffs of breath into the small nose and mouth until suddenly the infant had given a feeble cry. With every illness the physician had helped Kit survive, Hayden's reliance on him had grown.

"It does appear I am needed now." Dr. Bannister approached the bed and seized one of Kit's wrists. The child tried to pull away, but the physician was a big man and very strong. Kit's resistance quickly subsided into tremulous whimpering.

After a moment spent silently counting the child's pulse, Dr. Bannister clucked his tongue with an air of profound disapproval. "This will not do at all, my dear boy. You have excited yourself to the point where your heart is beating dangerously fast. If it gets much worse, I fear you might bring on a seizure."

The doctor's pronouncement sent a bolt of ice piercing Hayden's heart. Kit had suffered a seizure when he was only a few months old and nearly died from it. Only Dr. Bannister's skilled treatment had saved the little fellow. In his nightmares, Hayden could still see Kit's tiny body twitching uncontrollably. Never in his life had he felt so helpless. He could not bear the thought of his son suffering like that again, especially now that he was old enough to be aware of what was happening to him.

"He seemed so well only a little while ago." Hayden stroked the boy's head and looked toward Leah Shaw for confirmation.

Kit's governess had retreated to stand silently by the hearth. She appeared as shaken by the incident as Hayden felt.

The doctor opened his satchel. "As a precaution, it will be necessary to administer a calming draft."

"No!" Kit grew agitated again and tried to burrow under the bedclothes. "It tastes bad and makes me sleep and sleep. I shall not be able to do my lessons!"

"Lessons?" The physician unstopped a bottle and poured a quantity of rusty-colored liquid into a small metal receptacle that looked like a cross between a teapot and an overgrown thimble. "What is the child talking about, Your Grace?"

Hayden did not answer immediately for he knew what would have to be done next and he dreaded it. Only the desperate need to prevent Kit from suffering a seizure compelled him to accept the lesser of two evils.

At a nod from the doctor, he reached under the covers and pulled Kit into his arms. His son's head and back rested against his chest while he wrapped one arm around the boy, holding his arms still. With his other hand, he held Kit's head, to keep him from thrashing it from side to side.

"Here we go now." Dr. Bannister approached with the spouted cup. "If you would be more cooperative about taking your medicine, young man, this would be much easier on all of us."

Hayden braced himself for what would come next. The physician must force the cup's spout between Kit's lips and pour in the contents. Meanwhile, he would hold the child's nose so Kit must swallow the medicine or choke.

It had to be done, yet Hayden hated it.

"Stop this at once!" cried Leah Shaw, echoing the words trapped inside of him. "What sort of medicine are you forcing upon my pupil?"

Her outburst made the doctor hesitate and caused Hayden to relax his grip on Kit's arms. The child took full advantage of the distraction. With greater strength than his father had thought him capable, he broke free and batted the medicine cup out of Dr. Bannister's hand. The contents spilled all over the bedclothes, staining them reddish-brown and sending up a spicy-sweet aroma with a bitter undercurrent.

The doctor barked an oath and surged up like a great bear on its hindquarters to turn on Leah Shaw. "See what you have done, you fool woman! What are you doing here, interrupting Lord Renforth's treatment? If he suffers a seizure, you will be to blame!"

He stabbed his forefinger toward her as if it were the barrel of a pistol he longed to fire.

In spite of all Hayden owed the doctor, his protective instincts roused in defense of the lady who dared confront a powerful man whom she feared might harm her young pupil.

Before she could reply with some flippant remark that might only inflame the doctor worse, Hayden spoke up. "This is Miss Shaw, my son's governess. Everything happened so fast, I fear she may not understand we mean Kit no harm. Do not fret, Miss Shaw. Dr. Bannister knows what he is doing."

He cast her a look that he hoped would reassure her, together with a plea not to make the situation worse.

If she understood his wordless request, Leah Shaw chose to ignore it. "Does he, indeed? What *is* the good doctor doing, pray? From what I can see, he appears to be breaking his own rule about keeping your son from getting excited. If one may call abject terror *excitement*."

This was a kind of wit Hayden had not heard from her before—sharp, black and calculated to provoke.

The doctor was even less accustomed to having his actions questioned than Hayden. He responded accordingly. "I do not expect you to understand my treatments, Miss Shaw, since the science of medicine is too complex for the female mind to grasp. If it distresses you to see the boy administered a vital dose of laudanum, I suggest you step outside."

As Hayden watched Kit's physician and his governess confront one another, it felt as if his arms were chained to a pair of powerful draft horses, each pulling in the opposite direction. Thanks to Miss Shaw, his son appeared heartier and happier than he had been in a very long time. Renforth Abbey seemed a warmer, brighter place since she had taken up residence. But had her campaign to allow Kit more freedom given the boy dangerous ideas?

Dr. Bannister clearly thought so and Hayden owed the physician his son's life many times over. How could he cast aside that obligation and question the doctor's advice, which he had followed so rigorously for the past seven years?

"Laudanum?" Leah Shaw pulled a face, as if someone had thrust a vial of the medicine under *her* nose. "Tincture of opium, you mean? You may not think me clever enough to understand what you do, sir, but at least I know better than to give a child poison."

"Poison?" The doctor sneered. "Nonsense! Perhaps if you took a dose now and then, you would not be prone to hysterical outbursts, young woman."

"P-poison?" Kit whimpered, twisting himself around to burrow into his father's embrace. "P-please don't let him give me poison, Papa! I shall be good, I promise. I shan't get excited anymore."

"Hush, now." Hayden held his son close. "I will not let anyone poison you."

"Now see what you have done?" Dr. Bannister snarled at Kit's governess. "You have frightened the child for no reason. After this it will be twice as hard to dose him."

He advanced toward Leah Shaw and reached for her arm. She wrenched it away before he could get a proper grip.

"What do you think you are doing?" She did not

cower from the physician, though he was nearly twice her size. "Don't you dare lay hands upon me!"

"I intend to escort you out," the doctor growled, "before you make any more mischief. If that means I must pick you up and toss you out, so be it."

Hayden had no doubt Dr. Bannister would try to carry out his threat. And what might Leah Shaw do to prevent such an assault upon her freedom? Whatever it was would not be good for either of them, nor for the frightened child in Hayden's arms.

"Doctor, no!" he cried when the physician looked ready to lunge. "That will not be necessary."

Both of them turned to gape at him in a way that might have been comical under other circumstances.

"But, Your Grace…" the doctor protested.

"Miss Shaw," Hayden pleaded, "will you kindly excuse yourself?"

"Not until I have your word you will not let this man dose Kit with that foul brew." Her eyes flashed with the righteous defiance of a martyr willing to go to any extreme for her cause.

Another man might have told her what she wanted to hear to secure her cooperation, but Hayden could not bring himself to lie to her. "I promise I will take no such action until I have carefully considered your charges."

Dr. Bannister scowled, making Hayden realize how alarming his thick black brows and heavy features might appear to a young child. "Surely you are not going to indulge this dangerous nonsense, Your Grace."

For the first time in seven years, Hayden refused to

accept the physician's advice as law. It was a disturbing feeling, yet strangely liberating at the same time. "I assure you, Doctor, when it comes to my son's welfare I take *this nonsense* very seriously indeed."

The duke was prepared to hear her out?

Waves of surprise, relief and gratitude buffeted Leah. It was clear to her that his great, glowering ogre of a physician was accustomed to imposing his will upon everyone at Renforth Abbey. Was he the one who had persuaded the duke that Kit must be wrapped in cotton wool as if he were made of spun glass instead of flesh and blood?

That would have been bad enough, but the thought that he would drug a child into submission was one of the most abhorrent things Leah could imagine.

The duke drew back to look his son in the eye. "Now, Kit, I must speak with Dr. Bannister and Miss Shaw. Mr. Gibson will fetch Tilly to sit with you, but you must promise to rest quietly while we are gone. Can you do that for me?"

The fright he had suffered and the threat of being forcibly dosed with medicine seemed to have shaken the child out of his earlier defiance.

He nodded meekly and said, "Yes, Papa."

It outraged Leah to see a child intimidated into obedience. She had seen enough of that at the Pendergast School to last her a lifetime—young spirits crushed by bullying. It might have happened to Hannah and Grace, perhaps even to her if not for the moral support her circle of friends had provided. She must give Kit some of that same encouragement.

But what if Dr. Bannister insisted she be dismissed from Renforth Abbey? It was clear he exercised powerful influence upon the duke and equally clear that he wanted her gone. Could her fledgling alliance with His Grace stand a chance of prevailing against that?

Having secured his son's agreement, Lord Northam nodded to the butler, who had hovered silently just inside the door ever since announcing the doctor's arrival. Now Gibson hurried away to fetch the nursemaid.

While they waited for Tilly, the duke settled Kit back in bed and the doctor packed his satchel with violent movements and dark muttering under his breath. Leah tried to catch the child's eye and finally succeeded. She pulled a face in a droll imitation of the doctor's ferocious scowl. A subversive little grin twisted the child's lips but rapidly disappeared before his father or the physician had a chance to notice.

At last Tilly appeared, looking rather flustered. Leah was certain Mr. Gibson must have informed the girl of everything that had transpired in the nursery. The duke explained that he wanted her to sit with his son, as usual, and that she must summon him at once if Kit became upset or overexcited.

Then he looked from Dr. Bannister to Leah and nodded toward the door. The physician stalked off at once while Leah hung back. Lord Northam motioned her to go ahead of him. Cloaked in brittle silence, the three of them made their way down to the drawing room.

When they reached it, the duke turned to Kit's doctor. "May I offer you some refreshment?"

"I could do with a restorative after that wretched business." The physician scowled at Leah, who could scarcely resist the temptation to stick out her tongue at him, like a naughty schoolgirl.

Instead she addressed him in a tone of pretended solicitude. "You seemed rather overexcited just now, Doctor. Perhaps *you* would benefit from a liberal dose of laudanum."

"Of all the deuced impertinence!" he thundered. "Your Grace, will you suffer me to be addressed in that way by a servant in your house?"

Before the duke could order her to hold her tongue or, worse yet, apologize to this great bully, Leah was determined to get in one last jab. "What is so objectionable about my suggestion, pray? If tincture of opium is a harmless medication, why should you not be as quick to take it as you are to administer it to your patients?"

This was a skill she had mastered at school—asking the most outrageously blunt questions in a tone of pretended innocence, with just enough of a mocking edge to render figures of authority ridiculous. Such remarks were responsible for most of the scars on her palms, but it had been worth every lash to assert that her thoughts and her words were still free.

Her present inquiry whipped the physician into a frenzy of rage. With a wordless cry of vexation, he raised his hand to strike her. Leah steeled herself to meet the blow as she had so many others, defiant and unflinching.

But before it could land, the duke stepped between her and the physician. "You forget yourself, sir. I will not tolerate such behavior in my house."

Dr. Bannister looked as if smoke was about to pour out his ears. "Yet you would allow this...*creature*... to insult me with impunity after all I have done for your son."

"*For* him or *to* him?" the question popped out before Leah could prevent it.

The duke turned toward her. "That will be quite enough from you, Miss Shaw. Tormenting Kit's physician, a guest in my house, is not helping the situation."

His manner was controlled and his voice rang with moral authority that commanded Leah's respect.

Suddenly she felt ashamed of herself for deliberately goading the doctor. "Yes, Your Grace. Doctor, I apologize if I have offended you. My quarrel is not with you but with the medicine you dispense. I have seen its effects and I firmly believe it is a cure worse than the disease."

"Nonsense!" the physician huffed. Though he had regained control of himself, he seemed to resent Leah's apology as much as her earlier mockery.

"Doctor..." The duke spoke in a warning tone. "I reckon we owe it to Miss Shaw to hear what she has to say. Go on, my dear. You claimed laudanum is poison. What did you mean by that? How do you know of its effects?"

His questions seemed to paralyze Leah's tongue. It had been hard enough to talk about her time at the Pendergast School. But that had come pouring out almost before she could stop herself. Answering the duke now would require a conscious effort to reveal an even more painful episode from her early life. Difficult as it would be to tell Lord Northam, speaking of it in the doctor's hostile presence would render her unbearably exposed and vulnerable.

Yet, if this might be her only opportunity to prevent Kit from being drugged, what choice did she have?

Chapter Seven

Leah Shaw had been eager enough to speak when Hayden wished she would hold her tongue. Now that he'd bidden her explain herself, Kit's governess seemed suddenly reluctant. She appeared to struggle over whether to answer his question or not.

The doctor was in no humor to be patient. "Come, woman, answer His Grace. Truly, sir, I cannot imagine what possessed you to hire someone so disobliging."

Hayden shot him a warning look, but the doctor's words seemed to overcome Miss Shaw's reluctance. "I told you about my grandmother, Your Grace. In spite of her blindness, she was able to get about with my help and lead a full life. Even after she became rheumatic, we managed well enough. Then, one winter, a well-meaning doctor gave her tincture of opium to ease her aches and pains."

Hayden could tell how difficult it was for Miss Shaw to reveal this part of her past. Her usual flippancy and rebelliousness had deserted her. She seemed exposed in a way that made him feel more than ever protective toward her. He wished Dr. Bannister were not present so he could offer her a word or gesture of reassurance.

The doctor clearly had no such sympathy with her. "Laudanum is a perfectly reasonable treatment for the ailment you mention."

"Let her finish!" Hayden snapped.

Leah Shaw made it clear she did not need him to defend her. "Was it *reasonable* that my grandmother spent more time in a stupor from the medicine and less living her life? Was it *reasonable* that she craved more and more of that foul stuff and suffered when she was deprived of it? After she died, I overheard a neighbor say she had taken too much and it had killed her. Do you deny that can happen?"

"Medicine is meant to be taken in its proper dosage." The doctor sounded defensive. "Any substance will have ill effects when consumed in excessive quantities."

Miss Shaw gave a grim nod as if he had confirmed her suspicions. "I would call any substance capable of causing death and other such ill effects a poison."

The physician began to bluster.

Hayden ignored him. "Thank you, Miss Shaw. I would like a private word with Dr. Bannister now, if you would be so kind as to go check on my son."

Kit's governess looked as if she could not decide whether to be anxious or hopeful. He hoped his tone of voice might reassure her.

"Very well, Your Grace." She made a respectful

curtsey then withdrew, though Hayden sensed she was curious to hear what he meant to say to Kit's physician.

Once she had gone, the doctor sank onto the nearest chair with a loud exhalation. "Thank goodness that is over. The sooner you dismiss that impertinent creature, the better it will be for everyone."

Such criticism of Leah Shaw made Hayden's spine stiffen. He crossed his arms behind his back. "Are you expressing a medical opinion or a personal one?"

"Both." The physician gave a harsh chuckle that sounded almost menacing. "Surely you cannot have any intention of keeping her here after that preposterous display."

"Is it true the medicine you have given my son is capable of causing death?"

"As I said, *any* substance in excessive quant—"

"Is it true?" Hayden demanded. "Yes or no?"

"Not in the dosage I give the child. It would take ten times that much to be lethal."

Hayden had to exert all his self-control to keep from staggering. He had not wanted to believe it, but the doctor could not deny Miss Shaw's charges. Hayden was forced to acknowledge that he had assisted in subduing his son, so Dr. Bannister could administer a *medicine* capable of killing Kit.

"Leave my house." He forced his clenched jaw to move so he could utter the words.

"But Your Grace," the doctor protested, surging up from his seat, "you must know I would never allow any harm to come to the boy. Think of all I have done over the years to keep him alive."

Was that living? Hayden fancied he could hear Leah Shaw challenging the physician's defense. Before she came to Renforth Abbey, he had never questioned Dr. Bannister's edicts. But she had forced him to reconsider his long-held assumptions about what was best for Kit.

With difficulty, the duke sought to master his anger toward Kit's doctor. Putting all the responsibility on other shoulders would not absolve him of the decisions he had made. "Your treatment poses an unacceptable risk to my son. All this time I trusted you were doing everything in your power to safeguard his health. Yet while you have been away Kit has improved more in body and spirits than I have ever seen him."

The doctor's expression hardened. "If what you say is true, it is not *all* that has changed at Renforth Abbey in my absence."

"What are you insinuating?" Hayden demanded. "Out with it."

"You have come under the influence of that *governess.*" The physician's lip curled. "I suppose one can hardly blame you. She is young and attractive enough in her way, and you have been alone for a good many years. She has used the child to insinuate herself with you by indulging his every whim, no matter how dangerous. I must caution you against allowing such a dangerous practice to continue."

"Rubbish!" Hayden tried to ignore a traitorous quiver of agreement from somewhere deep inside him. "Miss Shaw has not the slightest design upon me. She barely tolerates my company. She only agreed to remain at Renforth Abbey for Kit's sake and then for no more than a year."

All that was perfectly true, yet he could not deny finding Leah Shaw more than a little attractive. And lately he had become more conscious of the loneliness he'd sought to escape by devoting himself to the care of his child. Was it possible his increasing approval of Kit's governess had begun to influence his attitude about what was best for his son?

What if she, like the physician he had trusted for so many years, turned out to be wrong?

Leah's breath came fast and shallow as she slipped out of the drawing room and shut the door behind her. So many intense, conflicting emotions churned inside her, she feared they might spew out in a violent effusion of tears. Much as she hated to admit it, perhaps the doctor was not entirely wrong about the ill effects of too much excitement.

One thing she knew for certain was that she hated feeling this way! It made her heart seem so precariously *open*. She would much rather hide her feelings behind an outrageous jest or vent them in a riot of laughter. But after her interview with the duke and Kit's physician, she found it impossible to mount any of her usual defenses.

Telling the two men how her beloved grandmother had been destroyed by the remedy that was supposed to help her roused painful memories Leah had striven for years to forget. Now she yearned for the kind of comforting embrace she had once received from Grace

Ellerby or Rebecca Beaton. But her friends were all so far away. Instead she found herself wondering how it might feel to receive such a gesture of consolation from Lord Northam.

The thought shocked her.

The duke was her employer not her friend, Leah chided herself as sternly as her teachers had once done. Yet she could not drown out a mocking whisper in the back of her mind. It reminded her that several of her friends' husbands had once been *their* employers.

Leah reacted as violently to that notion as Dr. Bannister had to her taunts. She did *not* want any nearer connection with the duke or any man! Pleased as she was to see her friends so happy with their new families, she had no more interest in marriage than ever. It was an institution after all, and institutions were designed to curb an individual's freedom for the collective good. She had vowed never to submit to that kind of regime again.

The murmur of voices from the drawing room was growing sharp, though Leah could not make out what the duke and the doctor were saying to one another. She longed to press her ear to the door and eavesdrop on their conversation, the way she had sometimes done at school, to the horror of her friends. Was His Grace telling Dr. Bannister he would no longer permit his son to be dosed with opiates? Or was he heeding the physician's demands to send her away? Dr. Bannister would have been right at home on the staff of the Pendergast School.

A swell of gratitude toward the duke rose within

Leah as she recalled how he had insisted her voice be heard and how he had placed himself between her and the doctor's raised hand. All he had asked in return was for her to go to his son's nursery. His recent conduct had persuaded her more than ever that she owed him her cooperation. Besides, after the frightening experience Kit had endured today, he would need her comfort and guidance.

Spurred by those thoughts, she hurried to the nursery, hoping her time as Kit's governess would not be cut short.

"How has he been, Tilly?" she whispered to the nursemaid with a nod toward the bed.

"Quiet as a mouse, Miss," the girl replied. "I asked if he wanted me to fetch any of his playthings, but he just shook his head without a word."

Leah wondered if all the upheaval might have tired the child and made him fall asleep. But when she approached the bed he looked up at her with wide, troubled eyes. Her young pupil might be quiet, but she could tell he was far from calm.

She settled herself on the bed beside him. "Shall I read to you for a while or would you rather read to me?"

Kit ignored her question. Instead, in a terrified whisper, he posed one of his own. "What did Papa say? Is he going to let the doctor poison me with that sleeping medicine?"

His choked voice and his stricken look smote Leah's conscience. What had possessed her to use that word in front of a child his age? No wonder he'd been so quiet all this time, stifled by terror that his father and the doctor were conspiring to do away with him.

"No one is going to poison you." She wrapped her arms around her young pupil and brought his head to rest against her shoulder. "I should not have said that about the doctor's medicine. I do not approve of its use, especially on someone your age, so I got rather carried away. You must know your Papa would *never* do anything he thought might harm you. You mean the world to him. Everything he does is for you."

The child let out a long, quivering sigh and Leah felt the tightly clenched muscles of his thin frame begin to relax into her embrace.

She was about to congratulate herself on allaying his fears when he challenged her assurances. "If that is true, why does Papa keep me from doing so many things I want? I feel like Gulliver when he was all tied up at first in Lilliput."

Was this her fault, too? A sharp flick of guilt stung Leah's conscience. In her quest to secure more freedom for Kit, had she only made him discontented and resentful of his father, who loved him so dearly?

"I understand." She stroked the child's fine dark hair in a comforting caress. "But it is really more like when the Queen of Brobdingnag kept Gulliver in his little traveling box. He may have wanted to get out and go where he liked, but there were so many dangers for him in that world. One of the giants might have trodden on him by accident. Or he might have drowned in a puddle."

"He still got carried off by the monkey," Kit argued

with something like his usual spirit. "And he had to fight the wasps, but he managed well enough. Besides, I am not tiny like Gulliver. There is no danger of anyone at Renforth Abbey stepping on me."

"That is true." Leah allowed herself a chuckle to lighten the mood. "But there are other dangers your father fears because your constitution is not strong and your legs do not work the way they should. When you started carrying on a while ago, he was afraid you might work yourself into a fit, which could have harmed you a great deal. He was so desperate to prevent it, he grasped at any measures, even one that might have been...excessive."

"I couldn't help getting upset," Kit said, though Leah sensed a note of shame in his voice. "Papa provoked me. He would not let me have my way."

"We cannot always have our own way in everything." As the words came out, it shocked Leah to realize she was echoing one of her teachers from the Pendergast School, though in a gentler tone. "We have to consider others, as well. What if Cook decided she did not feel like making your dinner or the scullery maid fancied sleeping in late rather than lighting your fire in the morning? Life might be more agreeable for them, but not for you...would it?"

Kit mulled over that idea, which might never have occurred to him before. Then his head brushed against Leah's shoulder as he shook it from side to side.

"Freedom is not entirely *free*," she continued, hoping Kit was clever enough to grasp an idea she had resisted understanding until she was much older. "It comes at a price of self-control and responsibility. If you want your father to grant you more freedom, you must show him that you are capable of controlling your behavior, even when you do not get your own way. Do you think you can do that?"

Kit heaved a sigh that suggested he knew it would not be easy. "I will try."

"I hope you will." Leah strove to sound confident he would succeed, though she was far from certain. She sensed the child's mounting frustration with the restrictions imposed by his father. The duke's habit of giving in to Kit over everything *except* his wish for greater freedom had left the child unaccustomed to exercising any self-control. "Remember how Gulliver kept calm and went along with the rules the people of Lilliput placed upon him? He could have raged and wreaked havoc upon their island to get his way. What do you suppose might have happened then?"

Kit drew back from her embrace, his forehead wrinkled and his eyes bright with the kind of interest he usually showed during his lessons. "They might have shot him with their arrows and tied him down again. And some of the Lilliputians might have been hurt when he fought them."

"I believe you are right." Leah wondered if her pupil might respond to more formal instruction in proper conduct. "But by showing the king he could keep his temper and act responsibly, Gulliver was able to gain his trust and secure greater freedom."

"So will I." Kit's mouth set in a resolute line that

reminded Leah of his father. "Gulliver was clever and brave. I want to be like him."

Just then the door opened and the duke entered. He seemed burdened with many heavy cares, the way he had looked when Leah first came to Renforth Abbey. At the time, she had been antagonistic, adding to his problems. Now her heart went out to him and she longed to ease his troubles, if she could.

He must have overheard the last of his son's words for he asked, "Who is it you wish to emulate? Me?"

It was a rather awkward jest, yet Leah appreciated his attempt to defuse the tension that lingered between the three of them.

When Kit shrank from his father with an anxious look that she knew must grieve the duke, she came to his aid. "Your son would do well to model himself after you, sir. But in this case, he was referring to Mr. Gulliver. He hopes to exercise the kind of self-control the character did when faced with his many challenges."

"A fine example to follow." His Grace gave a thoughtful nod and perched on the edge of the bed gingerly, as if he feared Kit might explode in another tantrum if he approached too close.

"Papa," said the child, his thin, frightened tone a marked contrast to his recent confidence, "where is Dr. Bannister? Is he going to come and give me that poi—medicine?"

That anxious question was foremost in Leah's mind, as well. What would she do if the duke decided to ignore her pleas? Threaten to leave Renforth Abbey? For all she knew, Kit's physician had succeeded in persuading His Grace to dismiss her.

To her overwhelming relief, the Duke shook his head. "Dr. Bannister has gone away and I do not expect him to return. I shall begin at once to look for a new physician to tend you—one who will never bring that sort of *medicine* into my house."

"Thank you, Papa!" Kit pitched toward his father, who opened his arms to embrace the child. "Thank you, thank you!"

As the duke cradled his son with such obvious affection, Leah recalled her fleeting wish to seek solace in his strong arms. When he glanced up, she cast him a wide, warm smile that she hoped would communicate her gratitude, admiration and some of the other complicated emotions he inspired in her.

But not all of them. She did not want him to glimpse signs of other feelings that confused and alarmed her.

"Kit does not owe me his gratitude for sending Dr. Bannister away," Hayden assured his son's governess during the next opportunity he had to talk privately with her. "Nor do you, Miss Shaw."

A few days after the upsetting confrontation, Kit had finally settled well enough that his father and governess were able to dine together after he went to sleep.

"The truth is, I owe my son an apology." Hayden concentrated on his plate to avoid Leah Shaw's frank, discerning gaze. "I should never have let Bannister dose him with laudanum."

He could not forget the vivid smile Miss Shaw had

offered him when it was all over. Her beaming countenance seemed to promise that in spite of his terrible mistake, all would be well again. It communicated admiration and trust—intangible but priceless gifts he had done far too little to deserve. He felt even more unworthy of her regard when he recalled the doctor's cynical warning that she might be using Kit to insinuate herself with him. He could not help wondering if it might be true.

"You did not know the harm it could cause." Kit's governess seemed prepared to excuse his actions more readily than he could. "And you must have believed it was the best thing for Kit at the time. I may not always agree with your choices, but I no longer doubt you have your son's best interests at heart. Dr. Bannister is the one who should have known better. He took advantage of your trust. You mustn't blame yourself."

"That is easier said than done." Hayden could not resist looking up at her, admiring her lively beauty and basking in her sympathy. "If I have learned one thing since my son was born, it is that being a parent means questioning every choice I make and always being afraid that I have made the wrong one. Dr. Bannister always seemed so certain *his* way was right. His treatments appeared to rescue Kit from death's door on more than one occasion."

Something powerful compelled him to justify his faith in the physician. Hayden told Leah Shaw about the night of Kit's birth and the time he'd suffered the seizure.

"I suppose it was easier to trust in his judgment

than my own," he concluded. "Following his advice absolved me of the final responsibility."

"Perhaps," she replied in a gentle tone. "But when you discovered the truth, you sent him away. I know that cannot have been easy for you, but I believe time will prove it was the right course. Now that you no longer feel obliged to follow all the doctor's orders, may I hope you will loosen some of your restrictions on Kit? Perhaps even allow a little excitement in his life?"

The winsome twist of her lips and the golden sparkle in her hazel eyes were nearly irresistible, yet Hayden could not entirely purge the poisonous suspicions Dr. Bannister had planted in his mind. "Would you have me blindly follow your system as I did the doctor's? I know you believe it is the right way to bring up my son, but he was every bit as certain. I do not wish to make the same mistake twice."

He thought Kit's governess might react angrily and spoil their pleasant dinner by arguing the point.

To his surprise, she greeted his pronouncement with a trill of laughter that carried only a faint rueful note. "I should have known it could not be that easy. Still I give you fair warning that I will continue to advocate for greater freedom for your son."

Hayden could not prevent the corners of his mouth from inching upward. "I would expect no less of you, my dear Miss Shaw. Indeed, if you stopped I might suspect an imposter had taken your place at Renforth Abbey. For now, let us give the matter a rest. Once we are finished eating, allow me to conduct you on a tour of the great hall. It was once the Cistercian's chapter house when this place was an abbey."

She nodded eagerly. "I look forward to it, Your Grace. As fulfilling as I find my work with your son, I must confess the time during my off-duty hours sometimes hangs heavy on my hands."

She was not voicing a complaint, Hayden sensed, but rather her appreciation for the diversion he offered. Still, the knowledge that she was not content at Renforth Abbey troubled him.

Chapter Eight

It might be slow going, but she *was* making progress at winning more freedom for Kit. Leah relished a growing sense of accomplishment as autumn turned the Somerset countryside golden.

In spite of the duke's warning that he meant to continue his cautious course, he no longer seemed quite so intractable. Leah had discovered that if she proceeded slowly and gave him a little time to consider each new request, he would often agree to it. If His Grace seemed more than usually resistant, she would counter by asking for something she knew he would consider outrageous. After he blustered himself out, she would sweetly offer to settle for a less drastic concession—the very one he had balked at earlier.

This manner of negotiating had won Kit the opportunity to eat his luncheon and tea at the table with Leah. The duke had permitted several new items to be added to his son's diet. When he saw how eagerly Kit consumed what he called "real food" and how the boy began to put flesh on his delicate frame, Lord Northam soon withdrew his objections to all but the richest dishes.

Leah's latest campaign was to get Kit out of his nursery now and then.

One evening, when the duke conducted her on a tour of the east range gallery, hung with a treasure trove of fine paintings, she seized an opportunity to raise the subject. "Renforth Abbey is such a magnificent house. It seems a shame your son cannot see more of it. I described your library to him and he said how very much he would like to see it. I wish I could take him there for some of his lessons."

"Perhaps in the spring," replied the duke, who had lately begun to put her off with delay rather than outright refusal. "As fine a library as it is, you must admit it is not well heated. I would not want Kit to take a chill."

He had her there, Leah was forced to concede. Perhaps to protect the books from the danger of fire, the library had only a small fireplace. But if Kit was not permitted downstairs until spring it would stall his progress and leave much more to be done before she departed Renforth Abbey.

"You may be right." She tried to soften the duke's objection by agreeing with him. "Perhaps it would be better to continue having lessons in the nursery and then take Kit for a carriage ride in the afternoon. The fresh air would do him good and I know how much he would enjoy a change of scene."

She braced for a blast from the duke, confident that

he would not be expressing hostility toward her, but concern for his son. Instead, to her surprise, he responded with a faintly mocking chuckle. "I know what you are trying to do, my dear Miss Shaw. I must warn you it will not work this time."

Lord Northam's use of the conventional pleasantry *my dear* flustered Leah to a ridiculous degree, as it did every time he addressed her that way. Averting her face to hide a foolish blush, she pretended to study a vast canvas by Canaletto. She told herself the duke meant nothing by it, even if he seemed to use those particular words more frequently of late. And if his voice seemed to warm and soften when he spoke them, it must be a vexing trick of her imagination.

"What will not work?" She feigned innocence. "What is it you suppose I am trying to do?"

He chuckled again, a sound that wrapped around her like a velvet cloak. "You know perfectly well what I mean and I should have recognized your strategy sooner. You expect me to be so aghast at the thought of Kit going for a carriage ride that I will immediately agree to the lesser evil of lessons in the library."

Leah spun to face him, though she was not certain the blush had entirely faded from her cheeks. "I refuse to concede that either of the ideas I proposed is *evil*. Have any of my previous suggestions done Kit harm?"

The duke thought for a moment, his earlier triumphant grin turning increasingly rueful. "Not yet, though there is a first time for everything and I truly believe Kit will be better off remaining in his nursery through the winter."

"But this is the south of England, not Greenland," Leah pleaded, vexed that His Grace had chosen this occasion to see through a gambit that had served her so well. "Besides you know Kit grows frustrated with being kept in his nursery. He has tried to be patient, but I fear if he must wait until spring to see more of the world, he may give way to another tantrum."

The duke's face blanched but his aristocratic features tensed in a resolute expression. "I will not be blackmailed with that threat, Miss Shaw. I vow, you ought to take up negotiating trade treaties. You would make this country a fortune."

"Not if you represented the other side," she quipped, unable to resist the temptation to tease him. "Come now, there must be some reason that would induce you to bring Kit downstairs."

"Perhaps…" He started to respond then stopped himself. "I mean…no. Not until spring. Somerset may not be Greenland but this house can still be damp and drafty in the winter."

"You were going to say something else." Leah sensed a point of weakness and sought to turn it to Kit's advantage. "There *is* a possibility you would consider. Do tell me."

"So you can break out your thumbscrews and persuade me of it against my better judgment? I think not." The duke tried to feign severity but he could not extinguish the rogue twinkle in his eye.

He had come to *enjoy* this give and take between them, Leah sensed with a flicker of amusement. And so had she. That realization provoked a bewildering clash of emotions.

Rather than examine and confront her feelings, she did what she had done so often in the past—sought a safe diversion. In this case, there was one close at hand. "If you will not tell me then I must *guess* what you were about to say. Could it be the dining room? You would allow Kit to take some of his meals there with us?"

The duke shook his head. "Out of the question."

Leah's thoughts ranged room to room through the house in search of possibilities. "The great hall? The drawing room? The chapel?"

A furtive flicker in Lord Northam's eyes told Leah her last guess had hit the mark.

"The chapel," she repeated. "Of course! You want Kit to be able to worship and hear the Word of God that has brought you comfort and strength. I think it is an excellent idea. Quite inspired, actually."

"Perhaps," the duke replied. "But not at this time of year. The chapel is the coldest part of the house. The Cistercian brothers clearly believed in the virtue of self-denial. Besides I already read the Scriptures to my son and pray with him."

"I know." A brooding sensation stirred in Leah's heart, as it did whenever she saw Lord Northam and his son with their dark heads bowed in prayer. "But there is something special about worshipping in a con-secrated place with other believers. It is like taking a single candle and putting it into a chandelier. The crys-tals reflect and magnify its light."

"That is why it will be the first place I take my

son when conditions are favorable to bring him down from the nursery. 'To everything there is a season,' remember."

Part of Leah wanted to continue insisting and cajoling until she secured the duke's agreement, but she feared her insistence might spoil the camaraderie that had taken time to develop between them. She would try again in another day or two and hope to catch him in a more receptive mood. Until then, there was another subject she wished to discuss. "It is hard to argue when you quote Scripture, sir. Speaking of time and season, Christmas will be upon us in five more weeks."

"So it will." The duke gave the Canaletto canvas a final glance then strolled on to the next painting, which depicted *The Adoration of the Magi*. "I have ordered more Lilliputian figures for Kit's present, as well as some of those connecting puzzles you told me about. Why do you mention it? I suppose you want me to take Kit on an expedition to collect boughs for decorating."

It was clear he intended the question facetiously, but Leah responded as if she believed he was sincere. "What a good idea! I am certain an outing like that would make Kit happier than any Christmas gift money could buy."

The duke looked so alarmed that Leah did not have the heart to rally him further. "But that was not what I intended to say at all. I only meant to tell you that I have received an invitation to spend Christmas with one of my friends. Grace…that is Lady Steadwell and her family who live in Berkshire. I wondered if you would permit me a fortnight's leave to take a little holiday."

Lord Northam continued to look troubled. Perhaps her change of subject had not fully sunk in.

"You wish to go away for Christmas?" he asked as if he had never heard of such a thing before.

"If you can spare me." Leah glanced at the painting of the nativity scene. "Grace is expecting a happy event before long and I believe she could use my help with her other children."

"Does the family not have a governess of their own?" The duke sounded strangely antagonistic.

"They do, but I understand she has requested time to visit with *her* family. If you cannot spare me, I will write to Grace at once so she can make other arrangements. I did not foresee any difficulty, since I assume you mean to spend the holidays very quietly."

She had been delighted to receive Grace's invitation, tactfully phrased as if Leah would be doing *her* a favor by accepting. In spite of the duke's occasional company in the evenings, Leah had begun to mind the isolation of Renforth Abbey. The prospect of Yuletide merriment at Nethercross beckoned her to Berkshire.

"That is true," Lord Northam admitted, his gaze fixed on the painting. "I hope you will pardon my selfishness, Miss Shaw. Of course you must have a holiday. Take as much time as you wish to visit your friend. Kit will miss you a great deal no doubt and look forward to your return in the new year."

"I shall miss him, too." Leah was dismayed to realize her words were more than a conventional response.

She had gotten along well with most of her former pupils, but never enough to make her regret moving on to her next post when the time came. Somehow, Kit had quickly won a special place in her heart. And she suspected he might not be the only member of the family she would miss during her absence.

That was all the more reason she needed to put some time and distance between her and Renforth Abbey.

"How much longer will it be until Miss Leah comes home, Papa?"

It was only New Year's Day, but already Kit's constant refrain had become as familiar to his father as the chorus of a Christmas carol.

"You are clever with numbers," Hayden said, striving to curb his impatience with the child. He could scarcely blame Kit for missing his vivacious governess when *he* felt her absence, as well. "Surely you can count up the days until Miss Shaw's return. She will not be setting off until after Twelfth Night and that is how many days away?"

Kit wrinkled his nose. "This is not a proper lesson. I cannot have any of those until Miss Leah comes home. I wish she would come tomorrow."

The peevish pitch of his son's voice grated on Hayden's nerves like a musician scraping his bow over out-of-tune fiddle strings. "You may wish all you like, but it will do no good. Besides, Renforth Abbey is not her *home*. Miss Shaw is employed here, like Tilly and Roger and Mr. Gibson."

Was he reminding his son of that fact, Hayden wondered, or himself?

"But none of *them* went away for Christmas." Kit picked up the figure of a Lilliputian lady that resembled his governess. "Why did Miss Leah have to go?"

"She did not *have to*." Hard as Hayden tried to keep his voice from sharpening, he did not succeed. "Miss Shaw wanted to spend the holidays with her friends."

"Are we not her friends?" Kit persisted. "Does she not like us anymore?"

His son's innocent question took Hayden aback. Did Leah Shaw not enjoy their company? She certainly seemed fond of Kit. As for him, Hayden was not so sure. He told himself it did not matter, yet deep down he knew it did. Perhaps if he'd made himself more agreeable, she might not have felt the need to go elsewhere for Christmas, leaving her young pupil bereft.

"I am certain your governess does not *dislike* you. But Renforth Abbey is not the most festive place to spend Christmas. I reckon Miss Shaw hankered for a bit more Yuletide cheer."

What sort of entertainments might she be enjoying at Lord Steadwell's estate? Hayden wondered. Music, games…possibly dancing? Would she be the family's only guest or might there be others—a brother or cousin of the baron, perhaps? The thought troubled him somehow.

"What does *festive* mean?" Kit asked.

Hayden tried to explain, but the activities that might be considered festive were outside his son's experience. That had never bothered him before. Such doings might have led to perilous excitement. Long ago, he had decided that what Kit did not know, he would not miss. Now he wondered if he had done right.

"Would you like to sit up at the table and put together one of your connecting puzzles?" he proposed by way of a diversion.

"I suppose." Kit did not sound as eager as he had the past few days.

Did the child secretly wish he could have escaped Renforth Abbey with his governess for the merriment of Nethercross? Hayden tried to think of an activity that might amuse his son. "It is snowing out, you know. Shall I carry you over to the window so you can see?"

Kit immediately perked up.

"Will you, Papa?" The child sounded as if he had been offered a treat of unimaginable delight.

A spasm of pity for his son wrung Hayden's heart—and not on account of Kit's infirmity.

He nodded and smiled. "You seemed to enjoy it that other time with Miss Shaw."

"But *you* didn't." Kit sounded puzzled by his father's willingness to do something previously forbidden. "You got angry with her and sent her away. She would never do it again, though I asked and asked."

Miss Shaw had respected his wishes even though she did not agree with them. That could not have been easy for someone so naturally rebellious. For some reason it touched Hayden's heart.

"Perhaps I was hasty in my judgment." He fetched Kit's warmest dressing gown and helped the child into it. "Perhaps I was…wrong."

It was not an admission he was comfortable making. If he owned to being wrong once, Kit might begin to question all his future decisions. But his conscience would settle for nothing less than the truth.

"Besides," he continued, "you are a good deal healthier now than you were last summer and I am strong enough to carry you safely without any danger of falling."

"Miss Leah would not have slipped if you hadn't shouted at her."

"Are we going to look out at the snow or sit here talking?" Hayden bent forward to scoop his son into his arms.

"Not that way," Kit protested. "Let me ride on your back like Miss Leah did."

Hayden hesitated. With the boy cradled in his arms, he would be fully in control of Kit's safety. Then he fancied he could hear Leah Shaw arguing that his son might need to feel more in control—the master of an imaginary steed rather than a babe in arms.

"Very well," he agreed, contrary to long habit and his better judgment. "But you must promise to hang on tight."

"I will." Kit fairly trembled with excitement as his father shifted him to his back.

This type of excitement was not the same as the violent tantrums he so dreaded, Hayden realized with a pang of regret. He should not have denied his son the former out of fear of the latter. "Here we go. Now, Kit, there is a difference between hanging on tight and actually throttling me."

"I'm sorry, Papa." The boy chuckled as if his father were joking, which he was, though not entirely.

When they reached the window, Hayden nudged back the curtains. Then he turned sideways so Kit could see outside. A light dusting of snow had carpeted the grounds and settled on the trees. More fat flakes drifted down from the sullen gray sky.

Kit gave a gasp of wonder. "It looks so different than it did before. Where have all the flowers gone?"

"They are sleeping for the winter," Hayden replied. "They will grow again in the spring and the trees will sprout new leaves. Birds that have flown away to warmer places will return again."

To everything there is a season. He recalled telling Leah Shaw that as an argument for keeping Kit snug and safe in his nursery, where one season was little different from the next. Now he wondered whether his long winter of grief and worry might have begun to thaw at last.

"What is snow?" asked Kit. "Where does it come from?"

Hayden explained as best he could about clouds and how the cold weather froze raindrops into delicate crystal flakes that melted again when warmed. As they stood staring out at the winter landscape and talking about it, the duke found himself gaining a whole new appreciation for the intricate workings of nature with its seasonal rhythm.

"I do believe Miss Shaw will have to add natural history to your studies when she returns," he concluded. "I believe you will find it very interesting."

"Is that her coming now?" asked Kit. "See the carriage."

The child's words sparked a flare of elation inside Hayden, as if someone had set off fireworks.

Reality extinguished them. "It cannot be her. That is a private traveling coach."

If Miss Shaw had returned early, she would have hired a pony cart from the village, not this elegant equipage.

"I wonder who it is?" asked Kit.

"I believe it might be your Aunt Althea." What could have brought his sister to Renforth Abbey, unannounced, on New Year's Day? And what trouble would she make?

"I hope the girls have not been too much trouble for you over Christmas, Leah." Grace handed her friend a cup of tea as they sat together enjoying a rare few moments of peace and privacy. "Miss Colbrooke is an excellent governess but she cannot begin to rival you for high spirits. Phoebe and Sophie have both asked if we can keep you on at Nethercross."

"But not Charlotte?" Leah inquired with a mischievous grin.

She had sensed that her friend's eldest stepdaughter did not approve of a grown woman who carried on like her younger sisters. In that respect Charlotte reminded her of the Duke of Northam.

"Do not mind Charlotte." Grace offered Leah a plate piled high with biscuits and sandwiches. "She takes time to warm up to new people, but when she does there is a no more devoted friend in the world."

"She is clearly devoted to *you*." Leah helped herself to several tempting morsels from the plate of refreshments. "That secures her my approval even if it is not entirely returned. The way she fetches you pillows and tries to keep you from being on your feet too long is quite touching. Once your baby is born I imagine she will be like a second mother."

It had not been easy, coaxing Charlotte to accompany her sisters on a visit to Admiral DeLancey's with their governess, who had returned the previous day from *her* Christmas visit. Only the promise of seeing Mrs. DeLancey's handsome son had finally persuaded Charlotte to go, giving Grace and Leah this rare time alone.

"I am relieved that all three of the girls are pleased about the baby." Grace laid a hand on her rounded belly with a sweet, brooding smile that reminded Leah of the Madonna in one of Lord Northam's paintings.

Far too many things made her think of the duke and Kit and Renforth Abbey. Leah had hoped this visit would weaken her growing attachment to them, but it seemed to be having the opposite effect.

"Enough about me and mine," said Grace. "I hope you have enjoyed spending Christmas at Nethercross as much as we have enjoyed your company. I could not bear the idea of you buried away on that remote estate at this time of year, with no merriment to speak of."

"I have had a splendid time at Nethercross!" Leah assured her friend. "Skating with the girls and helping them decorate the house. Not to mention that jolly party you hosted on Boxing Day for your tenants and neighbors. But the best part of all has been seeing you so happy with your new family. No one deserves it more!"

"I am not certain I deserve such happiness at all," Grace mused as she sipped her tea, "when I think how I secured my position at Nethercross under false pretenses and disguised myself from dear Rupert. But I am vastly grateful for the blessings I have received. Even if our circumstances were far more modest, I would count myself the most fortunate of women to have secured a loving husband and a happy family."

Pleased as Leah was for her friend, she told herself she did not envy Grace. In spite of her delicate condition the poor woman had scarcely enjoyed a single moment's rest during Leah's entire visit. If she was not overseeing the smooth running of the large household, she was helping His Lordship with plans for the Boxing Day party or mediating squabbles among her stepdaughters.

It had made Leah reflect on how many more responsibilities her friend had as lady of the house than when she was simply a hired governess. A wife with children did not have the benefit of half days off or the freedom to come and go as she wished. Too many other people depended on her…and was that not a form of bondage?

"I hope with all my heart you are happy, too." Her friend's solicitous words stirred Leah from her thoughts. "Teaching that poor bedridden little boy must be quite heartbreaking at times."

"Not in the least." Leah wondered why she felt compelled to defend her pupil from Grace's pity. "Kit does not feel sorry for himself nor do I. And he is no longer bedridden. He sits up every day for his lessons and meals. I am confident he can have a very fulfilling life if I can only persuade his father not to coddle him quite so much."

Though Grace nodded, Leah sensed her friend was not entirely persuaded. "It must be disagreeable to be constantly at odds with the duke about what is best for his son."

Leah laughed and shook her head. "You would not say that if you could hear our discussions. The duke and I have come to respect each other's beliefs. I know he adores his son and would do anything to protect him. His Grace knows that I have Kit's best interests at heart. The give and take between us has brought the boy greater freedom while protecting his health and safety. I look forward to making more progress this winter, then putting on a great push once spring comes."

As she spoke of the duke and his son, Leah could no longer deny how much she missed them. Her holiday at Nethercross had been highly enjoyable, yet she found herself eager to get back to Renforth Abbey.

"It does sound like a rewarding endeavor," Grace replied. "I hope you will succeed in winning more freedom for the boy. But speaking as a mother, I can sympathize with the duke's desire to protect such a vulnerable child. It must be a very lonely life for him, poor man."

Leah winced as if very strong, invisible hands had

gripped her heart and squeezed. Was Hayden Latimer as lonely as Grace suggested? Was that why he had exhausted himself caring for Kit—so he would not have the time or energy to notice? Was it why he had invited her to dine with him some evenings and given her tours of his house? Not because he had any particular liking for her, but because he was desperate for any sort of company.

His motives for the attention he paid her made no difference, Leah told herself and tried to pretend she believed it.

"I'm so pleased you allowed Miss Shaw to stay, dearest," Althea gushed as she and Hayden left the nursery after tucking Kit in for the night. "I was afraid you might dismiss the poor girl the minute she arrived."

"I very nearly did." Hayden tried to sound annoyed so his sister would not suppose he approved of her meddling in his life. Yet he could not bear to think what the past several months might have been like without Leah Shaw. "You had no right to engage a governess for Kit without my consent. And it was unfair not to warn Miss Shaw that her arrival would be unexpected."

Althea waved away his complaints in her usual highhanded manner. "I knew it was no use asking since you were bound to refuse. But I hoped you might give Miss Shaw a try if she turned up unannounced. Now you must admit that having a governess has not done Kit a bit of harm. The dear little fellow looks as well as I have ever seen him."

Much as he disliked conceding a point to his interfering sister, Hayden found he had no choice. "Very well. It was not your worst idea and you did make a good choice in Miss Shaw. She manages to make learning an enjoyable experience for Kit. I had no idea how clever he is until she began teaching him. Both Miss Shaw and I have been astonished at the progress he has made in his studies."

"You're welcome!" His sister beamed with satisfaction as they reached the dining room. "I know you detest it when I tell you what to do, but I only want what is best for Kit and for you."

An unexpected impulse of gratitude and love for his sister swelled in Hayden's chest. They were as different in temperament as two people could be. Consequently they had a history fraught with disagreement. But Althea did care for him and for Kit. She had been willing to risk his anger to give them what she believed they needed, the way he often did with his son.

As Gibson prepared to usher them in to dine, Hayden pulled his sister close for a brief but warm kiss on the cheek. "Thank you, Althea."

She seemed surprised by the gesture but responded with a tight squeeze before he drew back. "Your Miss Shaw must be a perfect treasure to have provoked such a display. I do wish she hadn't gone away for Christmas so I could have got a full report from her. But I can hardly blame her for going. She did not seem the sort of person to appreciate the seclusion of Renforth Abbey as you do."

She seized Hayden's arm as he escorted her in to

dinner. "One would scarcely know it was Christmas by the look of this place."

Althea shook her head in disapproval of the modest trimming of holly and ivy around the base of the candlesticks in the middle of the table.

A flicker of his accustomed impatience with his sister flared, but Hayden tamped it down. Much as he disliked the idea that some action of his might have caused Leah Shaw to spend Christmas elsewhere, he knew the charge was not unjust. "I see no reason to burden my staff with the tasks of decorating the house when there is no one to notice. If I'd had any warning you intended to drop in on us, I might have put them to the effort after all."

They enjoyed a surprisingly congenial meal. Hayden regaled his sister with a detailed account of Kit's studies, while she inquired about Miss Shaw's teaching methods. Hayden found that having an excuse to talk about his son's governess raised his spirits.

After dinner they retired to the drawing room and continued their conversation.

"I did hope Miss Shaw would have done more to get Kit out of that stifling nursery," Althea observed at last. "She seemed quite committed to it when I hired her."

Hayden felt compelled to defend Leah Shaw. "No one could have been more enthusiastic in their efforts. The blame rests entirely with me, but she has made progress. I have assured her that once spring comes we can begin to bring Kit out."

"I hope you will." Althea sounded doubtful that he

would follow through on his promise. "I am certain it will do the dear child a world of good."

Having witnessed the improvement in Kit's health and spirits over the past months, Hayden could not disagree. Yet when he thought of the perils that might come with increased freedom, his neck linen seemed to tighten around his throat, making it difficult to breathe.

"I have one more piece of advice for you," his sister continued, "since you appear to be more receptive than usual."

In the interest of family harmony, Hayden ignored the dig. "What might that be?"

Althea gave a self-satisfied little smile. "If you have any sense at all—and I know you have more than is good for any one man—you will do whatever it takes to keep this remarkable Miss Shaw at Renforth Abbey."

His sister's words reminded Hayden that the term of Leah Shaw's position would soon be half over. There was no question Kit had missed her very much since she'd gone on holiday. How might it affect the boy to lose his beloved governess permanently?

But what would it take to keep the lady at Renforth Abbey for as long as Kit needed her?

Chapter Nine

Conflicting feelings clashed in Leah's heart when she caught sight of Renforth Abbey again after a fortnight away. The sprawling, stately house looked as grand as when she had first glimpsed it in high summer. Indeed, with the ornamental waters frozen, the broad lawns crusted with snow and icicles sparkling on the turrets, the place reminded her of an austere beauty decked in white silk, lace and diamonds for her wedding.

Though it looked striking, the winter scene reminded her of the long dark days ahead. She would be all but buried alive on this secluded estate with no company but her invalid pupil and his solitary father.

Somehow thoughts of the duke and his son kept her from feeling quite so confined. She'd missed them in a way she had not missed anyone since taking leave of her school friends to make her way in the world. She was eager to see Kit's new playthings and tell him all about her holiday. She hoped Lord Northam had not exhausted himself caring for the boy during her absence.

She was touched that he had thought to send a carriage to the village to fetch her. Her return to Renforth Abbey promised a much warmer reception than her original arrival. As the carriage drew nearer to the house, she glanced toward the nursery window, where a splash of cheerful bright pink caught her eye. As she puzzled over what it might be, she caught a flash of movement. It took her a moment to recognize two faces staring down at her and a hand waving in wide vigorous arcs.

The duke must have held his son up to the window to watch for and welcome her. In spite of his fears that Kit might fall or take a chill, he had risked allowing the boy a rare taste of freedom for her sake. A warm smile set Leah's whole face aglow and made an unaccountable lump rise in her throat. Though she doubted Kit could see her, she waved back just as eagerly.

When the carriage reached the front entrance, Leah was flattered to find the household staff assembled outside to greet her. Some cast her smiles of welcome, while others clearly resented the imposition.

"What is all this?" she protested to the butler, her cheeks blazing with embarrassment. "You should not be standing out in the cold, especially not on my account. I am not a guest at Renforth Abbey."

"His Grace's orders, Miss Shaw." Gibson bowed to her, at which point the footmen and Lord Northam's valet followed suit and all the maids curtsied. "To celebrate your return. The young master has been counting the days."

"That is very kind, I'm sure." Leah waved them all

toward the door. "But you must get out of the cold at once."

"After you, miss," replied the butler.

Though she considered it ridiculous to precede the others when she was dressed for the weather and they were not, Leah hurried inside so the servants would follow without delay. From there she hastened upstairs to the nursery, removing her bonnet and gloves as she went. When she spotted a gilt-framed mirror on the wall of the nursery corridor, she paused to smooth her hair and approve the rosy color the winter air had nipped into her cheeks.

Upon reaching the nursery, she paused to tap on the door before entering. If Lord Northam was still holding his son at the window or carrying Kit back to his bed, she did not want to burst in and startle them.

"Is that you, Miss Leah?" Kit's eager cry penetrated the door. His voice sounded stronger than she remembered. "Come in!"

She was only too happy to oblige. Entering the room, she found the duke tucking his son back into bed. The sight of them both provoked a rush of happiness within her, far more intense than she was prepared for.

Clearly her young pupil shared the sentiment. His pale clever face positively blazed with joy at her return. "Welcome home, Miss Leah! Papa took me to the window so I could watch you drive up. Did you see me waving?"

"Indeed I did, though I could scarcely believe

my eyes." Leah flew to his bedside just as the duke straightened and turned toward her.

Something about his weary but welcoming smile made it difficult for her to breathe, suddenly. She managed to arrest her headlong flight far too close to His Grace. He raised his arms, making her wonder whether he intended to ward her off or enfold her in a welcoming embrace.

Instead, Lord Northam gave an awkward chuckle as he thrust out his hand. Grasping hers, he shook it cordially, though with rather excessive force. "Your return is most welcome, Miss Shaw. My son has been counting the days until your arrival. We have used it to practice his arithmetic. I hope you had a pleasant journey from Berkshire."

At the end of his somewhat lengthy greeting, the duke still had Leah's hand clasped warmly in his, pumping it up and down.

"As pleasant as any long coach ride can be at this time of year," she replied. "Thank you for sending your carriage to fetch me from the village. It was a delightful surprise and most kind of you."

When His Grace finally released her hand, as propriety demanded, Leah wished she could find some excuse to prolong the contact between them.

"It was no inconvenience." Lord Northam stared into her eyes as if his had been starved for the sight of her. "The coachman was happy to have some occupation. I may have to send you on drives to the village and back just to keep him in good humor."

Leah chuckled. She had missed the duke's wry wit.

Before she could reply, Kit piped up, "Pardon me."

He sounded a trifle vexed that the adults seemed to have forgotten him. "Did you see the banner we hung for you, Miss Leah? Papa helped me make it."

Leah forced her gaze away from the duke to his son, then to the window. An expanse of bright pink fabric hung from the top of the curtains. A message of welcome had been printed in yellow paint, surrounded by simple shapes of flowers in other vivid hues. She was surprised it had not drawn her gaze the moment she entered the room.

"What a neat job you made of it and what pretty colors!" She moved closer to the window to get a better look at the banner. "Never in my life have I had such a fuss made over my comings and goings. Thank you, both!"

Kit and his father seemed gratified by her response to their efforts.

"Consider it an attempt to make up for your original reception at Renforth Abbey," said the duke. "It ought to have been warmer. If I could have foreseen your invaluable contribution to Kit's well-being, I would have made you welcome from the beginning."

Was His Grace trying to say he wanted to make a fresh start, without his earlier resistance to her efforts? If so she would be happy to accept.

"Tell us about your holiday, Miss Leah." Kit patted the bed beside him, inviting her to occupy her accustomed spot. "What did you do at Nethercross to celebrate Christmas?"

"A great many things." Leah deposited her gloves

and bonnet on Kit's writing table then settled on the bed beside him. "Practically the moment I arrived, Charlotte, Phoebe and Sophie recruited me to go collect greenery with them to construct a kissing bough."

"Kissing bough?" Kit wrinkled his nose. "What is that and how do you make one?"

Leah cast the duke a rather reproachful glance as if to inquire how it would have harmed the boy to experience such Christmas traditions. She explained to Kit how evergreen boughs were wired into a spherical framework then decked with ribbons, fruit and other festive trimmings.

"It sounds very pretty," said Kit. "But what does it have to do with kissing?"

"It is a Christmas tradition. If a man and woman meet up beneath the bough, they are obliged to exchange a kiss." As she spoke, Leah found her gaze drawn toward Lord Northam, who stood before the mantel watching them.

For reasons she could not fathom, he looked quite severe.

Leah turned her attention back to Kit. "We entertained carolers on Christmas Eve, and attended lots of lovely church services. Lord Steadwell gave a party on Boxing Day for his tenants and neighbors. Later in the week we were invited to an assembly hosted by their neighbors, Admiral and Mrs. DeLancey."

Kit heaved a sigh. "I wish I could have gone with you to Nethercross for Christmas."

Again Leah's gaze flew to the duke. His son's words made him wince. She sensed how torn he was between thoughts of Kit celebrating such a merry Christmas and fears of the boy becoming overtired or contracting an illness.

Determined not let Kit fall into a destructive spiral of self-pity, Leah replied in as bright a tone as she could muster. "I am certain the Kendrick girls wished that, too. They plagued me with questions about you— Sophie in particular. She is nearly your age and a great lover of fairy tales. She has read *Gulliver's Travels,* and when I told her all about your Lilliputian figures, she was quite envious."

"*She* wanted to know about me?" The thought seemed to rescue Kit from his sulk before it had properly begun. "Tell me more about Sophie. What does she look like? What does she like to do besides read fairy tales?"

Leah exchanged a covert smile with the duke, who relaxed visibly. "Sophie is a little taller than you. She is the youngest of Lord Steadwell's daughters. She has lovely red-gold hair and blue eyes and she has a terrific imagination. She likes to write her own stories and draw pictures of the characters. She likes to dress up in old clothes and put on theatricals."

"I wish she lived nearer, so she could visit me," Kit mused. "I would let her play with my little people all she liked."

"As a matter of fact, Sophie said the same thing about you. So I suggested she write you a letter, which she promptly did. Shall I fetch it for you to read?"

If she had brought a chest of gold and jewels from Nethercross, Leah doubted Kit would have been more excited. The duke did nothing to discourage his son's enthusiasm. At the boy's eager bidding, Leah hurried away and returned bearing Sophie's letter. Kit opened it with great ceremony and proudly read it aloud to her and his father. He exclaimed over a self-portrait Sophie had enclosed, insisting it must be framed and hung where he could see it.

"I believe Sophie would like it very much if you wrote back to her," Leah suggested. "Would you like to begin writing a letter of reply tomorrow?"

She was anxious for Kit to make the acquaintance of someone his own age, even if it was only by post. Besides it would provide her young pupil useful practice with his reading and writing.

Kit did not greet her suggestion with the enthusiasm she expected. Instead his smile faltered and his shoulders sagged. "What will I have to tell her? I never go anywhere or do anything exciting."

Leah thought for a moment. When she replied, her words were addressed to the child, but also to his father. "Perhaps we shall have to do something about that."

The excitement of his governess's return seemed to tire Kit out, making it easier to get him settled for the night. That pleased Hayden, for it meant he would be able to dine with Leah Shaw. It seemed like a very long time since he had enjoyed the pleasure of her company and conversation.

"I am glad to hear you had such a fine holiday visiting your friend," he remarked as he held her chair. "I hope all that activity did not tire you out."

Miss Shaw gave a soft chuckle. "To be quite truthful, it did rather, trying to keep up with three energetic girls wanting to go in all different directions. There was never a dull moment."

Hayden took his accustomed seat opposite her. "I hope Renforth Abbey will not seem tiresome after all the festivity of Nethercross. Pray tell me more about your holiday. Did the Steadwells have any other guests to stay for Christmas?"

Leah Shaw shook her head as the soup course was served. "Grace has no relatives but a stepfamily, from whom she has long been estranged. Her husband's sisters have homes and families of their own."

Hayden tried not to show how relieved he was to hear it. Her explanation of the kissing bough ritual had made him wonder if she was speaking from experience. "The parties you attended, I suppose they involved a great deal of dancing."

She shrugged. "Some. Lord Steadwell and Admiral DeLancey were kind enough to claim a dance or two from me. The other gentlemen did not seem to know how to treat me—as a lady or a servant. The usual dilemma of a governess."

Though she spoke in a jesting tone Hayden found nothing amusing about it. He did not care to think of her plagued with dance invitations, yet it roused his indignation that she might have been snubbed by Lord Steadwell's neighbors.

"The loss was theirs entirely," he growled, "whether or not they possessed the wit to realize it."

"You are very kind to say so, Your Grace, but not everyone is as blind to social distinctions as you appear to be. Admiral DeLancey reminded me of you in that respect."

Hayden might have resented Miss Shaw's admiring observation about another man, but he recalled her mentioning that the admiral was married.

"What else did you do in Berkshire?" he prompted her as their soup bowls were removed and the fish course served.

"Are you not tired of hearing about it?" She gave an indulgent chuckle. "I should have thought the subject had been quite thoroughly explored in the nursery."

"Not at all." He enjoyed listening to her, whatever the subject. "Surely there must be a few details my son did not interrogate out of you."

"Perhaps one or two," she admitted then obliged him with a fuller account of some of her activities.

As she spoke, her tone and expression grew animated. She painted such a vivid picture of Christmas at Nethercross that Hayden could imagine Kit and him in attendance, as well—helping the Kendrick girls gather greenery, passing around mugs of piping hot cider to the carol singers, partaking in festive dinners. His sense of caution sternly warned him that such frivolity would carry a host of threats to his son—a fall, a chill, acute indigestion. Yet when he pictured Kit's smiles and sparkling eyes, the promise of his son's enjoyment outweighed the risks.

"Lord and Lady Steadwell sound like a fine couple." Anyone who treated Leah Shaw so kindly merited his approval, even if they had lured her away from Renforth Abbey for a whole fortnight. "You say her ladyship was a friend of yours at that dreadful school? How did they come to marry?"

By now they were well into a course of succulent game pie but Hayden scarcely noticed what he ate. Miss Shaw's spirited conversation provided a more nourishing feast for his mind and heart.

"That is a story fit for a fairy tale," she replied. "You see Grace was always a great beauty, though it brought her nothing but trouble at school, and later in her work as a governess."

When Miss Shaw told him how her friend had suffered unwelcome attentions from gentlemen in the houses where she'd worked, a blaze of outrage swept through Hayden. "I hope you were never subjected to any such liberties in your previous positions!"

She laughed at the idea though he found nothing amusing about it. "Fortunately, my looks do not begin to compare with Grace's. Neither is my disposition as sweet and gentle as hers. There was one young scoundrel who claimed to admire me. When he persisted after I tried to discourage him, he got a pitcher of cold water over his head to cool his ardor."

Hayden's relief vented in a hoot of laughter. It eased his mind to know Leah Shaw was capable of taking care of herself in such a situation. Yet he yearned to protect her if she should ever need it. He wanted no harm coming to the woman who was so important to his son.

"Poor Grace was not so fortunate," Miss Shaw continued. "By the time she accepted the position at Nethercross, she had resorted to disguising her looks with spectacles and a dowdy, old-fashioned cap. It turned out Lord Steadwell had hired her precisely because she appeared so plain. His daughters' previous governess had eloped and he did not want to risk them losing another one in the same way."

As she related her friend's history, Hayden hung on her every word. He could sympathize with Lord Steadwell's concern for his daughters, yet he wondered how the baron could have failed to recognize the beauty living under his roof. Much as Leah Shaw extolled the delicate golden loveliness of her friend, he preferred more vivid coloring, animated by a bright, lively spirit.

By the time pudding was served Miss Shaw had concluded the story. "After all their early difficulties, Lord and Lady Steadwell appear to be living happily ever after. Now that he has recovered from the grief of his first wife's death and is happy with Grace, his daughters are far happier, as well."

Her words sparked the beginning of an idea in Hayden's mind—an idea that part of him was reluctant to consider.

"There was one other thing that happened on my holiday," Miss Shaw continued. Was she perhaps puzzled by his lack of response to the conclusion of her story? "I am pleased to report, I have my next position already engaged."

"I beg your pardon?" Hayden knew what she must mean yet he shrank from acknowledging it.

"Admiral and Mrs. DeLancey are planning to take her son on a tour of the Continent and they have asked me to accompany them as Henry's governess." Miss Shaw's mobile features glowed as she spoke of the opportunity. "What could be more ideal? I shall be able to travel and see the sights at no expense to myself. Then when I have saved enough money for my own tour, I can return to those places I admired or visit others the DeLanceys missed on theirs."

It was clear she expected Hayden to share her enthusiasm for these plans, but that was impossible. He could not even pretend. The toothsome pudding turned to sawdust in his mouth.

"There is only one minor difficulty." Miss Shaw pretended to measure it between her thumb and forefinger.

Only *one* and *minor?* Hayden could foresee any number of significant difficulties with her leaving Renforth Abbey.

"What might that be?" he forced out the question in spite of his constricted throat.

"The DeLanceys hope to sail for Ostend by the end of June, which is a month earlier than I had intended to leave Renforth Abbey," Kit's governess replied in an offhand tone, oblivious to the tempest into which she had thrown Hayden. "But if we begin right away I am certain we can find a suitable replacement by then."

They might find a governess to fill the position, Hayden reflected as he tried to stifle a spasm of alarm. But would they ever find one as devoted to Kit as Leah

Shaw? Or one courageous enough to oppose the will of a stubborn duke to secure more freedom for her pupil? Even if they located a candidate with those qualities, would she be so adept at making Kit's studies a pleasure for him rather than a chore? Would she provide Hayden with such stimulating company?

Once again, it seemed Althea had been right. It was imperative he find a way to keep Leah Shaw at Renforth Abbey—by whatever means necessary. That conviction collided in Hayden's mind with an earlier thought he had been reluctant to acknowledge. Lord Steadwell had kept his daughters' governess at Nethercross by making the lady his wife.

Hayden wondered whether he ought to follow the baron's excellent example.

Chapter Ten

"Are you quite well, Miss Shaw?" The duke's question stirred Leah from her private thoughts as she stared out a tall window at the end of the west range.

Her view of the Renforth Abbey grounds was as drab and dreary as it could possibly be. In the two weeks since she had returned from Berkshire, the dusting of Christmas snow had been washed away by days of cold rain. Only once during that time had she managed to escape the house for a brief walk. Even then there had been nothing to see but sodden ground, bare trees and bushes. Her boots had gotten soaked and the hem of her skirt thoroughly spattered with mud.

Lord Northam's warm, caring tone seemed to pierce the winter gloom like a ray of May sunshine.

Leah turned away from the window and affected a cheerful air for his sake. How many long, isolated winters had he endured caring for his son? "Do not worry, Your Grace. I promise you, I am not ill. If I had a chill or a cough, I would make sure to keep away from your son and not risk him catching it."

"I know." The duke regarded her with quiet trust. "But I did not inquire only for Kit's sake. You may not be seriously *ill,* but you do not seem to be quite yourself of late. I hope you would confide in me if something were troubling you. I would very much like to assist you if it were within my power."

His solicitude made Leah smile. This time there was nothing feigned about it. "Unless you possess an uncanny ability to influence the climate, I fear there is little you or anyone can do. Winter always has a depressing effect upon my spirits when I am obliged to remain indoors so much. It reminds me of my years at school, which felt like one endless cold, damp, hungry winter."

What a blessed relief it was to be able to speak freely of her time at the Pendergast School. None of her previous employers had ever asked about her past or given any sign they cared. The sincere sympathy in the duke's gaze seemed to reach out and wrap around her.

"There is no excuse for you to be cold or hungry under my roof." Lord Northam held out his arm to her. "Dinner is waiting and we can move our places to the end of the table nearest the fire, which I will have stirred up to a good warm blaze."

"Those things will certainly help." Leah grasped the duke's strong arm and felt her spirits beginning to lift. "Though no more than the warmth and nourishment of your company. Your kindness never fails to lighten the winter gloom."

"You make it sound like a sacrifice on my part." Lord Northam cast her a sidelong smile as they headed off to the dining room. "I assure you nothing could be further from the truth. All the years I did little but care for my son, I did not realize how much I missed adult conversation on subjects other than estate business."

His remark reminded Leah of what her friend Grace had said about the duke being lonely. She was pleased to hear her company had helped to ease his isolation, though she wondered whether any other companion might have done just as well.

"Your wife…" The words burst out before she could stop them. "I suppose you miss her very much, still?"

She recalled one other time they had talked of his wife and how reluctant he had seemed to discuss the subject. What had made her raise it now? Grace had told her how long and how deeply Lord Steadwell had mourned his late wife before finally opening his heart to love again. Did the Duke of Northam expect to remain alone for the rest of his life, devoting all his affection to his son?

For his sake, Leah hoped not. And yet the thought of him remarrying did not sit well with her, either.

Lord Northam considered her question. Rather than changing the subject as she feared he might, the duke gave her an answer. "I suppose I do. I hardly know. By now I have been widowed longer than I was married. My time with Celia feels like a distant dream."

As she pondered his unexpected reply, the duke posed Leah a question she'd anticipated even less. "Speaking of marriage, Miss Shaw, have *you* ever been tempted to settle down? You told me once that you had never been asked, though recently you mentioned a suitor who got a pitcher of cold water over his head."

What made him ask such a question? Leah wondered. It flustered her, though she was not quite certain why. How could she refuse to answer after the duke had been so forthcoming in his reply to her?

"I would not dignify that fellow with the title of suitor, Your Grace. I doubt his intentions were honorable. If they had been, I would not have thrown cold water on him but neither would I have encouraged him. I have remained single less because I lacked proper suitors than because I have never had an inclination to wed." Somehow her declaration did not sound as adamant as it might once have done.

They had reached the dining room by this time, for which Leah was grateful. Now their conversation could return to more impersonal topics.

But after the duke had Mr. Gibson shift their places nearer the fire, and they took their seats, Lord Northam made no effort to change the subject. "Why have you not wished to marry, may I ask? Have you not met a gentleman who meets your expectations of a husband? Or do you find something objectionable about the institution itself?"

Leah tried to suppress her impatience, reminding herself it was she who had first raised the subject of marriage. "I cannot say I have ever entertained any particular expectations of a husband, Your Grace."

What qualities would she look for if she were to change her mind about marriage? This was the first time Leah had ever considered the matter. Humor would be a great asset, obviously, as well as kindness and strength of character. Any man who married her would need to be patient and understanding. A voice from deep in her mind warned her not to go any further with such an inventory.

"Then it is the *idea* of marriage you find repellent?" The duke did not appear to have much appetite for his soup. He kept glancing down into the bowl whenever Leah tried to meet his eye, stirring its contents with a furtive air. "On what grounds, may I ask?"

Had they not talked about this enough for one evening?

Leah tried to stifle her impatience. "From the time I was very young, my grandmother warned me that marriage meant the end of a woman's freedom. *The tender trap* she called it. She said she had once longed to travel abroad but instead she was persuaded to marry my grandfather. By the time she was widowed and her children grown, she had lost her sight. She hoped I would be able to see and do all the things she felt she had missed."

Leah chided herself for going on at such length. She stilled her tongue and put it to work consuming her soup.

"With all due respect to your late grandmother," the duke replied in a tone of cool disapproval, "it sounds as if she was not allowing you any more choice in the matter than she was given. Is not the ability to make decisions about our lives the most basic freedom there is?"

A calm whisper of reason told Leah that Lord

Northam had a point. But that whisper was drowned out by bellows of outrage from her heart.

Ripping the napkin from her lap, she surged to her feet and flung the square of crisp, snowy linen onto the table. "What right have you to question my grandmother's advice when you limit your son's choices so severely?"

The duke hastily struggled to rise, as propriety dictated a gentleman should. Though she knew she had already said too much, Leah could not control her impulse to lash out at him. "The longer you keep Kit ignorant and immobile, the fewer choices he will have as he grows up. Is that what you want for him?"

The look in Lord Northam's eyes gave her the bitter satisfaction of knowing she had provoked the same intense reaction in him that he had stirred in her.

Lightning seemed to flash in his gaze, not quite masking the deep shadow of pain. "I want my son to have the opportunity to grow up! I thought you understood that. I fail to see how my actions compare with poisoning the mind of an impressionable child against marriage."

Why could she not defuse this mounting antagonism with a jest? Leah hated the volatile feelings seething within her and rather feared them. They threatened to seize control of her words and actions, leaving her powerless to choose a different way. No one had ever made her feel so helpless to direct her emotions.

What gave Hayden Latimer that dangerous power? Part of her guessed the answer but she refused to admit it, for that would make it true.

"Poison my *mind?*" she echoed the duke's words, her tone bristling with scorn. "Gran did nothing of the kind. If she had, at least that would have been no worse than poisoning a child's body."

That was not fair. She knew it as soon as the words left her mouth. The duke had trusted the wrong person, but he had not fully grasped the danger of giving Kit laudanum. Though part of her took grim satisfaction in knowing she had struck a blow, her conscience reproached her. The staff of the Pendergast School had taught her little of true charity, but Leah thought she had learned something of it from her friends.

Pride and hurt refused to let her back down yet. But before the duke could say anything more to escalate their quarrel, Leah sensed the best thing she could do for both of them was disengage, giving them an opportunity to recover their composure.

"If you will excuse me, Your Grace, I fear I have lost my appetite."

Without waiting to hear whether he granted her leave to depart, Leah spun away and fled the dining room. Regrets nipped at her heels like a pack of hunting dogs as she dashed down corridors and upstairs. When she reached her room, she slammed the door behind her to shut them out, but they were too quick.

They pounced upon her, driving her to her knees where a bewildering storm of tears overwhelmed her.

Could his first faltering overtures toward Leah Shaw have gone worse?

As her rapid footsteps retreated into the distance,

Hayden collapsed back onto his chair. He was grateful for the discretion of his servants, who had melted away at the first sign of trouble. Still there was bound to be gossip below stairs in spite of Gibson's inevitable efforts to suppress it.

Such a scene had not played out at Renforth Abbey since the days of his marriage, unless one counted his son's tantrums. Even his sister, with whom he had been so often at odds, did not provoke him to such a show of temper. Was he misguided to consider wedding another woman whose priorities and disposition were so much at odds with his?

In poor Celia's case, he had not realized their differences until it was too late. Their marriage, which had begun with so much hope and promise, had been strained by the disparity between their temperaments and interests. He'd wanted to believe that he and Leah Shaw had settled all their differences and come to a tolerant understanding of one another. This jarring confrontation had proven him wrong. He reproached himself for escalating hostilities. Nothing he'd said to her was untrue, but some of it had been most unkind. Though the accusations she'd hurled at him had been hurtful, that did not make them false.

A subtle movement drew his gaze toward the dining room door where he spied the butler hovering.

"Shall I fetch the next course, Your Grace?" Gibson was clearly trying hard to ignore the empty chair opposite his master's.

Hayden shook his head. "Miss Shaw felt unwell and I must confess I have lost my appetite, too. Please convey my apologies to Cook and assure her it is no reflection on her skill."

"Very well, Your Grace." The butler managed to sound as if he believed every word, which Hayden highly doubted. "Is there anything else you require?"

Brandy, perhaps? Again, Hayden shook his head. He did not approve of the frequency with which many of his peers sought to drown their troubles.

"Nothing, thank you." Possessed of a sudden need for movement, he rose from the table and strode off without giving much thought to where he was headed.

His feet bore him to the cloisters, where he had often come in the past to clear his mind. The long enclosed walkway leading to the chapel was damp and rather chilly, which succeeded in cooling any lingering embers of anger within him. The soft, steady drip of water off the eaves was a soothing sound, though he wondered if Leah Shaw might find it dismal.

Between the isolation of Renforth Abbey in winter and his blundering efforts to sound her out about marriage, it would be a wonder if Kit's governess did not pack her bags and leave his household at first light. In spite of their confrontation, Hayden could not bear the thought of her going...for his son's sake.

It was *because* of their differences that Leah Shaw would make an ideal mother for Kit. Her compulsion to give the child as much freedom as possible balanced his caution and protectiveness. Between those opposite stances, with a certain amount of give and take, they had so far managed to strike a compromise that benefited his son. Hayden wanted that to continue.

But how could it if he drove the lady away? A shiver ran through him that was not entirely due to the damp chill of the cloisters.

It drove him back into the house, his pace hastening with every step. As he mounted the great staircase at a run, he met Leah Shaw descending almost as fast. They came to a halt on the landing and addressed one another at the same time, each in a breathless rush.

"Miss Shaw, I must apologize…"

"Please forgive me, Your Grace!"

Their words collided in the solemn stillness as their gazes met then quickly skittered away.

They tried again.

"There is no need, truly."

"I protest—the fault was mine."

Again their replies clashed.

Hayden's tightly wound nerves unraveled in an outburst of awkward laughter. Miss Shaw sputtered with answering mirth. Hayden's legs felt suddenly weak. In a lamentable breach of good manners, he sank onto the stairs. The lady did likewise, with no sign of offense.

Meeting her gaze again, he held it this time and raised his hand to signal his wish to speak first. With a self-conscious grin and a barely perceptible nod, she gave him leave to begin.

"I am sorry I offended you, my dear, in speaking as I did of your grandmother. When a person claims they mean *all due respect* I fear it is often an excuse to say something thoroughly disrespectful. I am certain your grandmother advised you as she did out of regard for your happiness. I of all people should know it is possible to do or say something harmful, even with the kindest of intentions."

Leah Shaw hesitated a moment before replying, perhaps to be certain he had finished. "I accept your apology as I hope you will accept mine, sir. I do not know what made me speak to you that way. I suppose I still feel compelled to defend my grandmother from anyone who would question her care of me."

"You do not need to apologize for such feelings." Hayden hunched forward, his forearms resting on his thighs. "Least of all to me."

"But I should have realized you were trying to defend the idea of marriage—a connection that made you happy and gave you your son. It is only natural that you should find Gran's views on the subject disagreeable."

It might serve his plans far better if Leah Shaw continued to believe his marriage had been idyllic. Yet Hayden could not bring himself to deceive her, even by omission. "I must admit, your grandmother's views do trouble me, but for the opposite reason you might think."

"I beg your pardon?"

Hayden twined his fingers together in a tight knot and brought his chin to rest upon them. "Since Celia's death, I have tried to deny it, but I fear my wife might have agreed with your grandmother."

"Oh." Leah managed to infuse that brief word with too many different feelings for him to be able to sort them out.

Had he just destroyed any hope of ever persuading her to accept an offer of marriage from him?

* * *

The duke's marriage had not been a happy one? That notion left Leah bewildered and saddened...yet oddly relieved, much to her chagrin. She recalled Lord Northam mentioning that his late wife's interests had differed from his, yet he'd also said how much he enjoyed spending time with her. Her treasured friendships had taught Leah that two people did not need to be exactly alike in order to share a deep, abiding affection.

"*My* grandmother never wanted me to wed Celia," the duke continued. "She thought her unsuitable to assume the mantle of Duchess of Northam and mistress of Renforth Abbey. Looking back, I realize Grandmother was right, but at the time I was too smitten to see it."

Was he confiding in her to atone for their earlier quarrel? Leah wanted to assure him it was not necessary to dredge up painful memories in order to appease her. Yet something deeper than simple curiosity kept her hanging on his every word.

"I did not fall in love with Celia in spite of our differences, but *because* of them." Lord Northam stared down at the wide gallery below as if he could picture his first wife scurrying past, laughing. "That Season was my first taste of London society and everything about it seemed to bubble and glitter. Only later did I realize how quickly bubbles burst and how easily things that glitter can shatter into dangerous shards.

"I was young," he continued, "and for the first and only time in my life, I felt a trifle rebellious. Grandmother's disapproval made me all the more resolved to marry Celia, as did the competition of several other suitors. I was beside myself with happiness when such an admired toast of society chose to accept *my* proposal."

All those years later, the duke still sounded surprised by his late wife's decision. Leah was not. How could any of those other suitors have compared to a man like Hayden Latimer? Not for his title and fortune or even his handsome looks, but for his many fine qualities of character that Leah had discovered since coming to Renforth Abbey. If Lady Celia had been the giddy butterfly she sounded, was it any wonder she'd been drawn to a man of quiet strength and prudence— one who could be relied upon to protect her from a harsh world that might take advantage of her reckless high spirits? Leah found she could sympathize all too well with the motives of the late duchess.

"We were happy at first." A gnawing edge of wistfulness in the duke's tone tugged at Leah's heart. "But I was unaccustomed to the hectic pace of London Society and soon tired of it. Celia miscarried twice. Her physician said it was because of the late hours she kept, the rich food and constant overexcitement. When my grandmother fell ill, I felt obliged to return to Renforth Abbey. I thought the wholesome country atmosphere would do Celia good. It seemed to for a time."

Leah began to understand why the duke was telling her all this. She wished propriety would permit her to make some gesture of consolation.

"While the weather was fine, Celia seemed content. She invited friends to visit, hosted picnics and went riding. She often visited a nearby estate, owned by a friend of my sister. But when autumn came and all her friends flocked back to London for the Little Season, Celia wanted to go, too. It was impossible for me to desert my grandmother when it was clear she had very little time left. Celia begged me to let her go to London on her own but I did not dare permit it. She was with child again and I knew if she fell back into her old ways, it could be dangerous for her and for the baby."

Leah could understand all too well how confining the fun-loving duchess must have found Renforth Abbey in the late autumn with no company and the weather cold and dull. How she must have resented her husband's preoccupation with his ailing grandmother, who heartily disapproved of her. And yet, Leah could not blame Lord Northam for his actions. He had only wanted to do what was best for his grandmother, his wife and his unborn child.

"Celia had far too much spirit to accept my decision tamely." The duke's jaw tightened and the fine lines that fanned out from the corners of his eyes seemed to deepen. "We had some terrible quarrels. You have seen how Kit can be when he is denied what he wants—Celia was nearly as bad. And you know from experience that I am far too easily provoked to anger."

A painful qualm of regret gripped Leah. Their argument over dinner must have reminded Lord Northam of the darkest times of his marriage.

"The accusation Celia most often hurled at me was that I had taken away her freedom when we wed. She said Renforth Abbey was like a prison and I was more a jailor than a husband. No doubt you and your grandmother would agree with her."

How hard it must have been for him to hear those same sentiments about marriage echoed over his dinner table so many years later. Leah wished she had held her tongue. And yet she would not deny her beliefs, which the Northam's marriage illustrated so painfully.

"It is not quite as simple as that, Your Grace."

"Is it not?" The duke turned his head to fix her with a searching stare.

Leah met it for a moment, hoping he would see she meant what she'd said. But she could not risk holding such a gaze in case he should glimpse how deep her sympathy ran and perhaps confuse it for something else.

"I do not blame you for acting as you did." She edged closer to the banister. The staircase was not the most comfortable place to sit. Yet it seemed to put them on a more level footing, not as master and employee, but simply two people with beliefs and feelings of equal importance. "I know you were not prompted by selfish motives, but by loving concern for those you felt bound to protect."

Lord Northam shook his head slowly. "That was what I believed at the time and what I have told myself often since then. But now I realize I have too often made the wrong choices in spite of my good intentions."

Leah gave a rueful nod. "That is what I meant when I said it was not simple."

The subtlest hint of a smile tugged at the corner of

his lips then quickly faded. "I have told you most of the story. I suppose you might as well hear the rest."

Why was he sharing so many private, painful memories with her? Simply because he regretted their quarrel? If so, he had done more than enough to atone already. She had been as much to blame for their argument as he, if not more. Yet Leah could not subdue her curiosity to learn the rest of the story.

Why did the subject of his past fascinate her so? Was it because it had been every bit as difficult as hers in its way, even though he was a wealthy peer and she a former charity pupil?

After a long pause, the duke continued. "My grandmother died, six years ago nearly to the day."

"I am very sorry." More than ever, Leah longed to rest her hand upon his.

No wonder his temper had been more easily provoked than usual. Anniversaries of painful events from her past always brought feelings of sorrow, guilt and anger closer to the surface than she usually allowed them. On top of that, to hear her talk about Gran, whose views had been so sharply opposed to those of the Dowager Duchess, could only have aggravated him further.

The duke acknowledged her sympathy with a brief nod. But before he could say another word, a door opened and closed on the ground floor and the decisive footsteps of the butler approached.

Without hesitation or consultation, Leah and the duke leaped to their feet as if they were about to be caught committing a crime.

"Thank you for that information, Miss Shaw." Lord Northam's voice sounded too loud and hearty for natural conversation. "Perhaps we can discuss it further at another time."

As he spoke, the duke began walking down the stairs. Clearly he was ashamed to be seen exchanging confidences with her. The thought stung Leah even though she felt the same way. Only she had her reputation to protect. Was he trying to protect it, too? That was the sort of behavior she had come to expect from him.

"Certainly, sir." She tried to keep her tone from betraying the fact that their conversation had been anything but ordinary and impersonal.

By unspoken agreement, Leah started *up* the stairs. "Good evening, Your Grace."

"Good evening, Miss Shaw," he called back.

A moment later she heard him talking to the butler.

What had the duke been about to tell her? Leah wondered as she headed back to her room. Whatever it was, she found herself far more curious than she had any right to be. Would Lord Northam tell her on some future occasion? Or might she never again catch him in so unguarded a moment?

Chapter Eleven

Had he been seeking to secure Leah Shaw as a future wife or trying to drive her away from Renforth Abbey? A full week after he had confided in Kit's governess about his marriage, Hayden was still vexed with himself for revealing so much about Celia's discontent. Did it not bear out Miss Shaw's critical ideas about marriage and cast doubt on his fitness as a husband?

In spite of that, he could not deny a strange sense of relief it had brought him to share those memories with her. Their weight no longer seemed such a burden on his heart and conscience. It helped that Miss Shaw had taken a charitable view of his actions. Her understanding meant more to him than he could ever convey.

For several days afterward she seemed to be avoiding him and Hayden did not try to impose his company upon her. He judged it best to allow the volatile emotions they had roused to ease awhile before making any further effort to advance his plan.

As a consequence, he found himself more than ever

looking forward to his opportunities to join her and his son for lessons. Today Kit was poring over an atlas Miss Shaw had borrowed from Hayden's library.

"This is Great Britain and here is Renforth Abbey." She pointed to a spot in the south of the country. "Can you locate Nethercross, where Sophie lives? It is to the northeast and lies along the banks of the River Thames."

Hayden wondered whether it was a good idea to teach his son geography. Learning about other places might only stir up discontent and a dangerous yearning to travel. But the boy clearly enjoyed the subject too much for his father to consider forbidding it.

As Kit searched the map, trying to locate Nethercross, Hayden's mind began to wander. He asked himself whether there were valuable lessons to be learned from his first marriage. Those lessons might help him persuade Leah Shaw that matrimony need not be the prison sentence she had been led to believe.

"There it is!" Kit's cry jarred Hayden from his drifting thoughts. "Look, Papa. I found where Sophie lives. It doesn't look far from Renforth at all. Perhaps someday I can go and visit her."

Hayden opened his mouth to quash such a dangerous idea. But before he could say anything, Leah Shaw caught his eye. Her gaze held a glittering green warning and a warm brown plea that prompted him to reply, "Perhaps Sophie and her sisters could come here to visit you."

Much to his satisfaction, his response appeared to please both his son and the child's governess.

"They could?" Kit beamed. "When can they come?"

Miss Shaw spared Hayden from having to make any irrevocable plans that very moment by saying, "Time enough to decide that later. Renforth Abbey and Nethercross may look close on a map, but the distance is a full day's ride. Lord and Lady Steadwell would never allow their daughters to make such a journey until the weather is warmer and the roads are free of mud. Now, are you ready for a more difficult search? Can you find Knightley Park way up in Nottinghamshire? Cissy and Dolly Radcliffe live there. Their foster mother is another old friend of mine."

The new challenge immediately commanded Kit's attention. His finger ranged upward over the map.

Hayden cast Leah Shaw a grateful smile and received one in return that made his chest ache with its radiance. Did he merit that simply because he had offered to invite the Kendrick girls for a visit? If so perhaps he would not find it as difficult to make her content at Renforth Abbey as he had Celia.

A pang of guilt drove the smile from his face. Had he ever truly *tried* to make Celia happy here? Or had he been so caught up in his worry for her, the baby and his grandmother that he could not loosen his protective grip against which she'd rebelled?

"I cannot find Knightley Park." Kit pushed the atlas away. "There are too many places on this map."

"Look for the town of Newark, in the middle part." Miss Shaw nudged the book back toward him. "It will be in bigger letters than some of the others."

Thus encouraged to continue, Kit narrowed his search.

Meanwhile his governess approached Hayden. "I have a suggestion that I hope you will consider."

When he encountered her hopeful look, Hayden wondered how he could possibly deny her. "Of course I will *consider* anything you suggest, my dear. Whether I can agree is quite another matter."

Her smile widened in response to his rallying tone. "I believe you might this time. You see I am a little anxious about Kit being carried from his bed to his chair for lessons and meals."

Hayden nodded. He was no stranger to such worries. In the past they had been strong enough keep his son bedbound. Lately he had learned to act more on hope and less on fear. But that still did not banish his concerns altogether.

"I thought it might be safer for Kit if we fix a set of wheels to the legs of his chair so it could be brought right up to the bed then pushed to the table once he is safely seated."

Before she even finished, Hayden began to nod vigorously. How could he refuse a suggestion that would allow his son more freedom without compromising his safety? "That is an excellent idea. I shall look into it immediately."

"I found Newark," Kit piped up. He seemed to have been too deeply engrossed in his search to have paid any attention to the exchange between his father and governess.

"Well done." Miss Shaw leaned over the table to

point out the location of Knightley Park. "I believe we ought to add Cissy and Dolly to your correspondents and perhaps Peter Romney.... I mean Lord Edgecombe. He is nearly your age, as are some of the young Chases. My friend Miss Fairfax is their governess."

Kit nodded. "Where do they live? I will write to them and perhaps they can *all* come to visit."

His son needed contact with other children. Hayden could not mistake the boy's tone of longing. But might that carry a different sort of danger? He recalled how mercilessly some of the boys at school had ragged anyone who was the least bit different—smaller than the rest, slower to grasp their lessons or with a speech impediment. Might a boy who could not walk be shunned or tormented?

Making friends by letter would provide Kit with many of the benefits but none of the risks. Hayden admired Leah Shaw for devising such a clever compromise.

Might there be a way he could learn from her? Were there things he could do to make life at Renforth Abbey more agreeable for her—providing a semblance of the freedom she so craved?

One possibility occurred to him. "If you will excuse me, I must go confer with the gardener...I mean the carriage maker in the village about wheels for Kit's chair."

His son looked up from the atlas with a hopeful sparkle in his eyes. "Wheels for my chair? Why?"

"Miss Leah will explain." Hayden ruffled his son's hair then headed off.

His lungs felt buoyant, like a pair of hot air balloons, lifting his spirits and lightening his step.

Halfway out the door he turned and called back. "You will dine with me tonight I hope, Miss Shaw? So we can discuss other ideas you might have for this young fellow."

"Of course, sir." She glanced up at him and Hayden was struck afresh by her vibrant beauty.

Though he needed to wed the lady for Kit's sake, it would be no hardship for him. Quite the contrary.

During the following fortnight, it seemed to Leah that Lord Northam was determined to make up for their earlier quarrel by being more than usually obliging. He wasted no time adopting her idea to get wheels fitted on a chair for his son, which delighted both her and Kit.

"It reminds me of the garden chair my grandmother used in her later years," the duke mused the first time he pushed his beaming son from the bed to the writing table.

Later on, when Lord Northam left them alone for their lessons, Kit begged Leah to push his chair around the room, which she was happy to do.

But when her pupil pleaded to make another circuit, she had to refuse. "We must get some work done. Otherwise your papa will guess what we have been up to. Would you like to write a letter to Sophie about your new chair? Perhaps you can draw her a picture to go with it."

"I wish you would push my chair out of the nursery so I could see other parts of the house," said Kit as Leah trimmed his pen. "Then I would have even more to tell Sophie. I want to do some of the things she writes about—riding ponies and boating on the river. I would not need strong legs to do those, only Papa's permission."

The edge of frustration in the child's tone reminded Leah what limited progress she had made on his behalf since coming to Renforth Abbey. She had freed him from his bed and expanded the horizons of his mind with education, but he was still confined to this one room, spacious and handsome though it might be.

"Try not to be angry with your father." She rested her hand on Kit's shoulder in a fond caress. "He is only trying to protect you from illness or injury because he loves you so dearly. He is learning to master his fear, but that takes time just as it has taken time for you to learn how to read and write."

Every word was true yet Leah felt as if she were being pulled in opposite directions. Was she making excuses for the duke because she had grown to like him so well? Had she slackened in her efforts to liberate Kit because she had come to sympathize with his father? If so, she was betraying her original purpose and the promise she had made to Lady Althea. Her feelings toward the duke were holding her back, preventing her from pushing harder for Kit's freedom.

Personal attachments constrained one's freedom of action, Leah reminded herself. She had learned that in school when the teachers sought to control her behavior by punishing her friends. Could the duke be playing upon her sympathy to turn her from his opponent into an ally?

Unstopping the ink bottle, she silently vowed to make Kit's well-being her top priority again. "Work on your letter for half an hour then I will push you around in your chair again."

"We have a bargain!" Kit seized his pen and began to write.

As Leah watched him work with such energy, her gaze strayed to the nursery door. Perhaps she and Kit needed to prove to the duke that expanding his son's boundaries was not as fraught with peril as he seemed to believe. To accomplish that, it might be easier to beg forgiveness after the fact than ask permission beforehand.

When the duke returned a while later, he seemed pleased to find Kit had been so productive with his studies, as well as being in good spirits. If he suspected his son's new chair was being used for more than conveying him safely from his bed to the table, Lord Northam gave no sign of it.

Kit must have guessed that telling his father about his new amusement might lead to it being forbidden. Though Leah had not asked him to keep it a secret, the child made no mention of his new activity to the duke.

They passed a pleasant afternoon, reading aloud, studying more geography then playing games after Kit's tea. Though the day outside was overcast and windy, Leah found it did not weigh quite so heavily upon her spirits. She and Kit and his father made their own sunshine.

"I hope you will join me for dinner," said the duke as Leah headed off. "There is something I would like to show you afterward."

"Of course, Your Grace," Leah replied, her curiosity piqued. They had dined together several times since the evening of their quarrel, but both had made an effort to avoid any contentious subjects. There had been no opportunity for the duke to confide anything further about his marriage. "May I ask what you wish to show me?"

"You may ask all you like." His eyes twinkled in a manner Leah found dangerously appealing. "But do not expect me to tell you. I want it to be a surprise."

"What sort of surprise, Papa?" asked Kit. "Can you tell me? I wish I could see it whatever it is."

The merry glint in Lord Northam's eyes faded. Did he regret raising the subject in his son's hearing when Kit could not share in the surprise? He rallied quickly however. "That depends. Can you keep a secret?"

Kit broke into a broad grin and exchanged a significant look with Leah. "Yes, I can! I promise."

"Very well, then." The duke pretended not to notice the byplay between pupil and governess. "I will tell you when I tuck you in for the night."

As she headed off to dress for dinner, Leah tried to guess what the duke had in store for her. The whole idea of a surprise seemed out of character for a man who liked to keep his world orderly, predictable and safe. Yet the contradiction intrigued her.

She took greater care than usual with her appearance that evening. Unbinding her hair from its plain governess knot, she tied up the loose flow of chestnut curls with a velvet ribbon instead. Then she donned a gown Grace had given her to wear during the Nethercross Christmas festivities. Its rich plum color complemented her hair and eyes and brightened her complexion.

Then she performed a little twirl before the looking glass and asked her starry-eyed reflection why she had gone to so much trouble. The younger-looking woman replied with an impudent grin, "Why shouldn't I? If Lord Northam took the trouble to arrange a surprise, the least I can do is look my best for it."

The duke seemed to regard the evening as some sort of occasion, as well, for he appeared very smartly turned out in a dark green coat and crisp, fresh linen.

Leah's heart gave a silly flutter when he regarded her with an admiring smile and offered her his arm. She could understand what had drawn the late duchess to her husband when they first met in an elegant London assembly room. Little had the high-spirited young debutante guessed that a handsome face and pleasing manner would lure her into a dull, restricted life, from which there could be no escape.

Part of Leah welcomed the reminder that a woman should not let a passing fancy get the better of her good sense. And yet her sympathy for the duke reproached her. She knew better than to think he had ever *intended* to make his vivacious young bride unhappy. He had only wanted to protect her and their baby from the consequences of her impulsive behavior.

"A penny for your thoughts, Miss Shaw." The duke's tone of gentle banter stirred Leah from her conflicted musings. "Are you trying to contrive a way to coax me into revealing my surprise prematurely?"

"Not at all." She was able to answer truthfully, "Though I would appreciate a hint to ease my curiosity."

The duke gave a delightful mellow chuckle as he held her chair. "On that score, I fear I must disappoint you, my dear. With your nimble wits, I suspect the smallest clue might lead you to guess what I have in store. And that would defeat the whole purpose of the surprise. Surely heightened curiosity and anticipation are a great part of the appeal."

"You have me there, Your Grace." Leah could not deny her anticipation. No doubt that was responsible for the heady froth of emotions that bubbled within her. They had nothing to do with the fact that Lord Northam had addressed her as his "dear" again.

"I *will* endeavor to divert your thoughts," he offered. "Pray tell me more about these children with whom Kit is corresponding. Apart from Lady Steadwell's stepdaughter, are they all pupils of your school friends?"

Leah welcomed the diversion. "My friend Evangeline is governess to the Chase boys and their sisters. Their father is a prosperous mill owner in the north. Cissy and Dolly *were* Marian's pupils but she is now wed to their cousin and guardian, Captain Radcliffe. Peter…Lord Edgecombe is the stepson of my friend Hannah."

The duke seemed to approve. No doubt he was relieved to hear the other children would be suitable acquaintances for his son. "I recall you telling me that most of your friends have taken husbands. I hope those other unions have proven as happy as Lord and Lady Steadwell's."

Dinner had been served and the duke conversed in a casual manner while they ate. Yet Leah sensed his last remark was more than an idle pleasantry.

"My friends certainly appeared very happy when we were together at Hannah's wedding." She tried not to sound suspicious of his motives for raising the subject. "Nothing in their letters has suggested otherwise."

"I am pleased to hear it," replied the duke with obvious sincerity. "I do not wish to provoke another argument, but I feel bound to point out the experience of your friends would appear to contradict your grandmother's views about marriage."

Must they discuss that particular subject again?

Leah inhaled a deep breath and tried to avoid taking or giving offense. "I do not believe it does. It is true my friends seem content in their marriages and for that I rejoice. But we are all very different women who need different things to make us happy. Rebecca has always craved security. Grace longed for acceptance. Hannah sought an appreciative outlet for her devotion. Marriage to a good, worthy man was able to provide each what she required."

The duke made no effort to interrupt her but listened intently. He seemed sincerely anxious to understand.

"But women like my grandmother and me," Leah continued, "…and perhaps your late wife, place a high value on our freedom. By its very nature, the most loving marriage would still limit that freedom."

Lord Northam chewed on a morsel of roast pheasant which was so tender it scarcely required such determined effort. Was he mentally gnawing on the tough bone of an idea she had offered him?

"But you are a woman of faith, are you not?" The duke's brow furrowed in an endearing manner that made Leah long to smooth it out. "How do you reconcile your wish for freedom with the obedience and trust the Lord requires of His followers?"

Usually Leah deflected such serious inquiries about her beliefs with a flippant jest. But with Hayden Latimer, somehow it felt natural to share such a vital part of herself. Perhaps if he understood her, it would help him to understand his late wife and make peace with the differences that had strained their marriage.

There might be more to it than that, a glimmer of insight warned her, but she chose to ignore it.

"The Lord may require many things of us." She chose her words carefully, wanting to explain in a way the duke could truly understand. "But He does not *compel* us against our will. We are not like those little play figures of Kit's that move and act however he makes them. We always have a choice whether or not to believe, to trust or to act in accordance with our faith. To me that freedom is the most precious gift of a loving Creator."

The duke did not respond immediately, but continued to consume his dinner in thoughtful silence. Could he begin to comprehend views so very different from his own?

At last he looked up as if suddenly reminded of Leah's presence. "Kit seems to like that chair of his. It was a clever idea. I am grateful to you for proposing it."

Had he made any effort to grasp what she had taken such pains to explain? Leah tried not to mind the sting of that doubt. "I only wish I could devise a means for him to go up and down stairs safely without being carried."

The duke shuddered. "That is one of my greatest fears for him."

Though not the only one, Leah knew. If she somehow found a solution, what barrier to his son's emancipation would Lord Northam put up next? Much as she had come to sympathize with this man and admire him in many ways, his overprotectiveness did try her patience.

It made her think again how certain women were less suited for the restrictions of marriage. Might it not also be true that certain men made their unions more confining than others? Lord Northam had proven himself that kind of man—much more than her friends' husbands. It was scarcely a wonder his marriage to a free spirit like Kit's mother had been strained.

The duke steered their conversation to an even safer subject—the history of Renforth Abbey—and the remainder of their dinner passed pleasantly. When it concluded and Leah prepared to take her leave, Lord Northam reminded her, "You have not seen your surprise yet."

"It slipped my mind entirely," she confessed. "Am I to see it now?"

His Grace nodded. "May I prevail upon you to close your eyes?"

"Why?"

"If I tell you, it will spoil the surprise," he replied in a playful tone. But his direct blue gaze conveyed an earnest plea that was far more compelling. "Humor me for a few moments."

Humor him? She could manage that, surely.

"Very well." Leah shut her eyes only to discover the lack of sight heightened her other senses.

She was suddenly aware of the muted clink of china and quiet voices as the servants cleared the dining room.

"Now give me your hands." The duke's voice, coming from nearer than she expected, made her start.

When she hesitated, he added, "There is only a little way to go and I promise to guide you faithfully. Trust me."

That would be a good deal more difficult than humoring him. But how could she doubt so protective a man would allow her to come to any harm? Leah raised her hands and held them out in front of her.

An instant later she felt the duke's strong hands lightly clasp her fingers.

"This way." He drew her forward.

Where was he taking her? Leah wondered. She had lost all sense of direction. Wherever it was, part of her hoped they would not reach their destination too soon.

The lightness of Lord Northam's touch suggested that he regarded her hands as precious objects, which must be handled with the greatest care. At the same time his grip was firm enough to convey his determination to safeguard her from any harm. Never in her life had she felt so highly regarded.

It did not take a great many steps to get where they were going, yet for Leah, time seemed suspended as she savored the unaccustomed luxury of placing her trust in someone else.

After two brief pauses to open and close a door, the duke murmured, "Only a moment now."

Conscious of cooler air upon her arms and neck, Leah guessed where they were, but an unexpected scent puzzled her.

"You may open your eyes now."

Leah fought a strange inclination to keep them closed and linger in the private space bounded only by his voice and his touch. After a brief struggle, she forced her eyes open and let out a soft gasp.

After weeks of wintery gloom, a perfect riot of the brightest colors beguiled her eyes while the heady aroma of new life offered a feast for her nose.

"What is all this?" She gazed around in wonder at the cloisters of Renforth Abbey, illuminated by the flicker of tiny brass lamps. Pots overflowing with spring flowers lined both sides of the tiled walkway. More greenery cascaded from baskets hung between the tall mullioned windows.

Some of the flower petals were closing for the night, but enough were still open to create a vivid living tapestry. Golden daffodils and narcissus. Deep yellow, purple and white crocuses. Tulips in a vast array of brilliant hues. Hyacinths in a rainbow of delicate pastel shades.

"You approve, then?" The duke's question drew her gaze back to him. His smile was the brightest thing in the room and his eyes by far the most beautiful color. "I thought you might appreciate an early taste of spring, so I consulted the head gardener. He assures me that by the time these have ceased to bloom, there will be plenty of snowdrops and crocuses budding outdoors."

"You did all this…for me?" Leah walked the length of the cloister, drinking in the beauty around her. She marveled at how Lord Northam had captured the essence of springtime, wrapped it in a bow and made her a gift of it.

A delightful shiver went through her that had nothing to do with the temperature.

The duke had no way of knowing that, however.

"Forgive me!" he cried. "I should have brought a wrap for you. The gardeners put out clay pots full of coals to keep the plants warm, but it is not enough for your comfort."

Leah heard a rustle and turned to assure His Grace that she was not chilled. Before she got all the way around, something warm slipped over her shoulders and she realized it was his coat.

She wanted to protest and insist he take it back, but she could not. The garment seemed to hold her in a warm but restrained embrace. The faint tang of Lord Northam's soap enveloped her, an intriguing counterpoint to the pervading floral sweetness.

The sight of him left her speechless, too. His snowy

white shirtsleeves billowed out from a dark-colored waistcoat embroidered with threads of gold. Without his coat, the duke looked like a different man—less cautious, more daring and dashing.

To compensate for Leah's silence, he answered her earlier question. "Of course I had it done for you. Who else? I know Renforth Abbey is not at its best in winter and that has weighed on your spirits. So I thought I might hurry springtime along."

Slowly the duke raised his hand until the backs of his fingers rested against her cheek in a featherlight caress. "I want you to be happy here, Leah."

It was the first time he had spoken her given name without adding "Miss" the way his son did. That, together with the familiarity of his touch kindled a blistering blaze in her cheeks. Did he realize what he was doing?

Of course he did. That insight struck Leah as she stood frozen in place, torn between contrary inclinations. New, strange feelings made her want this moment between them to grow sweeter still. Even when long-held beliefs urged her to put a safe distance between herself and any man.

Hayden Latimer knew precisely what he was doing because he had done it before. He had captured the heart of a lady and married her. Then, with the kindest intentions, had gradually restricted her freedom, as he later would with their child.

That thought made Leah flinch as if she feared he meant to strike her.

"It is lovely, Your Grace." She tore off his coat and

thrust it back at him, trying to ignore his look of shock and hurt. "I am obliged to you for going to so much trouble on my account but it is getting late and I should retire for the night."

"But, Leah," the duke called after her as she hurried away. "...I mean *Miss Shaw,* please let me speak."

She was nearly to the door by that time. Much as she ached to turn back Leah knew she dared not.

"We can speak tomorrow," she called back over her shoulder trying to feign a casual tone but failing miserably.

Though she knew he was too much of a gentleman to pursue her, she fled to her room as fast as her feet would carry her, her heart pounding with fear. She did not bolt her door behind her. That would do no good. Instead she wished someone would lock it from the outside to restrain her, in case her confused emotions got the better of her.

Chapter Twelve

He had been making such good progress at courting Leah, until his disastrous misstep had driven her
away. Now that he had addressed Kit's governess by
her given name, Hayden found it impossible to think
of her any other way.

All night he tossed and turned, recalling how well
the evening had been progressing. They had enjoyed a
pleasant dinner and managed to discuss their differing
views without animosity. The whole time, his anticipation had risen as he'd prepared to reveal his carefully
planned surprise. He'd pictured the look on her face,
trying to imagine how she would react to the foretaste
of spring he had assembled for her.

By the time he'd been ready to lead her to the cloisters, his heart was racing with a mixture of exhilara-
tion and anxiety. What if, contrary to all expectation,
Leah did not like what he'd done? He had pushed aside
that fear, urging her to close her eyes and trust him
to lead her. To *his* surprise and satisfaction, she had

agreed. Perhaps, for all her talk of freedom, she secretly yearned to have someone watch out for her—someone on whom she knew she could always rely. The sensation of her slender fingers clasped in his hand was so very pleasant Hayden had longed to lead her all over the house before reaching their destination.

When he'd finally told Leah to open her eyes, her reaction was beyond anything he could have hoped. The way her hazel eyes had widened with wonder, her soft intake of breath and the way her whole face glowed had overwhelmed him with tender happiness. Was there anything he would not be prepared to do if it promised to bring her such obvious delight?

When she'd shivered with cold, Hayden had chided himself for that overlooked detail. Yet he could not regret it altogether, since it provided a further opportunity for him to be of service. The coat he'd draped around her slender shoulders was a substitute for the arms which ached to enfold her—keeping her close and safe always.

Then in a tone of disbelief, she'd asked if he had prepared such a delightful surprise for her. Her question confirmed his earlier suspicion that Leah had never truly experienced the loving care she deserved.

At far too young an age she had been thrust into the role of guide, companion and caregiver to her grandmother. She had been forced to watch in helpless outrage as the old woman came to rely on something stronger, that would enslave and destroy her. Sent away to that barbaric school, Leah had tried to help her friends there by drawing their teachers' cruelty upon herself. Most recently, in her profession as a governess, she had guided and cared for her pupils.

No wonder she placed such a high value on self-reliance. Who else had she ever had to depend on? It was long past time she experience the freedom of having someone nurture *her*.

A conviction like that was too powerful to resist. Hayden had been compelled to act upon it, if only by grazing her cheek with his hand.

But that had been a grave mistake. Hayden rolled over and pummeled his pillow in an unsuccessful effort to relieve his anger with himself. Why could he not have been content with the promising beginning he'd made? How could he have disregarded the caution that was bred so deep in his bones?

Yet strenuously as he questioned his own actions, Hayden could not help questioning Leah's reaction, as well. He was certain she welcomed the liberty he had taken. After all, he was not some gangling boy out in Society for the first time, bewildered by the mysterious ways of women. He knew when a lady was receptive to his attentions, even if she might not be fully aware of it herself. Leah Shaw had given every indication she found his company more than agreeable. Her whole manner had appealed for a clear sign of his feelings.

What *were* his feelings toward her? Hayden asked himself as he rose to face the day and Leah Shaw.

He could not deny he found her very attractive and most stimulating company. He admired her indomitable spirit and sympathized with the many harsh experiences she had endured. His plan to wed her might be borne of necessity and concern for his son, but that did not mean marrying Kit's governess would represent any hardship.

But did he *love* her? Hayden's conscience persisted as his valet shaved him and helped him dress.

Perhaps not, he concluded after a rigorous examination of his heart. But surely that was best for all concerned. He had been wildly in love with Celia, of whom Leah reminded him in far too many ways. Perhaps if there had been less emotion and more prudence on both their parts, his marriage to Celia might have been happier. That was what he wanted, for Kit's sake—a stable, comfortable, lasting union.

He did not rule out the possibility that he and Leah would grow closer with the passing years. Indeed, he hoped they would. But in the beginning, less intense feelings would be safest.

That was all very well, Hayden's reflection seemed to chide him. After the way Leah had fled the cloisters last night, would he ever get the opportunity to propose?

Casting a final scowl at himself in the mirror, Hayden rushed away to intercept Leah before she reached the nursery. The things he had to say to her were not for the ears of his son. The last thing he wanted was to raise Kit's hopes that Leah would remain with them permanently.

He managed to catch up with her on her way to begin the child's morning lessons. "A word with you if I may, Miss Shaw, before you start your duties?"

"Can it not wait, Your Grace?" Leah seemed flustered by his sudden appearance and more than a trifle wary. "Kit will be expecting me and he does not like to be kept waiting."

Perhaps what he had to say *could* wait, but Hayden could not bear to cause her a moment's further anxiety. "I will not detain you long, I promise."

He glanced over his shoulder to make certain there were no servants nearby, quietly going about their work with open ears.

"Very well, then," Leah agreed, though she was clearly not happy about it. "What do you wish to say?"

Hayden suddenly found himself nervous as a schoolboy. "I want to beg your pardon if I offended you last night with my familiarity. I assure you with all my heart, you have nothing to fear from me, nor will you ever. I am nothing like those men who tried to impose themselves upon Lady Steadwell when she was employed as a governess. My feelings toward you are respectful and my intentions entirely honorable."

Leah shook her head vigorously and for a distressing instant Hayden feared she did not believe him. "I have no such fears, sir. I know you are a man of honor."

A wave of relief swept over Hayden, so strong it threatened to make his knees buckle. "I am delighted to hear it. But I cannot conceal from you what my actions surely betrayed. I have come to hold you in the highest possible esteem and I hope you will permit me to pay my addresses, not as your employer but as…a suitor for your hand."

Leah grew pale and appeared to sway a little on her

feet. Hayden could not tell whether she welcomed his declaration or despised it.

The lady did not leave him long in suspense. "I am honored you would think of me in such a connection, but I have made no secret of my attitude toward marriage."

"You have expressed it...in most vehement terms." The corners of his lips twitched in an unsuccessful effort to suppress a grin.

In spite of her protests, he sensed Leah was more receptive to his attentions than she claimed. She pressed her lips together to prevent an answering smile. But she could not keep her eyes from dancing.

"But I hope," Hayden continued, "that you might permit me to attempt to persuade you otherwise."

Her lips parted a little. But she caught the lower one between her teeth, as if to keep herself from saying something she might regret. Was that something encouragement or rejection? Hayden could not tell, nor was he certain she knew.

He wished he'd dare take her hands in his as he had last night, but he feared it might spoil any hope of securing her agreement.

"You did not douse me with cold water last night," he reminded her as a possible indication of the feelings she might not fully fathom. "I take that as a hopeful sign."

Her tension vented in a bubble of laughter that unlocked her lips. Clearly humor was a means of reaching the part of her that might want what he offered.

"Perhaps that is only because there was no cold

water at hand," she teased, further easing the tension between them.

"Was that the only reason?" A note of sincere curiosity infused Hayden's question.

Leah reflected for a moment then shook her head. "A gesture of such kindness deserved a more considerate response. I do not believe my opinion of marriage is likely to change, but perhaps it would be worth… testing to be certain."

This was more encouragement than Hayden had expected. His grin blossomed into a delighted smile. "A very enlightened view. I can ask no more than that."

His obvious satisfaction with her answer seemed to cause Leah some dismay. "I hope you will make no more of it than I have said. I should be very sorry to injure your feelings if, as I expect, I cannot give you the answer you wish."

He should tell her his heart would be in no jeopardy, Hayden's conscience urged him. Of course he would be bitterly disappointed, for Kit's sake, if he could not induce Leah to accept his eventual proposal. But that was all.

Still, it might not be the best strategy to inform a prospective bride that he intended to guard his heart. "Let *me* worry about my feelings. If you endeavor to keep an open mind, I will be content to take my chances."

"As you wish," Leah replied with an air of someone accepting a challenge. "Now I must see to my duties. Regardless of what happens between the two of us, your son will be my first priority."

"In that, we are perfectly agreed." Hayden extended his hand as if to shake hers. But when Leah reached for it, he clasped her fingers and bowed to brush his lips over them.

What principle of anatomy could account for the sensations she was experiencing? The question plagued Leah as she tried to concentrate on teaching Kit that morning. Whenever she recalled the duke grazing her fingers with his lips or her cheek with his hand, a warm tingle flared in the place he had touched.

What would her former teachers say if they knew a duke wanted to make her his wife? They could not be one bit more astonished than she.

Of course she had sensed Lord Northam's feelings toward her growing more cordial of late, as had hers for him. From time to time she'd had hints those feelings might be more than friendly, but she chose to ignore or deny the warning signs. In the past, her profession had seldom brought her into close contact with gentlemen, which was how she'd preferred it. Reading of Grace's unfortunate experiences had reinforced her belief that she was not missing anything by avoiding the perils of romance.

After her first unfavorable acquaintance with Kit's overprotective father, it had never occurred to her that she might grow to respect or like him, let alone develop any warmer attachment. For that reason, she had neglected to mount any defenses against such feelings.

Now she wondered whether it might be too late.

"Have I spelled this word right, Miss Leah?" Kit's

question roused her from thoughts that were both disturbing and inviting.

Thrusting them to the back of her mind, she strove to concentrate her full attention on her pupil. "You have indeed. Well done. You have been working very hard this morning. Would you care to take a little break and go for a ride in your chair?"

"Out of the nursery, you mean?" asked Kit in a tone of excitement Dr. Bannister would have done everything in his power to discourage. "Yes, please!"

There was not a great deal to see besides paintings hung on the walls of the corridors and different suites of guest bedchambers that had not been used for years, but at least it would be a change of scene for the child.

As Leah wrapped a shawl around his shoulders and tucked an extra blanket over his legs, she wished Kit could visit the great hall, the library and especially the cloisters with their indoor spring garden his father had devised for her benefit. Was it possible she could take advantage of the duke's interest in her to win greater freedom for his son?

"There. I do hope you will be warm enough," said Leah as she crouched by Kit's chair. Vital as she believed it was for him to experience more freedom, she did not want to risk him getting chilled.

Before she could rise fully, Kit flung his arms around her neck. "Thank you, Miss Leah! I am glad that you came to be my governess. I like you best in the world next to Papa!"

The child's declaration and warm squeeze brought a lump to Leah's throat. An answering surge of affection led her to press a fond kiss upon his forehead. "I am glad I came to Renforth Abbey, too."

Would she be sorry to leave it in a few months? Her heart suffered a strange, hollow ache at the thought. Perhaps she would not regret leaving the estate itself, so quiet and isolated. But she would miss Kit a great deal, if her holiday in Berkshire was any indication. She would miss his father, too, she could not deny it.

Had Lord Northam already begun to alter her opinion about marriage even before he tried?

Carefully she pushed Kit's chair out of the nursery and down the long gallery. The way the boy reacted to such a small taste of freedom gladdened Leah's heart. It made her more determined than ever to secure as much liberty for him as she possibly could in her remaining months as his governess.

When she wheeled him past the staircase, Kit craned his neck and leaned over as far as his chair would permit. If it had not been equipped with arms, he might have fallen off, but that possibility did not seem to bother him. "The room where you sometimes eat dinner with Papa is down there isn't it, Miss Leah? And the place he brought all the flowers for you? Will you take me there someday?"

The notion of Kit exploring the wealth of varied rooms on the ground floor appealed to her greatly. But it was blighted by disturbing visions of the duke losing his footing as he carried his son down that long flight of stairs. "I have spoken to your father about it and I will keep on until I persuade him."

The way he meant to keep courting her until she

agreed to marry him? Was it possible their efforts to persuade one another could end up benefiting them both—*and* the child they cared for?

Leah had fallen so deep in thought, and Kit was so attracted by all the new sights, neither of them heard quiet footsteps approaching until it was too late.

"What have we here?" The duke's voice made both Leah and her pupil start. "I do not recall giving permission for my son to make excursions outside the nursery."

He did not raise his voice but there could be no mistaking his tone of disapproval. It roused Leah's spirit of rebellion.

"I do not recall you *forbidding* me to take Kit out of the nursery, either." Would her impudent quip play upon his feelings for her to lessen his opposition? Or would it rouse his old antagonism and make him reconsider his desire to wed her? Leah was not certain, though either one might have its benefits.

But which of the two did she hope for?

Leah was not certain until Lord Northam gave a wry chuckle. "You have me there, my dear. After this, I must make sure to be quite specific about the limits I place on my son for his protection. At least you took the trouble to wrap him up well against the cold."

"It isn't very cold, Papa," Kit protested. "I'm glad you aren't cross with Miss Leah for bringing me out."

The duke dropped to crouch before his son. "I cannot understand why you want to be out here when your nursery is so comfortable and stocked with all your books and playthings."

"Because…" Kit gestured around the wide, plain hallway "…it's new."

His son's simple explanation made the duke rock back on his heels.

"Very well, then." He rose slowly. "You may continue with your…explorations for a little longer, on the condition that I am allowed to accompany you."

"Of course you can, Papa." Kit held out his hand to his father, who enveloped it in his and gave it a squeeze.

They passed a further half-hour poking about the upper floor of the new range. Kit greeted everything he saw as if it were an amazing discovery.

The child's enthusiasm soon began to rub off on Leah, who found herself looking closer at paintings and items of furniture she had scarcely spared a second glance, seeing things she might otherwise have missed. Would the sights of the Continent truly be more remarkable than ordinary places seen with fresh eyes in the company of those she cared for?

She sensed that similar thoughts might be going through Lord Northam's mind. As he answered Kit's eager questions, the duke sometimes cast a glance over his son's head to catch her eye. Often he smiled and she could not help smiling back. Other times his handsome features remained solemn but his eyes shone with affection for his son that seemed to extend to her, as well.

Every time it happened, her heart seemed to perform a cartwheel in her chest.

Was she falling in love with Hayden Latimer? That question and others that followed brought her a quiver of wonder and a qualm of unease. Had she been gradually falling in love with him from the moment they'd met? And was it too late to stop?

Halfway through dinner that evening, Leah put down her fork and gazed across the table at Hayden. "If you mean to scold me for taking Kit out of his nursery without your permission, do get it over with, please."

Her tone was defensive and a trifle impatient, as if she suspected him of deliberately withholding his censure to spring on her when she let her guard down. Those feelings mirrored his so closely that Hayden could not help sputtering with laughter, much to Leah's annoyance.

"What is so amusing, may I ask?"

With difficulty Hayden mastered his mirth. It felt good to laugh as often as he had in recent months. That simple release had been missing from his life for far too long. He now appreciated what a treasured blessing it was. A surge of gratitude toward Leah swelled within him, for it was she who had brought laughter back to Renforth Abbey.

"Forgive me." He suppressed a final chuckle. "But I was about to ask you to say you told me so, and get it over with."

"Told you *what?*" Relieved from the prospect of his anger descending upon her at any moment, Leah gave an answering chuckle.

"The same thing you have been telling me since the day you arrived here." Hayden prepared to follow a course of turbot in white sauce with a generous slice of *humble pie.* "That the benefits of allowing my son more freedom outweigh the risks."

"Oh, that." Leah cast him a teasing grin sweetened with unmistakable affection. "Why should I continue to wheeze that old tune when you seem to be learning it very well on your own?"

They both chuckled over that, the pitch of her laughter and his creating a harmony as agreeable as any duet performed in an opera house.

"All the same, I doubt Kit will be satisfied for long investigating the upper floor." Hayden grew serious. "Have you come up with any clever ideas about how we can get him safely up and down the stairs? His rolling chair will be no help making that trip and I do not trust anyone, myself included, to carry him without risking a fall."

"One possibility does occur to me." Leah did not sound confident that her idea would find favor with him.

"Go ahead," Hayden prompted. "What is it?"

"I agree it would be hazardous to carry Kit up and down the stairs frequently. And the difficulty will only increase as he grows bigger."

Hayden nodded as she spoke. It was clear Leah understood the perils involved and was no more willing to risk harm coming to Kit than he. More than ever, he knew he must persuade her to become his son's new mother.

"I suggest removing the obstacle," Leah continued. "Move Kit's bedchamber down to *this* floor so he will be able to take part in everything that goes on down here. That way he would only need to be carried down the stairs once, very carefully."

"Put Kit's nursery on the ground floor?" Immediately Hayden could foresee all manner of difficulties. "But I could not have him sleep so far from me. What if he needed me in the night?"

"Install a bell between his room and yours, like the ones to summon servants," Leah suggested.

When she saw he was about to object she forestalled him. "Or move *your* bedchamber to the ground floor, as well. Goodness knows, there are enough unused rooms that could be converted to that purpose with a little effort."

"With rather a *lot* of effort I believe you will discover," Hayden corrected her.

As usual Leah refused to be daunted. "All Kit's life you have spared no effort to do what you felt would benefit him. Is that truly what would prevent you from trying my idea or are you still afraid to give your son more freedom?"

Hayden knew he owed it to her and Kit to examine his heart and give a sincere answer. After a long thoughtful pause he replied, "A little of both I suppose."

Leah nodded as if his answer tallied with what she had expected. "You do not need to decide right away. But for all our sakes I hope you will consider my suggestion carefully and not dismiss it out of hand."

That was only reasonable, Hayden had to admit. Leah had moderated her efforts since her first stormy days at Renfoth Abbey. She had cultivated patience with his slow pace of change. She had demonstrated her concern for his son. The least he could do was try to meet her halfway.

The lady seemed to feel he needed more encouragement. "You know, if you show me you are willing to grant your son more freedom, it might help to alter my opinion about…that other matter."

She glanced toward the butler and footman who hovered silently near the sideboard, awaiting Hayden's signal to serve the next course.

Leah was referring to the subject of marriage, he realized. If he allowed Kit more freedom, it would show her that marriage to him might not be the prison sentence she feared.

If she did agree to marry him, Hayden suspected she would be motivated as much by tender feelings for the child as for him…perhaps more. Though he told himself it would be for the best if Leah's reasons for marrying were the same as his, somehow the thought still troubled him.

Chapter Thirteen

"It sounds quiet downstairs today," said Kit as Leah pushed his chair through the upper gallery, an outing that had become a highly anticipated part of his daily routine. "Are the workmen all finished what they've been doing?"

"I believe they might be." Leah tried to think of a subject to divert her young pupil's curiosity.

For three weeks now, the mysterious sounds of footsteps, hammering and distant voices from the ground floor had intrigued Kit no end. When he questioned them, Leah and his father put him off with vague references to renovations. Hayden feared his son would grow impatient with the pace of the work if he knew what it would mean for him. Leah did not want to let the truth slip out in case Hayden changed his mind at the last minute, which she worried he might.

She approved the effort he was making to master his fears and take this daunting step toward greater freedom for his son. She took it as a touching indication of his feelings for her that he had decided to act upon her suggestion.

"Shall we play skittles?" she asked Kit, certain the activity would take his attention off what was going on downstairs.

It was Hayden who had first mentioned the game, remembering how he and his sister had played it in the upper gallery when they were children. Kit enjoyed the opportunity to be active and make some noise by knocking down the pins. At first his arms had been too weak for him to roll the ball far, let alone hit any pins, but with practice he had improved a great deal.

"Yes, please!" Kit sat up taller in his chair. "I hope I can knock down six pins with one roll today. I want to be able to play skittles with Sophie when she comes to visit. Do you suppose Papa could teach me some more games?"

"He might," said Leah as she set up the wooden pins. "You will have to ask him when he comes."

Hayden still spent far more time with his son than any father Leah had ever known. But with the approach of spring, he had become more involved in running the estate, not to mention supervising the construction downstairs. In spite of being so busy, he appeared better rested, more relaxed and happier. He and Kit seemed to enjoy their time together more.

Leah handed Kit the ball and watched with satisfaction as he knocked down several pins.

"Only four." He sounded disappointed, clearly forgetting it had not been long since he'd been happy to hit even one. "But I will do better with the next roll."

"I am certain you will continue to improve if you keep that attitude." Leah encouraged him as she reset the pins for his next try.

She pictured Hayden and his sister playing the game when they were children. No doubt he had been careful to observe the rules and not disturb their grandmother by making too much noise. Althea would have jumped and shouted when she made a good score and perhaps not been above the occasional bit of cheating.

In recent weeks, Leah and Hayden had often talked of their childhoods, which made her feel closer to him than ever. Unlike her, he had been old enough to recall the fever epidemic that carried off his beloved parents, grandfather and younger brother. Was that devastating loss part of the reason he clung so tightly to those he loved? While she could sympathize with such feelings, Leah was not certain she dared wed a man who would always want to hold her too tight.

"There now," she returned the ball to Kit. "Take your time, aim carefully and put all your strength into your roll."

The child's features settled into a determined expression so like his father's that Leah could not help but smile. Hard as she tried to keep her feelings for Hayden Latimer from running away with her, she sensed her resolve slowly crumbling. If he had continued to argue against her views about marriage, it would have aroused her antagonism, like the traveler in Aesop's fable who pulled his cloak tight against the raging wind. Instead, the duke's attentiveness and sincere efforts to change had worked on her like the sun's beaming rays, loosening her grip.

Kit did as Leah had suggested, his eyes narrowed and the tip of his tongue stuck out in a look of intense concentration. The ball flew from his hand and barreled into the pins.

"Seven!" Kit bounced up and down in his chair in the throes of excitement that would have alarmed his former doctor. "I never thought I could knock down that many with one roll."

"Well done!" Hayden's voice startled both Leah and the child as he strode into view. "Keep at it and you will soon be better than I ever was."

"Papa!" Kit held up his arms for an embrace.

Leah wished she could do the same.

All she had to say was one little word, the voice of temptation whispered, and she would be free to give and receive such gestures of affection from the duke.

Free? A more familiar voice countered. *With such a fiercely protective man and a child who required so much special care?* There were sure to be far more things she would *not* be permitted to do.

Unaware of Leah's troubled thoughts, Hayden stooped to hug his son.

"Playing skittles is making me stronger." Kit flexed his arm to show how it had put on flesh. "Miss Leah says so. And it is great fun. Would you like to play against me, Papa?"

Hayden nodded toward the scattered pins. "A few hits like that and you would humiliate your old father.

Give me a chance to practice first so I can offer you a little competition."

"Besides," he continued, casting a significant glance toward Leah, "if you can take a recess from your game, there is something I would like to show you."

Kit gave a vigorous nod. "What is it, Papa?"

Hayden bent over the child and hoisted him into his arms. "You will see soon enough."

As he headed toward the stairway with careful steps, a footman appeared and rolled Kit's chair away toward the servant's stairs.

"Whatever it is, can Miss Leah see it, too?" Kit asked his father.

"Of course," Hayden replied. "In fact I want her to see, since it was her idea."

"Come on, Miss Leah!" the child called. "You don't want to miss it."

"I certainly do not." She scrambled after them, her heart galloping with anticipation of Kit's reaction.

Or was it pounding with dread of her frail young pupil being carried down that tall flight of stairs? Images of Hayden falling with Kit in his arms flashed through her mind in a disturbing sequence. She could only imagine how he must feel after years spent zealously guarding his son from the slightest bump or sniffle.

"Let me walk ahead of you," she offered as Hayden hesitated at the top of the stairs.

She would hold tight to the banister and if any mishap did occur, hopefully she would break their fall.

"Are we going downstairs?" Kit sounded as amazed

and delighted as if he had been informed of a voyage to the Orient.

"We are." Hayden's features creased with anxiety. "Now keep still like a good boy and hold tight to my neck."

Leah cast him a smile that she hoped communicated encouragement and confidence. Then she turned and proceeded down the stairs with care almost as great as if *she* were carrying the child.

Behind her, she heard Hayden's firm but cautious tread. When they rounded the landing, she looked down to see Kit's chair waiting for him, along with a welcoming committee comprised of Mr. Gibson, Tilly and several more housemaids and footmen.

By the time she reached the lower floor, Leah's breath was coming so fast and shallow, she felt a trifle faint. She joined the others to watch Hayden descend the last few steps. Did anyone else notice the faint sheen of sweat on Lord Northam's distinguished brow?

The servants burst into applause when the duke lowered Kit into his chair. The child grinned and bowed from the waist, clearly delighted with the whole proceedings. "Is this what you wanted to show me, Papa?"

"Part of it." Hayden sounded winded as if he had just climbed a mountain rather than walked down a flight of stairs. "Now let us see the rest."

It was a kind of mountain he had scaled, Leah reflected as she followed the parade toward Kit's new quarters. This obstacle to his son's freedom had long seemed overwhelming, but Hayden had battled his paralyzing caution to conquer it at last. This one step would open up whole new vistas for the child—the library, the music room, the cloisters and chapel, even the grounds outside.

When she had first come to Renforth Abbey, Leah would have considered this a simple task that should have been accomplished right away. Now she knew better. It had been anything but easy for Hayden. Yet he had done it, because he loved his son and because he wanted to prove something to her.

He was capable of change and willing to undertake it for the sake of those he cared for. If Hayden could change, perhaps she could, too. Perhaps she could conquer her fear of confinement, learn to be content in one place and allow herself to form lasting attachments... even if they threatened to tie her down.

Walking down that long staircase with his precious son in his arms was one of the most terrifying ordeals Hayden had ever attempted. Afterward when he thought back on it, his innards twisted into tight knots and his palms grew damp. A single misstep and he could not bear to imagine what might have happened. All his worst nightmares would have come true.

Yet, as the dismal days of winter warmed to spring, and he watched his son blossom, he could not deny the reward had been worth the risk. Four wheels attached to the legs of a chair and Kit's bedchamber moved to the ground floor—who would think two such simple changes could have such a profound effect on the boy's life? But they had opened up a new world to Kit that he had embraced eagerly. Every day he seemed to grow stronger, happier and more independent.

One evening in early April, as Hayden and Leah emerged from the nursery after hearing his son's prayers and saying good-night, he shook his head and gave a wry chuckle. "Did you hear Kit at dinner, informing me he is too old for a nursemaid and asking for a valet of his own? What will be next?"

"It is a rather precocious request," Leah agreed. "But perhaps worth considering. He is growing so fast. He will soon need someone with good strong arms to help him get about. Besides, Kit might feel less coddled if he is attended by a man. I would suggest someone fairly young who could also be a companion for him—take part in his games and so on."

"I should have known you would have an opinion on the subject." Hayden offered Leah his arm, which she took with only the slightest hesitation.

In the weeks since Kit had taken up residence on the ground floor, Hayden sensed a growing change in Leah, too. She seemed more content at Renforth Abbey, less restless. They had not discussed the subject of marriage for some time, but he suspected it was as much on her mind as his. Unless he was mistaken, she seemed to be warming to the idea, or at least getting used to it.

"Does that mean you will think about Kit's request?" She cast him a sidelong glance, her lips arched in the beginnings of an impudent grin that had become so familiar to him. "Surely you cannot still be afraid that every bump or chill will cause him terrible harm?"

Hayden shook his head ruefully. "It is not easy to

abandon the habit of worrying about him. No matter how big and strong and capable he becomes, part of me will always think of him as that frail little mite I first held in my arms and swore to protect."

He could tell by the dewy, brooding look in her eyes that Leah did not think less of him for voicing such feelings—quite the contrary. Yet he must give the lady her due, as well. "On the other hand, when I think of the restricted life Kit had before you came to be his governess I pity the poor child with all my heart and blame myself for my blindness."

"Do not be too severe upon yourself." Leah gave his arm a heartening squeeze. "You deserved every bit as much pity as your son. Pleased as I am to see him enjoying his newfound freedom, I am equally happy to see you reclaim a life of your own. You will be a better father to Kit because of it, I am certain."

Without paying much attention to where they were going, they had arrived at a side door that opened onto the gardens.

Hayden nodded toward it. "The evening is mild and there is still some light. Shall we walk out before dinner?"

"I would like that," Leah responded readily. "In fact, there is something I would like to show you and a question I want to ask."

A question? *He* was the one with a question always on his mind. More than once it had risen to his lips only to be suppressed by fear that her answer might not be to his liking. The longer he was able to wait, the more optimistic he would feel about his chances. Yet his sense of caution urged him to be certain of Leah.

"Lead on." Hayden opened the door and ushered her out.

The sun had already sunk down below the horizon, illuminating the western sky in vivid bands of red, orange and purple. Hayden could not recall the sunsets being so intense and beautiful in the past. Was it Leah's company that made them appear that way? He suspected so, just as food had more flavor when she dined with him. Every experience, however commonplace, seemed heightened somehow when he shared it with her.

Even as he savored this sharper awareness of life's joys, he could not stifle a qualm of uneasiness. It was growing harder and harder to prevent his heart from becoming engaged, as had been his prudent plan. After all, he could not be certain Leah would agree to wed him. She still might decide to go off to Europe with that admiral and his family. Hard as he might try to prevent it, he must try equally hard to keep his heart from being torn apart if it did come to pass.

When he felt his emotions slipping out of his control he reminded himself of his marriage to Celia, which had begun on such a pinnacle only to erode under the pressures of time and their differences.

"What is it you want to show me?" he asked as they walked further and further from the house.

Here, a series of walled gardens that provided fresh produce for the estate stood near a fringe of woodland.

Those trees separated the grounds of Renforth Abbey from the surrounding tenant farms.

"This." Leah tugged him toward one of the enclosed gardens and pushed open a wooden door that led inside. "Why was it left to go to seed when every other part of the estate is so well cared for?"

Hayden stared around at unpruned trees and weed-choked flower beds. "I'd forgotten all about this little garden. My grandfather had it made for my grandmother when they were first married. After he died, she ordered it shut up and left as it was. I never understood why. Althea once asked but Grandmother refused to answer. It was the closest I ever saw her to tears. Why does it matter?"

"Because." Leah let go of his arm and wandered toward a tall oak tree. A rope swing with a wooden seat hung from one of its sturdy branches. She sat down on it. "I would like to bring Kit out here when the weather is fine."

Instinctively Hayden began to marshal his arguments, but Leah seemed to anticipate them before he could speak.

"He could ride in your grandmother's garden chair. I already asked the coachman about making any repairs it needs. Later it might be nice if you bought Kit a cart and a big good-tempered dog to pull it."

"A large dog?" Hayden forgot his objections to the garden as he contemplated that alarming notion.

"Don't you think it would be good company for him?" Leah gave herself a little push to set the swing moving back and forth.

"Careful!" Hayden strode closer to catch her if she fell. "Are you certain that branch is strong enough? The rope could be rotten, too."

Leah laughed. "The branch is as sound as can be. But you're right. It might be a good idea to replace the rope with new before Kit uses it."

"Are you mad?" Hayden seized the ropes and brought the swing to an abrupt halt. "Or only trying to drive me that way? I will not have my son flying through the air and cavorting with beasts twice his size!"

Leah looked up at him with a mixture of pity and exasperation he had come to know so well. He found it strangely appealing. "A few months ago, you did not want Kit to leave his bed, but now you chide yourself for keeping him there so long. Other children play on swings. Other children have dogs and are none the worse for either. Kit wants more than anything to be like other children even if he cannot walk. Those are two ways he can. Do not let *your* fears hold him back."

Was that what he'd been doing all Kit's life? Leah's charge rocked Hayden as if he were the one on the swing rather than she. Had he let his fears hold his son back more than the child's physical infirmity? Was *he* Kit's greatest handicap?

"Do you never get tired of being right?" He gave Leah's swing a gentle push, hoping his outburst had not set back his campaign to win her hand. What greater proof could there be that he and Kit needed her to advocate for the boy's independence?

"Tired of being right?" Leah gave a gurgle of melodious laughter that reassured him she was not offended. "Hardly! It makes a very agreeable change as a matter of fact. Does that mean you will let me bring Kit here and you will think about getting him a dog?"

Hayden tried to banish the images of possible disaster and the feeling of alarm they engendered. "With certain conditions. That tree limb must be inspected for soundness and the swing replaced with a new one. And any dog I acquire must be the most docile tempered of its kind to be found."

"Very prudent measures," Leah said, nodding. "Believe me, I do not want to risk any harm coming to Kit, either. But I worry *more* about the consequences of keeping him too sheltered. That reminds me, there is something else I believe Kit will like about this garden."

"And what might that be?" Hayden gave the swing another push. The branch and rope had held so far. Perhaps both were sturdier than he'd given them credit for. Did the same apply to his son?

"I happened to be out walking earlier this week." Leah seemed to enjoy the movement of the swing. Had she ever taken part in such childhood pastimes? Or had she been too busy caring for her grandmother? Hayden doubted there had been any swings or games at the Pendergast School.

"I heard voices from within these walls," Leah continued. "It seems some of your tenants' children sneak in here to play."

"Do they, indeed?" Now that he looked, Hayden could see where some weeds had been pulled and scattered about and earth in the flower beds had been newly turned.

"Please do not be angry with them." Leah glanced over her shoulder at him with a beseeching look he was powerless to resist. "If the garden has been deserted for so long, why should someone not make use of it? I believe your grandfather would approve of others amusing themselves in a place he and your grandmother were once happy."

"I believe he would," Hayden mused. It would be better than having the place shut up and going to seed.

"I am glad we agree." Leah jumped off the swing in midflight, squealing as she almost lost her balance.

Hayden flew toward her and caught her arms, steadying her on her feet. She made no effort to pull away, so he hung on longer than propriety allowed.

"I would like Kit to meet the tenant children." Leah stared deep into his eyes, willing him to approve. "I believe it would be good for them to work together to bring this old garden back to life."

Hayden heaved a sigh. "You do not believe in taking one step at a time, do you? Or even two. Will you next suggest I ought to get Kit his own hot air balloon?"

Leah laughed at his exaggeration. "If you have already agreed to let him come here, what could it hurt to have the company of other children? He loves exchanging letters with my friends' youngsters but that is no substitute for flesh-and-blood playmates."

"What could it hurt?" Hayden repeated. "You are right to say there are worse things Kit could suffer than illness or injury. What if those children want nothing to do with him because he cannot run and play as they can? What if they ridicule him or impose upon him?"

"Those were not the difficulties I foresaw," Leah replied, challenging him yet reassuring at the same time. "They are 'dangers' any child may face and hopefully overcome. Would they be so much worse for Kit than boredom or loneliness?"

By now the vivid colors had faded from the horizon leaving a plump yellow moon master of the night sky with thousands of tiny twinkling stars for company.

"Are you afraid your son might make new friends and you will be obliged to share his affections?" Leah asked.

Her question managed to do what propriety could not. Hayden abruptly released his gentle grasp upon her arms. "Don't be ridiculous! I love Kit. You know that. I do not want to see him hurt. Surely you must know from that wretched charity school how cruel children can be to any they perceive as weaker than themselves."

"I do," Leah admitted with a sigh that pierced his heart. "Did I ever tell you about the big girls who used to stand around the fire warming themselves and blocking heat from reaching the little ones? If we did not wolf down our food at meals, they would take whatever we had left once they finished their own portions."

Outrage swept through Hayden like fire fanned by a strong wind. "Your teachers should have protected the smaller girls!"

Protectiveness was the ruling trait of his character. He could not fathom how others could stand by and permit the big and strong to run roughshod over the small and weak.

"They should," Leah murmured, "but the big girls curried favor by telling tales on the rest of us for any misbehavior, no matter how trivial."

How much of that had she come in for? By the grief in her tone Hayden suspected Leah had been a prime target. It made him feel unbearably helpless that there was nothing he could do to change what had happened to her.

His feelings were too powerful to deny some outlet. Before he knew what he was doing, his feet bore him back toward her. He fumbled in the shadows for her hands. Then he raised her palms to his lips and anointed them with tender kisses. If only he had the power to take those scars away—the ones on her hands and even deeper ones upon her heart.

Any misguided warning her grandmother had planted in her mind about the institution of marriage must have been reinforced a hundredfold by that other wretched institution. Was it any wonder she feared giving anyone power over her for fear they would abuse it—even the power of love?

A faint gasp escaped Leah's lips when he began to kiss her hands. The sound struck Hayden like a blow and made him realize what he was doing. In some ways this gesture was more intimate than a kiss on the lips—it certainly felt that way to him.

"Forgive me for taking such a liberty!" he pleaded. "I only meant to…"

His voice trailed off. How could he explain what he scarcely understood himself?

But when he tried to release her hands, Leah kept hold of his. "I know what you meant and it was kindly done. But do not pity me too much. I may have learned painful lessons about cruelty at the Pendergast School but I also learned of generosity, loyalty and kindness. Those lessons were well worth the price. Do not deny Kit that opportunity. Love cannot prevent all harm but it can provide strength and solace to triumph over whatever trials life may bring."

Her words carried a ring of truth that even his deeply ingrained protectiveness could not deny.

"It will not be easy." That was an almost ridiculous understatement.

"Of course it won't." Somehow Leah's frank acknowledgement of the difficulty reassured him more than any glib words of encouragement. "But I do not believe it will be as hard as you fear, either. Not long ago you asked me to close my eyes and trust you to lead me. Now I must ask you to trust *me*. Can you do that?"

Could he? Trust was far too close to other vulnerable feelings he strove to repress until he could be entirely certain of Leah. He feared his efforts were not going so well.

"I can try." Even that tepid admission came out with painful effort.

Yet he felt amply rewarded when Leah raised his hands and grazed her lips over his knuckles. "Then perhaps I can, too."

Chapter Fourteen

"**I** will not say I told you so," Leah teased Hayden gently a month later as they stood in the walled garden watching Kit playing with the tenant children. "But I cannot deny I might be thinking it."

Some of the children were digging in the earth, pulling weeds and sowing flowers from the Renforth plant nursery. One boy was pushing his brother on the swing, while Kit and a girl were taking turns throwing a stick for his dog, Goldie, to retrieve.

"You would have every right to." Hayden's voice peeled with sweet satisfaction. "Not only is Kit happier than I have ever seen him, he is better tempered, too. Not being the focus of everyone's attention has made him less willful. That was a boon I did not expect."

Leah nodded, her gaze lingering on the boy with unmistakable affection. "I was afraid you were going to call a halt to the whole thing that first day when the other children crowded around, asking Kit about his chair and why he couldn't walk."

"If you had not held me back and reminded me to trust you, I might have whisked him into the house and sent the other children away." Hayden's tone betrayed the effort it had cost him to restrain his protective urges and how grateful he was that she had helped him succeed. "Now I see they were only curious. Once Kit explained his condition to them, they seemed to take it for granted."

Knowing how difficult all these changes had been for Hayden over such a short period, Leah could not help admiring him all the more. He had braved his deepest fears for the sake of his son…and for her sake, as well. After he had gone to such lengths to change in the way she needed, how could she not try to do the same for him?

During the past weeks, as she watched Kit take step after step toward greater liberty, Leah had sought to give free rein to her feelings for Hayden. She had allowed herself to imagine a future at Renforth Abbey as wife, mother and duchess. At first the prospect of those ties had frightened her with the permanence and weight of responsibility they carried. But when she considered the alternative, leaving this place and the man and child for whom she had come to care so deeply, marriage seemed the lesser of two evils. Perhaps she would discover that the benefits of wedlock far outweighed the risks.

Now the time was fast approaching when she must make her choice. She could not postpone it any longer.

"I received a letter the other day." Her mouth felt dry as she spoke and her chest constricted, as if by an old-fashioned corset. "From Admiral DeLancey's wife about the position she offered me at Christmas. It seems they have decided to leave for the Continent a fortnight earlier than expected. She wants to know if I will still be able to accompany them."

Hayden reacted as if she had informed him of the admiral's intention to attack Renforth Abbey.

Turning toward Leah, he seized her hands in a grip so tight it was almost painful. The gaze that bore down upon hers was much alarmed. "Surely you do not mean to agree. Kit still needs you and so do I. We would be quite lost without you!"

What would become of them if she left? Leah tried to imagine. Might Kit catch a cold or might one of his new friends call him a name? If such a setback occurred when she was no longer there to support Hayden, would his doubts and fears get the better of him? Would he tighten restrictions upon Kit until they ended up in the same intolerable situation where she had first found them?

"I suppose I could make my apologies to the DeLanceys and renew my position as Kit's governess for another year." A spasm of regret gripped Leah at the prospect of abandoning her dream of traveling abroad.

Hayden's grasp eased a little, but he gave a decisive shake of his head. "That would be preferable to losing you, but it would only delay the day of reckoning. So many times during these past weeks I have wanted to propose to you, but each time I put it off because I feared it might be too soon and you would refuse."

He glanced toward the children, who were all so engaged in their own activities that they paid no attention to Kit's father and governess. "I was planning a special evening with the proper atmosphere to ask for your hand, but I find I cannot wait another moment to speak. Please, my dearest Leah, put an end to my anxiety and say you will do me the great honor of agreeing to become my wife! I promise I will devote the rest of my life to making you happy."

Leah had no doubt he would do everything in his power to keep that promise. She had never known a man willing to give so generously of himself. The prospect of having someone to care for her and protect her was vastly appealing after a lifetime of fending for herself. More than that, she longed to care for him in ways no one else could. She would fill the void in his heart carved out by so many losses. She would encourage him to let hope for the best rule his actions rather than fear of the worst.

"Thank you for being so patient." Her gaze ranged over his features, which had become so dear to her. Hayden appeared years younger than he had when they first met. The shadows of exhaustion beneath his eyes had been banished. The fine lines of worry etched upon his brow had eased. His mouth was far more apt to curve into a warm smile than settle into an anxious frown. "And for the honor of your proposal. Just as you have made the effort to overcome your fears for Kit, I have fought to overcome my…reservations about marriage."

"Have you succeeded?" Hayden looked from her face to their clasped hands and back. Such was the power of his gaze that everything around them seemed to dissolve. The voices of the children receded as if they were much farther away. The beating of her heart grew louder in Leah's ears than anything outside the snug sphere that seemed to enclose them.

"Perhaps not as well as you have," she confessed. Then before the shadow of disappointment darkened his gaze more than she could bear, she added, "But enough that I feel able to accept your proposal."

"You do?"

The outpouring of relief, gratitude and joy Leah sensed from him drowned out her last few nagging doubts. When he leaned toward her, she lifted her face and tilted her head as instinct urged her, until their lips met in a kiss of tender affection that knew no bounds.

For a span of time measured only by the beating of their hearts, she and Hayden lingered in their own private garden, where trust and love had blossomed and fears were no more than troublesome weeds to be plucked up and cast out.

Often during the following fortnight, Hayden was tempted to pinch himself to be certain he had not imagined that afternoon in the garden when Leah had at last accepted his proposal. During the wondrous kiss that sealed their betrothal, it felt as if one final burden had fallen from his shoulders, leaving his spirit free to soar.

Leah would not abandon him and Kit. She would stay and together they would build his son a happy future that balanced his safety and health with increasing independence. He would care for Leah, too, as no one in her past had done properly. He would do everything in his power to make up for all the deprivations she had suffered. He would apply the important lessons she had taught him about his son's need for freedom to his relationship with her, as well.

Today he strode through the cloisters with such a bounce in his step that he wondered if he ought to add weight to his boots to keep from floating up to the vaulted ceiling. With the wedding date only a month away, Renforth Abbey was bustling with life as it had not done for many years. The servants were busier than many of them had ever been—scrubbing floors, airing rooms, beating rugs, polishing windows and chandeliers. But rather than grumbling about the extra work, they all seemed reenergized. Gibson was fairly bursting with industry.

The chapel doors had been thrown open, allowing Hayden to peer in and check on the work going forward there. The stone floor was being scrubbed by several fresh-faced housemaids who chattered away as they worked. A pair of nimble young footmen perched on ladders polishing the finely carved rood screen with linseed oil. Hayden reminded himself to ask Leah what sort of flowers she wanted to decorate the chapel for their wedding ceremony.

Hearing the approach of swift, light footsteps— clearly a woman's—he glanced back down the cloisters, expecting to see Leah. His smile faltered only a little when he recognized his sister. He and Althea might have had their differences over the years, but she was responsible for sending Leah into Kit's life and his. For that service he would be forever grateful.

"Althea!" He opened his arms to her. "This is a pleasant surprise indeed. What brings you down to the country when the Season is at its height? The wedding is not for another month."

"Thank goodness for that!" His sister avoided Hayden's embrace. "It gives me thirty days to talk some sense into you. To think I should have to urge caution upon *you*—what is the world coming to?"

"Talk sense to me?" Hayden shook his head, bewildered. "Urge caution? What are you on about? Do you disapprove of my marriage plans?"

Althea threw up her hands. "You talk as if you expected me to be delighted. I do not know what has come over you."

Her glance strayed toward the chapel, making Hayden look, too. The maids appeared frozen in place, their scrub brushes stilled and their heads lifted, staring toward him and his sister.

"We need to talk," said Althea as if that was not what they were doing already, "somewhere *private*."

Her voice rose in volume on that last word. As if on cue, the maids began scrubbing again, harder and faster, perhaps trying to make up for their lapse.

"Very well." Hayden nodded to indicate the way she had come. "The library should be quiet, since it does not need to be prepared for wedding guests."

His sister gave an inexplicable shudder then turned and marched back down the cloisters at a pace Hayden was hard-pressed to match. On the way to the library he tried several times to inquire why she objected to his marriage plans. Each question was met with bristling silence and a baleful glare.

He could not fathom what had come over Althea. After all, she was one of Leah's greatest admirers. At Christmas she had practically demanded he propose to Kit's governess.

The instant she swept into the library and he pushed the door closed behind them, his sister rounded on him and let fly the tirade she had clearly been bursting to unleash. "Have you taken leave of your senses, Hayden? Can you imagine what Grandmother would say if she knew you were planning to make a common governess the next Duchess of Northam?"

This sudden disapproval of his engagement was perverse, even for his sister. "When did you ever give a fig for what Grandmother would say? Besides, there is nothing *common* about Leah. She is one of the most uncommon women it has ever been my pleasure to meet. It was by far the greatest favor you ever did me when you sent her to Renforth Abbey. She has changed Kit's life and mine. I cannot understand why you should object to my marrying her. I would not be the first nobleman to wed the woman who has taught and cared for his children."

Hayden's reasoning did nothing to pacify his sister—quite the contrary. "Unfortunately, that is true. There has been a perfect epidemic of peers wedding governesses in the past few years. First there was Viscount Benedict, but he always was rather odd. Then Lord Steadwell followed his deplorable example and just last summer, the Earl of Hawkehurst. The dowagers of the ton are saying they should save themselves the expense of a Season by putting their marriageable daughters to work as governesses instead. Once word gets about that a *duke* has fallen prey to this madness, the gossip will be perfectly violent!"

As had been the case for most of his life, his sister's opposition only strengthened Hayden's resolve. He crossed his arms in front of his chest and stared Althea down. "Then it is fortunate I live a quiet country existence and do not care a whit for Society gossip."

"I do not have that luxury." His sister began to pace the perimeter of the library gesturing wildly as she spoke. "I should have seen this coming. Of course you would be starved for companionship, buried for years out in the midst of nowhere. I should have engaged a plainer governess, not one so much like poor Celia. But I thought you had learned your lesson. I thought you intended to dedicate the rest of your life to Kit."

Was Leah really so much like Celia? His sister's words took Hayden aback. He had to admit, there were many similarities. Did he have a weakness for spirited, impulsive women because they added zest to his quiet, cautious life? And did those intriguing differences carry the seeds of future discord?

"Why are you bringing all this up now?" he demanded. "You were the one who told me I should do everything in my power to keep Leah at Renforth Abbey. I was only trying to follow your advice for a change."

"By proposing *marriage?*" Althea fairly shrieked. "I

only meant for you to offer her a higher salary or promise to redecorate her room, not make her your duchess!"

"Those things would never have worked," Hayden insisted in an effort to silence his sister and the doubts she had begun to raise in him. "Leah would not care about them enough to give up her freedom."

The moment those words were out, they turned to plague him. Would marriage to him inflict the loss of liberty Leah most feared? If she did feel confined and rebelled against it, would he be compelled to tighten his hold on her as he had on Celia?

"You were right when you said Kit needs Leah," he continued, determined to persuade Althea and himself that he had done the right thing. "Once we are married there will be no fear of him losing her. I am sorry if the resulting tattle inconveniences you, but surely Kit's welfare is worth a little sacrifice."

"What about Miss Shaw and the sacrifice she will make?" Althea demanded. "Is she prepared to assume all the responsibilities of a duchess and the mistress of this house? Will you keep her hidden away in the country for the rest of your lives or will you bring her to London one day and subject her to the scrutiny of Society? Does the poor girl realize you only want to marry her for the sake of your son?"

Until the instant Althea fell silent, Hayden was not aware of how loud their argument had grown. But her questions were not ones he could readily answer. He had not considered the additional restrictions Leah might endure as the wife of a duke and the object of cruel gossip. As for whether she knew he was only marrying her for Kit's sake, he was far from certain whether that was true.

During the shaken silence that followed his sister's questions, a faint high-pitched sound drew Hayden's attention to the library window he had not realized was half open. He recognized it as the whimper of a creature in pain. Had Kit's dog been injured?

But when his gaze flew toward the sound, it was not a wounded animal he saw, but the stricken face of Leah Shaw. He had never imagined her features could look so deathly pale, nor her hazel eyes so full of anguish. How much of his quarrel with Althea had she overheard and what had she made of it?

Leah gave a violent start, as if she'd just realized he was aware of her presence. Then she turned and fled, confirming Hayden's fear that she had overheard far too much. In that wretched instant, all his plans and hopes for the future seemed to shatter and collapse into dust.

She *must* get away from this place. She could not bear to remain another night under Hayden's roof!

Those thoughts spurred Leah as she ran down the lane that led away from Renforth Abbey. Desperately she concentrated on that objective and on putting one foot in front of the other. If she slackened her pace or allowed her thoughts to drift, memories of the past half hour would surely ambush her. She could not bear it if they did.

To think how happy she had been such a short time ago. Savoring her success in setting Kit free. Looking forward to being more than just his teacher. Anticipating a kind of life she'd once thought she could never want, only to discover that she *did*...provided she could share it with the right man. What a gullible fool she'd been to believe a man like Hayden Latimer could want her for herself.

"Leah!" His voice rang out behind her. "Where are you going? Please stop so we can talk."

"No!" She pushed herself to move faster so he would know she meant it. "I don't want to listen to you anymore. I have heard quite enough!"

She'd been out in the garden with Kit, his dog and the young footman who was training to care for the boy. One of the maids had come looking for Hayden, saying his sister had arrived and was anxious to see him. Immediately Leah had wondered if Lady Althea had come to talk her brother out of his mad whim to wed his son's governess. If so, she could not abide the thought of being talked about behind her back. Whatever Hayden's sister had to say, Leah had been determined to hear it for herself.

And she had, as she'd hurried past the library.

"You heard *too much*." Hayden's voice sounded closer. He was gaining on her, drat him! "But there is still more you need to hear, and you will hear it if I have to chase you all the way to London."

Coming from some people, that might have been only a ridiculous overstatement, but Leah knew Hayden's resolute nature. If he said he would pursue her as far as necessary, then he would. Not that he would be obliged to go all the way to London. Already her legs felt like jelly and every sharp gasp of air stabbed her lungs when she inhaled. Yet she resisted the urging of her body to stop and have it out with Hayden. If she must speak to him again, she needed time for her heart to heal enough that she could make a bitter jest of her feelings and pretend they had not run so deep. But clearly he was determined to humiliate her further by forcing her to betray feelings he did not return.

Very well, then. She stopped abruptly and spun about to confront him. If he was resolved to make her listen to whatever excuses he could contrive, she would make certain he got an earful, as well.

When she saw how close Hayden had come to catching her, Leah was glad she had decided to face him on her own terms. The only thing she wanted less than being forced to talk to him would be having to submit to his touch. It humiliated her to think how he had used it to stir her feelings for him while he remained unmoved.

"What is your plan now?" She employed every ounce of will to subdue her ragged breath. "Do you intend to fetch me back to your house by force and lock me away so I can never leave?"

"Don't be...ridiculous." Hayden skidded to a halt, chest heaving beneath his well-cut blue coat. "I have no intention...of keeping you...against your will."

They had reached the top of the rise where the lane began to wind through the trees. Nearly a year ago Leah had first glimpsed the beauty of Renforth Abbey from this spot. In January she had returned from Berkshire to a warm welcome. Today, was she seeing

Hayden's house for the last time? With ruthless force Leah quelled any traitorous feelings of regret. Better never to see the place again than be imprisoned there.

"Do you not?" she challenged Hayden. "But I thought you would do *whatever it takes* to keep Kit's governess at Renforth Abbey. Now that your despicable *marriage mission* is exposed, a lock and key is what it will take."

He flinched from her scathing indictment as if from a series of hard cudgel blows. "I am sorry you heard… what you heard. The truth is not nearly as bad as it must have sounded if only you will listen."

"The *truth*." Leah pronounced the word as if it belonged to some incomprehensible foreign language. "That would be a refreshing change. Are you certain you would recognize it? You do not seem to have a close acquaintance."

"I suppose I deserve that," Hayden admitted. "But I swear I never meant to deceive you. It is true I wanted you to stay and continue the fine progress you have made with Kit since you came to Renforth Abbey. Marriage was the only means I could conceive for keeping you with us…permanently. But if I deceived anyone, it was myself more than you."

He looked so guilty, repentant and miserable that Leah was hard-pressed not to pity him. Sternly she reminded herself of everything he had told his sister— things he had begun to confess. She had let down her guard and allowed herself to care for him when he only wanted her skill and her service, not her heart.

"How did you contrive to deceive yourself?" She narrowed her eyes.

Hayden hung his head. "By virtuously pretending I was only marrying you for Kit's sake when the truth is I wanted to prevent you from leaving *me*. I began to sense it a while ago but it was only when I saw you running up this lane that I knew for certain I could not abide the thought of losing you. I fell in love with you, Leah, something I never intended—something I persuaded myself I did not want. Too often for me love has ended in loss. With your penchant for freedom I knew you were the last woman in the world I should allow myself to care for because I was bound to lose you. But my heart had its own ideas in the matter."

His words were a siren's song that could draw her in so easily if she let them. But *in* to where? A tender trap of the kind her grandmother had warned her against? Many women might leap at the opportunity to wed a kind, handsome duke and become the mistress of a great house, but Leah had overheard Lady Althea as well as her brother. In many ways the life of a nobleman's wife was *more* constrained than other women's, trussed-up by bindings of duty and propriety that increased the higher one climbed on the ladder of society. The only ladies with less independence than a duchess were those of the Royal Family. What advantages of rank or fortune could compensate for that loss?

Even *if* Hayden truly loved her, something of which she was still not persuaded, would it be enough?

"How can I be certain you mean any of that?" It

would be far easier to walk away if she could cling to the belief that he did not truly care for her. "There is nothing you would not do or say to benefit your son. The irony is that Kit does not need me as much as you believe. He only needs you to keep on opening his world and you can do that if you set your mind to it."

"How can I prove I love you?" Hayden's features clenched in a look of deep perplexity.

In spite of herself, Leah ached to soothe away his troubles. Part of her longed for him to persuade her of the feelings he professed. The longer he stood there with his brow furrowed, searching his mind and heart for the answer, the more she wished he would simply open his arms and invite her to discover the truth of his feelings in the depth of his embrace. But he did not.

"Well?" she prompted him after what seemed like an eternity of suspense. "Can you think of nothing at all?"

It seemed perhaps he had, for his eyes widened and his mouth fell slightly open. But that instant of illumination was followed by one of intense anguish, the like of which Leah had only seen when he feared for the welfare of his beloved son.

"I reckon there is only *one* way I can show how much I care for you." The corners of Hayden's lips curved upward, but the shadow of heartbreak in his eyes made it a smile of profound regret.

"What is that, pray?" Leah did not like the sound of it.

"By letting you go, of course."

The moment he spoke, she knew he was right. Recalling what his sister had said about the sort of wife he needed, she feared the kindest thing she could do for Hayden was to grant him his freedom, as well.

Chapter Fifteen

The grief of every love he had lost over the years besieged Hayden's heart at once, begging him to recant his intention to let Leah walk out of his life. They urged him to cling to her with all his might—not only for his own sake but for Kit's.

And what about *her* sake? The whisper of a newborn resolve inquired. Must that not count for something? If he truly loved her, as he claimed, should he not place her happiness above every other consideration, including his own?

If he continued to stand there staring into her eyes, which he wanted to believe held a plea to change his mind, his determination would surely crumble beneath a weight of fear and longing it could not sustain. He forced his feet forward, one step at a time, away from the safe solitude of Renforth Abbey.

"W-where are you going?" asked Leah.

Did he fancy a plaintive note in her query or was

that only left over from the distress of hearing how he had tried to trap her into marriage?

"I mean to walk you to the village," he replied in a gruff, choked voice that he feared might break at any moment. He refused to let it—not out of pride but because he knew too well the tender heart Leah hid behind her facade of impudent defiance. He did not want her insisting she would stay and wed him out of pity. If she tried, he was not certain he would be strong enough to refuse.

"I will see you safely situated at the inn for the night," he continued with the same dogged determination that kept him walking. "Tomorrow I will fetch your possessions from Renforth Abbey and bring Kit to say goodbye."

He heard her scurry to catch up with him. "Wouldn't it make more sense to go back ho—to the house and let me do my own packing? I could leave tomorrow and say goodbye to Kit then."

Leah was right as usual. Her suggestion did make more sense in all respects except one. "If I get you back under my roof, I am not certain I could master my selfish inclinations and let you leave tomorrow. Besides, I thought you would be pleased to have Kit make an excursion to the village, whatever the reason."

"I…am, of course." She did not *sound* pleased. "I hope it will not distress him to have me go away so suddenly."

Hayden could see her out of the corner of his eye as they trudged along the wooded lane. The trees were all in full leaf. Lacy ferns edged the narrow path, their greenery relieved by scattered wildflowers in shades of white, yellow and pink. A gentle breeze rustled the leaves while a high, clear trill of birdsong pealed from some secret perch.

If he had walked this lane with Leah yesterday, all the colors would have appeared more vivid and the sounds would have created pleasing harmonies. Now his whole world seemed to have fallen into shadow, and he wondered if it would ever emerge into sunshine again.

"I expect it will upset Kit to see you leave." What was the point in pretending otherwise? "But you have shown me my son is not made of spun glass. He is quite capable of surviving a bump or a chill or a disappointment. Besides, he has other resources now—his dog, his playmates, his correspondents. And I will engage another governess or a tutor for him."

No doubt Kit would weather Leah's going far better than he. Hayden wondered how he had managed for so long to deceive himself that he must keep her at Renforth Abbey for his *son's* sake. "I do not want you to fret that I will return to my former ways simply because I do not have you around to push me."

"That is reassuring." Leah sounded more subdued than Hayden had ever heard her.

"I cannot pretend it will be easy." He forced himself to keep talking in an effort to persuade Leah and himself that everything would be all right when his heart warned him otherwise. "But nothing of any lasting value ever is."

Did that apply to their feelings for one another, as

well? He wondered. His brief courtship with Celia had been blissfully smooth, leaving their love unprepared to weather the shoals and storms it would later face. His love for Leah had developed slowly and warily, building upon a strong foundation of respect, gratitude and sympathy. Now it faced the greatest test of all—one that experience warned him would not likely yield the result he wished.

This time Leah did not reply, leaving Hayden to wish he could see into her heart to know what she was feeling. Did she believe his declaration of love, coming as it did with a contradictory insistence that she must go away?

"Do you recall I once started to tell you what happened after my grandmother died? We were interrupted and I never had the chance to finish."

Later, he had considered it unwise to raise the subject with a woman whose hand he was trying to win. Now that no longer mattered. Besides he had come to view those past events in quite the opposite way.

"I remember," said Leah, but she did not invite him to tell her more. Perhaps she did not want to hear.

Hayden refused to be put off. This might be his last opportunity to tell her. "Though my grandmother was old and had been failing for some time, her death affected me more than I expected. She had been one constant fixture in my life. I had hoped if she could hang on until her great grandchild was born, it would revive her somehow."

Leah made no effort to stop him talking, so he continued. "I can only imagine how gloomy Renforth

Abbey must have been for Celia that winter with no company but a morose, grieving husband. One day when she could not bear it any longer, she ordered the carriage and started for London. It was hours before I discovered she was gone. I rode after her and fetched her back, which she did not take well. By the time we arrived home, Celia was in labor, though the baby was not due for some weeks."

By now Hayden sensed attentiveness in Leah's silence.

"My wife was so exhausted from the journey, she did not survive Kit's birth. It is a wonder he did, poor little mite. For years, I blamed myself for not keeping a closer watch on Celia to prevent her from traveling in her condition. I used that regret to justify my efforts to protect my son at all costs, even the cost of his happiness. Now I realize I *was* to blame for what happened to my wife and child, but not in the way I believed all these years. If I had not clung so tightly to Celia, she might not have been driven to escape. I cannot risk anything like that happening to you. I would rather give you up than destroy whatever feelings you have for me by clinging to you."

"You were not to blame for what happened to your wife!" The words burst from Leah's lips almost before Hayden finished. "She had a choice and she chose unwisely. You cannot be certain what she might have done if you had acted differently. And you cannot let the past hold your future hostage!"

He knew she meant it kindly, and indeed she was probably right. But for some reason her words struck him the wrong way. "You are a fine one to talk. Has your past never held you back? We have both suffered losses, Leah. I reckon mine have made me cling too tight to those I care about, but yours have made you reluctant to care at all. You call it *independence* and *freedom,* but are you certain those are not brave sounding names for *running away?* How free are you, truly, if you cannot allow your heart the freedom to love?"

The only answer he received was a short, sharp hiss as Leah sucked in her breath. She stiffened, too, but she did not reply. Was that because she could not believe he was correct for a change? Or had his harsh insight wounded her too deep for words?

By now they had reached the point where the lane to Renforth Abbey joined the village road. The inn was within sight. There were not many villagers out and about but enough to shatter Hayden and Leah's privacy. Especially since the sight of the duke going about on foot was apt to stir curiosity.

Hayden pitched his voice lower. "I will arrange for you to receive a sum of money that should allow you to travel wherever you wish to go."

Leah shook her head. "I cannot accept that. Not from you. Not after everything that has happened between us."

"Nonsense." Hayden scowled. "You *must* allow me to do this. All you have done for Kit…and for me is worth far more than any amount of money I could give you. Besides, if you have an opportunity to experience the freedom you yearn for and see all the distant wonders you wish, perhaps you will find yourself inclined to settle down one day."

If she did, he doubted Leah would choose a man so encumbered as he—a man who had destroyed his best chance of happiness with her by failing to acknowledge his true feelings until it was too late.

Had Hayden meant the things he'd said to her when they had parted, about proving he loved her by giving her the freedom she craved? Or had he simply been trying to atone for hurting and deceiving her? Leah had asked herself those questions every day for the better part of a year as she traveled through France, Switzerland, Austria and Italy. The answers she received had varied from one day to the next depending upon her mood. Now, as she stared toward the familiar house and gardens of Renforth Abbey, they still gave no sign of having reached a firm conclusion.

The past year had been the most stimulating of her life by far. She had seen so many wondrous sights, met interesting people and learned more than she'd ever imagined. The experience had enriched her beyond measure and she would never regret having made the most of the opportunity. And yet...

Scarcely a day had gone by when she had not wondered what Hayden and Kit were doing. Was the child well and happy? Had Hayden continued to expand his son's horizons or had his fears driven him back to his old ways? Whenever she gazed upon some stirring new sight, part of her had ached to share it with the duke and his son. One of the happiest moments of her entire journey had been just last week when she'd glimpsed the coast of England again after so many months abroad.

Was her heart entrapped by her feelings for Hayden, or had he helped her set it free to find love at last?

Leah suspected the latter and hoped she would know for certain when she saw him again. Anticipation had built inside her with every mile she'd traveled closer to Renforth Abbey. Now she could scarcely contain it.

As she alighted from the pony cart that had brought her from the village, she strained to catch the voices of children at play or the deep, resonant bark of Kit's dog. The stillness troubled her. Was all well at Renforth Abbey? The fear that it might not be made her stomach plunge.

Surely Hayden would have found a way to contact her if anything had gone wrong, if any harm had come to his son. But why should he? She had not been part of Kit's life for nearly a year, though she had sent him cheery letters from many of the places she'd visited.

Anxious to make certain they were well, Leah plied the brass door knocker with urgent vigor. It felt odd having to knock for entry to Renforth Abbey.

After two or three very long minutes, the door swung open and Mr. Gibson peered out. The moment he recognized her, his solemn countenance gave way to a broad, welcoming smile. "Miss Shaw, what a pleasant surprise! I was not aware you had returned to England. I trust your tour of the Continent was satisfactory in every way. Pray come in."

"Thank you, Mr. Gibson." As she stepped across the threshold, into the familiar entry hall, a strange but very agreeable feeling came over Leah. Was this what homecoming felt like? If so, it was the first time in her life she had ever experienced it. What had she been missing? "My travels were very satisfactory indeed. Any inconveniences were more than made up by the many new things I had an opportunity to see and do. I collected a few presents for Kit…I mean Lord Renforth and I thought I might deliver them in person."

The look of regret with which Mr. Gibson greeted the explanation for her visit roused Leah's anxiety once again. "I am sorry you were obliged to come all this way, Miss Shaw. I am certain Lord Renforth and His Grace will be even sorrier to have missed you. But they are away from home at present. Your friend Lady Steadwell invited them to visit her family. They left last week for a fortnight in Berkshire."

A sharp spasm of relief made Leah's eyes water at the same instant a joyful laugh burst from her lips. "A holiday at Nethercross? What a fine idea!"

The butler nodded. "Who would have imagined such a thing when you first came to Renforth Abbey? Not I, certainly."

Gratified as she was to hear of the progress Hayden had made, another thought occurred to Leah. She struggled to maintain her smile and willed her voice not to contradict it by wavering. "I suppose Lord Renforth's new governess accompanied them to Nethercross?"

"Tutor, I believe you mean, Miss Shaw," the butler corrected her. "In fact, His Grace gave the young man a holiday to visit his family, as he did not wish to impose upon Lord and Lady Steadwell by bringing a large retinue."

The butler invited her to stay for tea. Though Leah appreciated his kindness, she declined. Her thoughts were racing and she needed to sort them out.

On the way back to the village, she mulled over the surprising news about Hayden and Kit's travels. Clearly they had managed far better without her than Hayden had once believed they could. Had *he* realized that, as well? Would he still want her to be part of their lives if Kit no longer needed her?

"Thank you for bringing me to visit Sophie, Papa." Kit gave his father a squeeze around the neck as Hayden helped him onto the saddle of a stocky brown pony. "I do like it here."

"So do I." Hayden marveled at his son's strength and rejoiced in his obvious happiness. "The Kendricks have been very kind to us. I feel quite at home at Nethercross."

There was a bittersweetness to their visit, though Hayden made every effort to conceal it from his son. Because their acquaintance with the family had begun with Leah, there had been frequent reminders of her. Each one brought Hayden a pang.

He sought to ignore the present one by concentrating on Kit.

"Have you got a good solid seat?" He checked that the child's feet were inserted firmly in the stirrups. "Don't forget to keep a tight grip on the reins."

"I won't forget, Papa." Kit chuckled in a way that

sounded exasperated but indulgent. "Don't worry so much. Phoebe says I am a fine rider and this pony has never gone faster than a walk in its life."

"I am well aware of that, thank you." Nevertheless, Hayden checked over the harness and made certain the saddle was properly cinched.

He had not abandoned all caution when it came to Kit's welfare and he doubted he ever would. But he had learned not to let his worries interfere with his son's happiness and independence. Seeing Kit's delight in being able to ride, just like any able-bodied child his age, was well worth any unease he might suffer.

"Look!" Sophie pointed toward a carriage coming down the lane between two rows of linden trees. "More company. I wonder who it can be."

She rode her pony to the edge of the paddock. Her elder sister Phoebe followed, raising her hand to shade her eyes from the sun. "It's a lady. I believe she is by herself. Is it…Aunt Leah?"

The name smote Hayden hard in the chest. He had to lean against Kit's pony to keep from staggering. That did not help for long.

"Miss Leah?" Kit jogged his pony's reins, urging it toward the fence, beside Sophie and her sister. "Is she back from abroad? Why did you not tell me, Papa?"

Hayden tried to inhale a deep breath of air, but the Nethercross paddock seemed to be in short supply at the moment.

"Perhaps there is some mistake," he warned Kit as he trailed after the boy. "It may not be her at all."

Was he trying to protect the child from disappointment…or himself?

"It *is* her," Phoebe insisted. "I recognize her hat. It is the same one she wore the last time she came to see us, just before she went abroad."

"Aunt Leah!" Sophie called and waved as the lady climbed out of her carriage. "Welcome home. You'll never guess who has come to visit us."

As the lady approached, Hayden hastily smoothed back his hair and wished desperately that he had worn a newer coat.

"I'm sure I never will." The familiar lilt of Leah's voice made it impossible for him to deny her identity any longer. "I hardly recognize you two girls. You have both grown at a perfectly scandalous rate since I saw you last."

"Do you recognize me, Miss Leah?" Kit sounded anxious that she might not.

Leah pretended to look puzzled. "There is something rather familiar about you, young man. You remind me of a very dear boy I know, but he is not nearly so big and robust as you. And he certainly could not ride a horse."

"It's only a pony." Kit laughed, clearly reassured that his former governess had not forgotten him. "And you know I am that boy. You're only teasing."

"Partly," Leah admitted, reaching over the fence to grasp his hand. "It is true that I can scarcely believe how you've grown."

Until that moment, Hayden might have been invisible for all the heed she had paid him. But now Leah's glance flitted toward him. Did he glimpse a depth of vulnerability beneath her usual show of high spirits? Or was he only seeing what he wished to? There could be many reasons she had come to visit Nethercross, none of which had anything to do with him.

"Have you come home to stay?" Kit asked her. "Or have you only come to visit for a while before you go traveling again?"

Though Hayden longed to know the answer to that at least as much as his son, he gently reproached the child. "You mustn't be such a busybody, Kit. Le—*Miss Shaw's* plans are her private business."

"But I want to know," Kit persisted then directed his next words to Leah. "I did not like it when you went away last time, but Papa said if we truly love you we should be happy that you were doing what made *you* happy. I tried to, but I missed you quite a lot and so did Papa. So I hope you can be happy to come back home again."

Before Hayden could muster his breath to protest, an even better idea occurred to the child. "Or perhaps you could take us traveling with you!"

When Leah replied, it was not to the boy but to his father, "You said that?"

Hayden gave a self-conscious nod. "I hope you have been happy on your travels. Your letters to Kit certainly made it sound that way. It was kind of you to write to him."

Phoebe, bless her heart, seemed to recognize the need for Hayden to have a private moment with Leah.

"Sophie and Kit, why don't we show Aunt Leah how well you can ride?"

Until now, Hayden had insisted on leading the pony when Kit rode, but Phoebe added, "It will be all right, Your Grace. I promise to stay close to him."

Hayden cast the girl a grateful smile, only faintly shadowed with worry. "Thank you, my dear. I have every confidence in you."

As the three young riders headed off at a careful pace, Hayden stepped closer to the paddock fence.

"Kit will be fine," Leah reassured him. "So you read my letters, did you?"

"We read them together. It was good practice for him." That was all Hayden intended to say, but more words followed in spite of his efforts to contain them. "After Kit grew tired of reading the latest letter over and over, I kept on until the paper nearly fell apart."

He patted the breast of his coat, over the inside pocket. "I still have your last one here. It is in tatters."

Would she make a jest of his lovelorn fancy? Hayden did not care.

"There were times I would have given anything to have a letter from you to read over and over." A wistful note in Leah's voice gave him more hope than he had permitted himself since she went away.

"You're not watching!" called Kit, prompting his father and Leah to wave and exclaim over his and Sophie's horsemanship.

That seemed to satisfy the child, who turned his attention to the girls.

Leah lowered her voice for Hayden alone to hear.

"The two of you have managed admirably without me. It seems Kit does not need me as much as you thought he would."

She sounded pleased and proud of their self-sufficiency, yet somehow forlorn.

Her gloved hand rested on the top rail of the paddock fence. Hayden covered it with his. "Kit may not need you, but I do—more than ever! My feelings for you have not changed in your absence, except to grow deeper. At the risk of being rude, I must repeat my son's question. *Have* you come home to stay?"

"That depends…" Her gaze locked upon his, giving Hayden the feeling that *he* had come home at last after a long, lonely sojourn. "…on whether it is too late for me to reconsider your proposal."

"Never!" Reaching over the fence, Hayden grasped Leah under the arms and swung her into the paddock with him. "It will never be too late for that, if you mean to accept."

Leah gave a squeal of surprise that turned at once to joyful laughter.

Throwing her arms around his neck, she clung to him as if she never meant to let go. "I do accept, with all my heart!"

Epilogue

Nearly two years to the day since she had first entered Renforth Abbey, Leah waited with her dear school friends at the entrance to the cloisters, on their way to the chapel.

"I am so happy to have another wedding in our group." Marian adjusted Leah's veil one last time before the ceremony. "It gives us all such a welcome opportunity to gather together with our families."

"Thank you all for coming to share my special day!" Leah embraced each of them in turn—Rebecca, Marian, Grace and Hannah, grateful for the precious blessing of their friendship. "I do wish Evangeline could have been here to complete our circle, but I know how busy she must be with plans for the new school. Did I tell you Hayden insists on making a large contribution to the endowment fund?"

"That is excellent news!" Hannah clasped Leah extra tight. "The larger the endowment, the better school we can build to replace that horrid Pendergast institution. Evangeline is eager to get started, but she cannot bring herself to leave her present position until she finds someone capable of filling her shoes."

"No wonder it has taken her so long." Rebecca gave a chuckle and shook her head. "Those will not be easy shoes to fill. I wonder what her employer thinks of Evangeline hiring her replacement. You must admit, it is rather presumptuous, even for our intrepid leader."

"I'm not certain she means to hire a new governess for Mr. Chase's children," Hannah confided, "so much as find the gentleman a wife."

That set all five of them talking at once, until Grace's stepdaughter, Charlotte, pulled open the door to the cloisters. "Are you coming or not? Poor Lord Northam is looking awfully anxious that he might be left at the altar."

After the way she had bolted a year ago, Leah could hardly blame him.

"We must not keep him waiting any longer." She motioned her friends to go off and join their families in the chapel. "I delayed this wedding once already. I don't intend to do it again."

"I am quite amazed you are going through with it." Rebecca winked at her. "If I were a gambling woman, I would have wagered Leah Shaw would never willingly give up her precious freedom."

Leah did not mind her friend's good-natured teasing, for she knew she would have done the same if their

places were reversed. Still, she could not let the gibe
go unanswered. "But I am not *giving up* my freedom,
you know. It is only since coming to Renforth Abbey
that I have *found* true freedom from my fears and from
my past. Now I am free to love Hayden as he deserves
and make a happy life with him."

"Well said, my dear." Grace brushed a tear from
the corner of her eye. "I believe we can all echo that
sentiment."

The others exchanged nods and smiles of agreement
as Charlotte hustled them off to the chapel.

After giving her friends a moment to take their
places in the chapel, Leah followed. Morning sunlight
streamed in the windows on the south face of the cloisters, making the stonework inside glow like gold. The
perfume of Renforth Abbey roses enveloped Leah as
she glided along the ancient walkway between pots of
flowers that lined both walls.

They reminded her of the night when Hayden had
given her the wondrous gift of springtime in the middle
of winter. Though there might be cold, dark moments
in the years ahead, she trusted their love would bring
them through to springtime again.

The chapel was decorated with still more flowers
and bathed in softly colored light from the great stained
glass window behind the ornately carved rood screen.

Inside the chapel door, Kit sat waiting in his wheeled
chair with his tutor standing behind it. He grinned up
at Leah when she entered and held out his hand, in
which she placed hers. As a harpist and flautist began
to play a pastoral air, Kit's tutor pushed his chair down

the aisle while Leah walked alongside, holding the child's hand.

Somewhere in the congregation, Leah knew Hayden's sister sat watching with ill-disguised disapproval as the duke wed his son's former governess. She hoped Lady Althea would feel differently once she saw how happy they were together.

When they reached the front of the chapel, Leah stooped to press a kiss on Kit's cheek before taking her place beside his father.

The vicar opened his prayer book to begin the ceremony that would unite them. Hayden leaned toward Leah and whispered, "I hope you are not too nervous about getting married at last, my love."

"I do have a few butterflies fluttering about inside me," Leah confessed with a grin. "However, they are not from apprehension but excitement."

"So you have no qualms at all about settling down?" The tender devotion that radiated from his eyes assured her that he would call the whole wedding off in an instant if she was the least bit uncertain.

"I do not think of it as *settling down*." She clasped his hand and raised it to her lips, much to the amusement of their wedding guests. "I believe that making a new life with you will be the most thrilling adventure I could ever undertake!"

* * * * *

Dear Reader,

This story has unique significance for me because, like its hero, I am the parent of children with special needs. And, like its heroine, I once taught children with special needs. Every day, with God's help, I seek the right balance between an instinct to protect and a need to promote independence.

Hayden Latimer, Duke of Northam has devoted his life to caring for his bedridden son. Feelings of guilt and the bitter experience of loss compel him to protect the child at any price. Spirited governess Leah Shaw is hired by Hayden's sister to teach the boy and encourage his father to allow him more freedom.

The duke and the governess learn difficult but valuable lessons from one another. But when their hearts are stirred, they must liberate themselves from the burdens of their troubled pasts so they can be free to find love.

Deborah Hale

QUESTIONS FOR DISCUSSION

1. Leah Shaw comes to Renforth Abbey "on a mission" to secure more freedom for Kit. Why do you think this assignment has such personal significance for her? Are you involved in any causes that affect you strongly because of past events in your life?

2. When Leah first arrives, she is very critical of the way Hayden is raising his son and he becomes defensive. Yet her words make him begin to reevaluate his actions. Have you ever given or received criticism that was hard to hear, but contained some truth? How did you or the other person react?

3. Leah has a negative opinion of Hayden in the beginning. What actions or events help her begin to see a different side of him? Have you ever had a similar experience? How did you react to it?

4. At first Leah uses humor as a weapon against Hayden. Why do you think she does that and what is his reaction? Can you think of instances in the story where she later uses humor in a more positive way? Are there others you could suggest to her?

5. When it comes to many things in his life, Hayden is ruled by fear and worry. How does it affect him

and his loved ones? What passages of Scripture could you recommend that might help him overcome this problem?

6. Hayden's attitude toward Leah begins to soften after she shows him the scars on her hands. Why do you think that is? Have you ever had kinder feelings toward a difficult person after becoming aware of their spiritual scars?

7. Hayden's excessive protectiveness and Leah's burning need for freedom seem so opposite, yet both have roots in their experience of loss. How might loss or other painful experiences affect two people in different, even opposite, ways?

8. Hayden sees God as a constant source of strength, in whom he can confide. Leah treasures the free will God has given her. What blessing from the Lord do you most treasure and why?

9. Some of Hayden and Leah's disagreements lead to anger and hurt between them, while others are more productive, resulting in healthy compromise. Can you think of an example of each from the story? Why do you think the result is different in each case? Are there any lessons you might draw from them about how to settle disagreements in a positive way?

10. Hayden and Leah recognize that they both need to change if they hope to be happy. They make

REQUEST YOUR FREE BOOKS!

2 FREE INSPIRATIONAL NOVELS
PLUS 2
FREE
MYSTERY GIFTS

Love Inspired.
HISTORICAL
INSPIRATIONAL HISTORICAL ROMANCE

YES! Please send me 2 FREE Love Inspired® Historical novels and my 2 FREE mystery gifts (gifts are worth about $10). After receiving them, if I don't wish to receive any more books, I can return the shipping statement marked "cancel." If I don't cancel, I will receive 4 brand-new novels every month and be billed just $4.74 per book in the U.S. or $5.24 per book in Canada. That's a saving of at least 21% off the cover price. It's quite a bargain! Shipping and handling is just 50¢ per book in the U.S. and 75¢ per book in Canada.* I understand that accepting the 2 free books and gifts places me under no obligation to buy anything. I can always return a shipment and cancel at any time. Even if I never buy another book, the two free books and gifts are mine to keep forever.

102/302 IDN F5CN

Name	(PLEASE PRINT)	
Address		Apt. #
City	State/Prov.	Zip/Postal Code

Signature (if under 18, a parent or guardian must sign)

Mail to the Harlequin® Reader Service:
IN U.S.A.: P.O. Box 1867, Buffalo, NY 14240-1867
IN CANADA: P.O. Box 609, Fort Erie, Ontario L2A 5X3

Want to try two free books from another series?
Call 1-800-873-8635 or visit www.ReaderService.com.

LIH13R

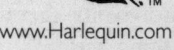

Bygones's intrepid reporter is on the trail of the town's mysterious benefactor. Will she succeed in her mission?

Read on for a preview of
COZY CHRISTMAS
by Valerie Hansen, the conclusion to
THE HEART OF MAIN STREET *series.*

Whitney Leigh rolled her eyes. "Romance! It's getting to be an epidemic."

Because she was alone in the car, she didn't try to temper her frustration. Fortunately, this time, the editor of the *Bygones Gazette* had assigned her to write a new series about the Save Our Streets project's six-month anniversary. If he had asked her for one more fluff piece on recent engagements, she would have screamed.

Parking in front of the Cozy Cup Café, she shivered and slid out.

As a lifelong citizen of Bygones, she was supposed to have been perfect for the job of ferreting out the hidden facts concerning the town's windfall. Too bad she had failed. Instead of an exposé, she'd ended up filling her column with news of people's love lives. But she was not going to quit investigating. No, sir. Not until she'd uncovered the real facts. Especially the name of their secret benefactor.

She stepped inside the Cozy Cup.

"What can I do for you?" Josh Smith asked.

Whitney was tempted to launch right into her real reason for being there. Instead, she merely said, "Fix me something warm?"

"Like what?"

"Surprise me."

She settled herself at one of the tables. There was something unique about this place. And, truth to tell, the same went for the other new businesses on Main. Each one had filled a need and become an integral part of Bygones in a mere five or six months.

Josh Smith was a prime example. He was what she considered young, yet he had quickly won over the older generations as well as the younger ones.

He stepped out from behind the counter with a steaming cup in one hand and a taller, whipped-cream-topped tumbler in the other.

"Your choice," he said pleasantly, placing both drinks on the table and joining her as if he already knew this was not a social call.

"I see you're not too busy this afternoon. Do you have time to talk?"

"I always have time for my favorite reporter," he said.

"How many reporters do you know?"

"Hmm, let's see." A widening grin made his eyes sparkle. "One."

Will Whitney get her story and find love in the process?

Pick up COZY CHRISTMAS to find out.
Available December 2013
wherever Love Inspired® Books are sold.